Dear Friends,

Welcome to Pilgrim Cove, Massachusetts!

On the surface, Pilgrim Cove is much the same as any little seaside town. Picturesque and peaceful with long stretches of unspoiled beach, fresh ocean breezes and sense of time passing slowly. But things aren't always as they seem. And the people of Pilgrim Cove—including a colorful group of characters known as the ROMEOS—have stories to tell.

Matthew Parker, his two young sons and his dad have shared a home since both men became widowed several years before the story opens. And now they're convinced no women are needed in the Parker domain. But when Matt meets Laura McCloud, who has healing of her own to do, he discovers that his life is missing something vital—a woman's love.

THE PILGRIM COVE series evolved when I combined personal experience—like me, Laura McCloud has a bright future despite a battle with breast cancer—with my love of New England.

So laugh, cry and enjoy yourself as you become part of this coastal community. Watch as Laura and Matt discover that love can be as powerful as the ocean outside their door. Happy reading!

Linda Barrett

P.S. I love hearing from my readers! Send a letter: linda@linda-barrett.com or P.O. Box 841934, Houston, TX 77284-1934. Check out my Web site at www.linda-barrett.com.

CAST OF CHARACTERS

Laura McCloud: Boston career woman; leases Sea View House

Matt Parker: Single dad, owns Parker Plumbing & Hardware

Bart Quinn: Realtor for Sea View House
Father of Maggie Sullivan and Thea Cavelli
Grandfather of Lila Quinn Sullivan
Great-grandfather of Katie Sullivan

Brian Parker: Matt's eleven-year-old son

Casey Parker: Matt's seven-year-old son

Maggie Quinn Sullivan: Bart's daughter, Lila's mother
Partner in The Lobster Pot
Married to Tom Sullivan

Thea Quinn Cavelli: Bart's daughter
Partner in The Lobster Pot
Married to Charlie Cavelli

Lila Sullivan: Bart's granddaughter and partner

Dee Barnes: Manager of Diner on the Dunes

THE ROMEOS:

Bart Quinn: Unofficial leader of the ROMEOS

Sam Parker: Matt's dad, works part-time with Matt

Joe Cavelli: Thea's father-in-law

Rick "Chief" O'Brien: Retired police chief

Lou Goodman: Retired high school librarian

Max "Doc" Rosen: Retired physician

Ralph Bigelow: Retired electrician

Mike Lyons: Retired engineer

The House on the Beach
Linda Barrett

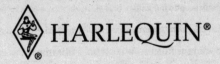

HARLEQUIN®

TORONTO • NEW YORK • LONDON
AMSTERDAM • PARIS • SYDNEY • HAMBURG
STOCKHOLM • ATHENS • TOKYO • MILAN • MADRID
PRAGUE • WARSAW • BUDAPEST • AUCKLAND

ISBN 0-373-71192-1

THE HOUSE ON THE BEACH

Visit us at www.eHarlequin.com

Printed in U.S.A.

To my husband, Michael, who received the dreaded phone call and had to convey the bad news. Then he said, "I'm here for you, sweetheart." And he was. And still is.
"I love you, Mike."

With deep gratitude to...

—Dr. Eric Bernicker, Dr. Joseph Dossi, Grathan Walls, Janan Destaphano and Cathy McClellan, R.N.'s. You grace the profession with your humanity.

—my family and friends, most of whom live far from Houston...for their unstinting love, support, advice and a zillion phone calls! And just as many prayers.

—my GED students, whose very existence kept my mind occupied during this hard time—and to the staff at SEARCH for many tasty lunches and great conversation.

Together, you helped me become a steel magnolia when I needed to be one, and I thank you from the bottom of my heart

Books by Linda Barrett

HARLEQUIN SUPERROMANCE

971—LOVE, MONEY AND AMANDA SHAW
1001—TRUE-BLUE TEXAN
1073—THE APPLE ORCHARD
1115—THE INN AT OAK CREEK

Don't miss any of our special offers. Write to us at the following address for information on our newest releases.

Harlequin Reader Service
U.S.: 3010 Walden Ave., P.O. Box 1325, Buffalo, NY 14269
Canadian: P.O. Box 609, Fort Erie, Ont. L2A 5X3

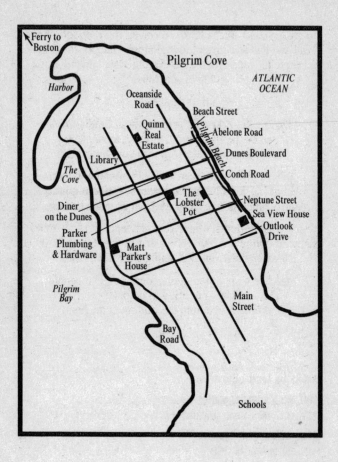

Ferry to
Boston

Pilgrim Cove

*ATLANTIC
OCEAN*

Harbor

Oceanside
Road

Beach Street

Quinn
Real
Estate

Abelone Road

Pilgrim Beach

Dunes Boulevard

Library

Conch Road

*The
Cove*

The
Lobster
Pot

Neptune Street

Diner
on the Dunes

Sea View House

Outlook
Drive

Parker
Plumbing
& Hardware

Matt
Parker's
House

*Pilgrim
Bay*

Main
Street

Bay
Road

Schools

CHAPTER ONE

"I'M SORRY, Ali, but I'm not ready to make such a big decision." Laura McCloud sat at the kitchen table across from her sister the morning after their mother's funeral, sipping coffee and nibbling a piece of dry toast. Her Boston home had overflowed with visitors the evening before, but she and Ali were alone now. The house was almost back in order. Leftovers filled the refrigerator shelves—not that she had much of an appetite.

"But you know how much we'd love for you to join us in Atlanta," continued Alison. "Charles especially wants you to know that the invitation comes from him, too. And the kids would adore having their Aunt Laura close by."

"I do know it, and I love you all for it, but—"

"And we have fabulous medical centers, too," interrupted Alison. "As good as here. Not that you have anything to worry about anymore," she added quickly.

Right. Nothing except the knowledge that there were no guarantees. "I'm not concerned about finding medical care. It's just that I have another idea."

"You do? What?"

"Remember Pilgrim Cove? Remember the beautiful beach?" Laura watched her sister's eyes widen and a grin light up her face.

"Do I remember? Of course I remember. What great summers we had. So, what's your idea? A summer vacation at the beach?"

"Not exactly," replied Laura. "I'm not going to wait that long."

"You're going to the beach in the middle of winter?" Alison asked in disbelief as she hugged herself. "Brr. Not me."

Laura laughed at her sister's antics. They'd always gotten along well, and Laura had really missed Alison when she'd left Boston. Suddenly Laura had to blink back tears. Alison was now her only family.

"I'll think about what you said regarding Atlanta, but I've got a career here and...I need some time. Time for myself."

Alison's hand reached for hers. "I'll support any decision you make, sis, but are you sure you really want to be alone?"

"With the sand and the ocean and my work...don't worry, Ali. I'll be very busy."

"Yeah, yeah. The sand will blow in your eyes, the ocean will crash against the seawall and the ferry won't run. So much for winter at the beach!"

Laura smiled. "I'll wait until next month. March should be somewhat better. I wonder what Pilgrim

Cove is like during the off-season. At least the rent should be cheaper.''

"Wait a minute. Why are you concerned about rent? A few dollars one way or another for a week's vacation shouldn't make a difference."

"I'm thinking about more than a week," Laura said in a slow, deliberate tone. "I'm thinking about a three-month lease, maybe through Memorial Day. A small house might not be too expensive, not too hard to keep up, but I'd want it right on the beach."

She stood as the image crystallized in her mind. "I need a change, a complete change of scene. And I need it now. Fighting with the weather will be much easier than fighting for Mom's life and my own."

She reached up and tousled her short blond curls. "Look at me, Alison. Look at these ringlets. I'm delighted to have hair again, but I don't recognize myself when I pass a mirror. Where's the sleek blunt cut that was so easy to manage?"

"You're adorable in those curls! In fact, you look wonderful, Laura, just wonderful." Laura could hear the passion in her sister's voice.

"Donald didn't think so," she responded.

"Donald Crawford was a jerk!"

Laura shook her head. "No, Alison. Don wasn't a jerk. He was just human. He had a girlfriend with a huge responsibility to an ill mother—and he handled that—but my getting sick was just too much. He wasn't prepared for all the emotional turmoil. Who can blame him?"

"I can," replied Alison.

"Be fair," said Laura. "We weren't engaged. He didn't owe me anything."

"He wasn't worthy of you!" Alison insisted. "You're the most outstanding person, the most beautiful, wonderful woman…"

"You're hardly objective." Laura laughed. "But can you really blame Don for wanting a normal life? What man wouldn't have second thoughts when he heard the words 'breast cancer'?"

"A man who loves you," came the quick reply.

"Well, I'm not going to count on that happening," said Laura in an even tone. "So I'll have lots of time and energy to rebuild my interrupted career." She leaned across the table. "I'm thirty-three. It's now or never. And you heard my agent last night. 'Work is therapy, Laura,'" she mimicked Norman Cohen's low voice. She relaxed in her chair. "Norman is a dear friend as well as a businessman. And he's got some radio ads lined up for me."

Alison would have protested again, but Laura held up her hand. "I'm not discussing men anymore, Ali. I'm not sure there's a man in the world who could look past this. Anyway, it's too soon. All I can do is take one day at a time. *Capisce?*"

"Sure," Alison replied. "I understand, but I don't have to like it. I love you and I want you to have…"

"I know," Laura said in a hoarse voice. "You want me to have everything you have…loving husband, healthy children…but that's probably not going to happen for me. What *is* going to happen, however, is a nice long stay in Pilgrim Cove."

Alison remained quiet for a long moment. "I recognize that expression and that tone," she finally said. "You've made up your mind. But my invitation remains open—will always remain open."

Laura looked at her sister's face, at the sincerity clearly written there. "Thanks, Ali, thanks a lot. But I've got to figure it out my own way."

She reached for the phone. "I'm calling Bartholomew Quinn, the man who arranged the summer rentals when we were kids. I remember going with Daddy to Mr. Quinn's real estate office. And I remember him. A head of thick white hair."

"White? And that was how many years ago? Close to twenty? He might be dead by now!"

"Hope not." She picked up the receiver and dialed directory assistance.

BARTHOLOMEW QUINN STOOD at the large front window of his Main Street office in Pilgrim Cove. His hand cupped the bowl of the empty pipe in his mouth, a comfortable habit he hadn't bothered to break even though he'd given up the pleasure of filling the beauty with fine tobacco.

Promises. He'd made promises. A promise to his daughters and to his beloved granddaughter and to her precious daughter. Four generations of Quinns, three of whom had said, "No more smoking, Dad, Granddad, Papa Bart!" He shook his head remembering how they'd ganged up on him. Foolish girls to worry so much. He was as strong as ever and as sharp as ever, and maybe just as hardheaded, too. He sighed. Except these days he chomped an empty pipe.

His eyes focused on the late-model blue Honda Accord pulling into a visitor's spot in front of his building, then he glanced at his watch. If this was Laura McCloud, she was right on time. He'd been astonished to hear from her last week. Astonished that she remembered him. But then again, he grinned to himself, he was a pretty memorable guy. Just ask his kids. Or anyone in Pilgrim Cove. Everyone knew Bartholomew Quinn!

The car door opened and a woman emerged, golden hair tossing in the wind. Bart tsked. She should have worn a hat. Wasn't she aware that February was the worst of the winter months in New England? He straightened his silk bow tie and adjusted the comfortable woolen cardigan he wore. Bart Quinn knew how to adapt to weather and to life. After seventy-five years on the planet, he'd had plenty of practice.

He watched the young woman check the sign—Quinn Real Estate and Property Management—and walk to the front door. He went to greet her.

"Well, as I live and breathe," he said, shaking Laura's hand. "The young McCloud girl. All grown up."

She had a delightful laugh, but it didn't quite hide the sadness in her dark blue eyes. Strain showed in the too-thin face.

"Come in and have a hot cup of Earl Grey." He ushered her to a small round table. After calling to an assistant for the tea, he took a seat opposite Laura.

"You've had a hard time of it, haven't you?" Bart began. "A fine woman was Bridget McCloud, and your dad, too. I remember Connor well. Two good people, and now their daughter's come to see me." He sat back in his chair and waited.

Laura nodded. "Yes, I've come to you, Mr. Quinn, with a request." She moved her chair a fraction closer. "My question is, can you help me find a house to rent immediately? A house right on the beach. I want to be able to open my eyes and see the ocean."

Her voice had the clarity of a bell. A musical quality, Bart thought. She was so lovely despite her distress. He cocked his head as he listened.

"You see," Laura continued, "I need to get away for awhile. I need to be here, near the water. Can't wait for summer. I need to…to…"

"Lick your wounds? Heal a little?" suggested Bart.

Her eyes widened. "That's part of it. Mom's illness…she was in remission for so long and then three years ago, the nightmare began again! Her nerve cells deteriorated. In the end, she couldn't walk, couldn't talk… I need some time to recover and to adjust." She paused in thought. "Long walks on the beach, fresh air, time to read and to cook simple meals. And with some basic recording equipment, I can work here as well as in Boston."

"And what exactly does Laura McCloud do to earn her keep?"

A dimple appeared as she shot him a small grin. "Laura McCloud earns her keep on the radio and telly with her commercial announcements."

Her language and Irish lilt matched his, and he roared with laughter. "Oh, you've got it down, girl." Bart was pure American, but his parents had emigrated from County Cork at the turn of the last century and a bit of their flavorful speech had taken hold in him.

She nodded. "I've always been good at languages. I seem to have the ear and the voice. In college, I majored in Speech and Theater and found work in narration and voice-overs. But—" she turned away from him then and stared through the window "—my career has fallen apart in the last few years. I've been…distracted. And now I've got to rebuild."

Her eyes glowed as she turned to him again, and Bart saw the strength behind them. This girl would make it somehow, with or without his help. But he wanted very much to help her. He thought about a property he managed—a unique beachfront property—with a sliding scale rental fee for people in difficult circumstances. His gut told him Laura qualified, and his gut was rarely wrong. He nodded his head. "Sea View House."

"Excuse me?"

"You'll be wanting Sea View House." Bart stood up, selected a key from among many on his key ring and walked to his big old-fashioned rolltop desk. He opened a small drawer and withdrew a set of duplicate keys. He reached for some papers. As he relocked the drawer, he picked up the phone and pressed the intercom. "Lila, come in and meet a special friend of mine." He winked at Laura, then opened his office door just as Lila rushed through.

Bart chuckled. Lila never walked.

"Laura McCloud," he said, "I'd like you to meet my partner, Lila Quinn Sullivan, who also happens to be my granddaughter."

BART'S GRANDDAUGHTER WAS lovely, Laura thought as she extended her hand. Twenty-something. Bright blue eyes, with an intelligence behind them.

"I'm looking for a place to rent," Laura said. "Your grandfather suggested Sea View House."

A wistful expression came over the young girl's face as she turned to Bart. "Sea View House?"

"Yes," he confirmed. "Laura's a special guest. And Sea View's a special house. He looked at Laura. "You spent about ten consecutive summers here, didn't you?"

She nodded. "What's so special about this particular house?" She needed a quiet place, nothing out of the ordinary.

Lila stared over Laura's shoulder, her eyes unfocused. "Sea View House has this reputation," she began. "Good things happen to everyone who stays there…" She paused, then shook her head. "Well, no, I guess not everyone…but I'm sure you'll be happy there. Welcome back to Pilgrim Cove.''

And she was gone.

''Moves at the speed of light, my Lila does,'' said Bart as he led Laura to his car. ''She's the joy of my life, she and her little Katie. But…well, there's a sorrow on her heart, too.'' He sighed. ''Everybody has troubles, but I can't think of a better place to be than Sea View House while you figure them out.''

Laura murmured noncommittally. She scanned the town as they drove, excitement mounting as she recognized some of the businesses. From Bart's office on Main Street, they passed a bank, then a barber shop called The Cove Clippers. She'd gone there with her dad each year for his ''summer cut.'' And there was The Diner on the Dunes! Happy times and delicious meals with her family.

''There's Parker Plumbing and Hardware,'' Bart pointed out. ''They carry everything. I'll call Matt to turn your water on. My friend, Sam Parker, started the business but now his son, Matthew, runs it. Good family. Not without their share of heartaches, too. But they carry on.''

Laura sighed. If Bart thought he was giving her a lesson in life, he was wasting his time. She was already an expert. She didn't interrupt him, but instead continued to look at the town, trying to recognize landmarks from her childhood.

''Is Neptune's Park still here?'' she asked.

Bart grinned around his pipe. ''Sure it is. Can't

imagine Pilgrim Cove without it, but it's only open in the summertime, mind you."

She nodded. Carousels and Ferris wheels were the stuff of sunshine and warm nights. Too bad she wouldn't be in town long enough to enjoy them. She refocused on the route Bart was taking and memorized it. He made a left from Main onto Outlook Drive.

"The whole peninsula is six miles long and less than two miles across, so we'll be at Sea View House in just a couple of minutes. Main Street divides the town. We have a beach side and a bay side. There's always a breeze when you're a finger in the ocean."

"That's why you have so many summer people every year," Laura said. "The news is out. Pilgrim Cove is the place to be during the season."

"For me, it's the place to be every season," said Bart. "Look ahead now. You'll see the front and side of the house."

Laura complied and felt herself grinning. Sea View House. Weathered wood, a big sloping roof, two stories with a third window above—maybe an attic— and a big brick chimney in the center. A white picket fence surrounded the front yard on Beach Street. "Wow! What a wonderful house. And only a vague memory to me. I didn't know anyone living here when I was a kid."

Bart pulled the car into the driveway. "It's a saltbox, the kind built in the 1700s. John Adams, our second president, was born in a saltbox. And William

Adams, a shirttail cousin of John, founded our town in 1690. A hundred years later his great-great grandchild, also named William, built this house. Of course, it's been remodeled several times and now it's been converted to two apartments. There's a lot of history here, but for a later time.''

Laura nodded and got out of the car. "Let's walk around the house first," she said.

"You go. I'll open her up," replied Bart. "The sun is bright enough, but that ocean breeze is whipping big today."

True, but Laura reveled in it as she followed the paved driveway to the back of the property, past a deep covered porch leading to a backyard bordered by a low cement wall at the sand line. Inserted into the cement wall were tall boards standing upright. Laura studied the strange arrangement and saw loose sand blowing against the boards. Sand that would otherwise be hitting the house. She smiled, appreciating the simplicity of some solutions.

And then she was on the beach, the powerful Atlantic in front of her, surging and ebbing as far as her eye could see. The heels of her boots hardly dented the hard-packed sand as she walked closer to the water. She could have stood for hours mesmerized by the rhythmic motion of the waves. She turned, eventually, to look back at Sea View House.

For the first time in too long, a frisson of excitement flowed through her. A sense of anticipation. Suddenly she knew exactly what she was going to do.

She hurried to the front door, ran down the center hallway and found Bart Quinn in the kitchen. "Where do I sign?"

CHAPTER TWO

A WEEK LATER, on the first of March, Laura drove her packed Honda down Main Street in Pilgrim Cove, turned right on Outlook Drive and headed toward Sea View House. The late-afternoon sun seemed pale but promising for the days ahead, and Laura felt the corners of her mouth start to turn up.

She had actually done it! Had arranged for her mail to be forwarded and her house in Boston to be checked by a service. She had staked out three months for herself—time to come to terms with her life and her losses. Alison had called it a retreat, and maybe it was. Laura saw it more as an opportunity to spend three months in a friendly place, on the beach at the water's edge, with no schedule or deadlines. The only appointment she had was a breakfast date with Bart the next morning. The Realtor had insisted on welcoming her to town when she'd spoken to him earlier in the week.

She stopped at a red light, and glanced around the inside of her car to admire her packing skills. With her computer, her books, her clothes and her groceries, there wasn't a spare inch left over. Norman Cohen had given her two scripts to study. They were in the car, too. She'd cautioned her agent, however, not to be too aggressive on her behalf yet. Her goal was to take life nice and easy for a while.

Fortunately, her cash reserves wouldn't be as taxed as she'd feared. Bart Quinn had explained that the William Adams Trust Fund provided the bulk of the upkeep on the house. Laura's responsibility was computed on a sliding scale based on recent income. Other factors included personal history and circumstances.

"Sometimes the Adams Trust Fund collects full rent on both apartments because money might not be the overriding issue," Bart had explained. "The trust focuses on the whole person."

She'd been stunned at the unusual arrangement, and Bart had laughed. "Aye. It is unusual, but it's part of what makes Sea View House and Pilgrim Cove special." He'd become serious again as he revealed more. "No one in town but me and a few others know who's paying what rent at Sea View House. Your privacy is protected." His eyes had twinkled. "Any complaints?"

Complaints? Not a one! Luck was with her, and she hadn't asked too many questions.

The traffic light changed, and she continued down Outlook Drive before turning left onto Beach Street. Sea View House sat on the corner, big, solid and welcoming. A blue van was parked in front of the old beauty. Laura pulled around the vehicle, glanced at the Parker Plumbing emblem, then turned into the driveway. She quickly shut the ignition, suddenly anxious to start unloading and begin her new life.

She hefted a bag of groceries from the car and checked the van as she walked to the front door. The vehicle was empty. She shrugged, turned the doorknob and let herself inside without having to use the key Bart Quinn had given her. She walked down the hall to the kitchen.

"Hey, Brian," came a masculine voice from under the sink, "hand me the pipe wrench. The shutoff valve is leaking."

Laura walked around a pair of large, tan work boots attached to long jean-clad legs, placed her groceries on the table and found the tool the man had asked for. "I'm not Brian, but here's your wrench."

"What the…? Ouch!"

Laura muffled her giggle with her hand. Or tried to.

"I know that voice," said the unseen man as he started to maneuver himself up. "And the laugh. They're unforgettable."

"Then you listen to too many commercials," replied Laura.

She watched the masculine body emerge and lever itself to a standing position. And then she looked up. And up. The face looked familiar. Dark wavy hair, eyes as black as coal with long lashes any woman would envy. Fifteen years evaporated as she stared at him.

"I remember you," she finally said, feeling herself blush as recognition dawned. The memory of a single kiss a lifetime ago.

He grinned and his eyes twinkled. "I kissed you under the boardwalk the last night of summer vacation way back when. You were about sixteen, and it's taken you all this while to come back. I must have messed up."

"You've obviously managed to survive," Laura replied dryly. "And how old were you?"

"Seventeen." The man extended his hand. "Matt Parker," he said, "and you're Laura McCloud."

She nodded and shook his hand. "Bart mentioned a Matthew and Sam Parker, but I'd forgotten about your plumbing business, so I wasn't expecting you. But surely Bart Quinn told you I'd be here."

"Not a word on your identity. Scout's honor. But when I heard you speak, I was seventeen again."

"Really?" she asked, wondering if he was as sincere as he sounded.

"You were 'the girl with the voice.' All the kids called you that," Matt said.

"That's crazy," Laura replied in astonishment. "The voice? I don't even sing!"

"Doesn't matter. I have a good ear—my whole family does—and you have a memorable voice. Tone, pronunciation, clarity." He offered his opinion as a casual statement of fact.

"Let's change the subject," Laura said, "Who's Brian and what's wrong with my pipes?"

Matt rolled his eyes and looked innocently at the ceiling. "Kitchen sink or vocal?"

She had to laugh at his expression. "I give up. Help me out here. I'm moving in right now. Does this house have running water or not?"

"It will in a few minutes." Matt Parker grabbed the wrench and got back on the floor, head under the sink. "Brian is my eleven-year-old son who's supposed to be helping me. I've got two boys. And my dad lives with us, also. It's a real bachelor household."

"Oh."

"My wife died four years ago."

Subject closed. Laura could read vocal nuances, too. "I'm going to the car. I've got lots to unpack," she said.

"Hang on a minute," Matt said. "The valve's tight now. No more leaking. I've already checked the two bathrooms, so you're all set." Matt spoke as he stood up again. "And I can help you unload your car as long as I'm here."

Laura heard the front door open, and a young voice called out, "Hey, Dad, you need me?"

Footsteps pounded down the hall and suddenly a miniature, coltish version of Matt Parker appeared and stopped in his tracks. The boy looked at his dad, then at Laura, his dark eyes questioning, suspicion lurking. "Who's she?"

"Brian Parker! Where are your manners? You

know better. Now apologize to Ms. McCloud."
Matt's voice was firm and low.

The boy looked quickly at Laura. She could see the
fear behind the suspicion. She watched him step
closer and slightly in front of his father as though
protecting him. His fear touched her heart. Poor kid.

"Hey, Matt," said Laura. "Thanks for fixing the
sink. I can handle the unpacking. In fact, I'd prefer
to do it alone, a little at a time." She turned to Brian
and held out her hand. "Nice meeting you, Brian.
You can take your dad home now."

Brian shook her hand, then looked hopefully at
Matt, but Matt didn't move. The child turned back to
Laura. "Sorry. Glad to meet you."

Laura smiled at him. The kid knew how to be polite. She'd urge them to leave for all their sakes.
"Thanks again. See you around."

She stepped toward the hallway.

"Wait a second," said Matt.

Laura paused and watched him walk toward her.

"I love my kids," Matt said, "but they're not in
charge."

"Oh?" she replied with a laugh. "Don't you believe in family democracy? One person, one vote?"

His eyes twinkled. "With two boys under twelve?
I don't think so."

"I don't blame you. My own niece and nephew
run me ragged. Although I have to admit I love every
minute of it."

"Laura." Matt sounded hesitant, but continued,

"Are you involved with anyone right now? Because if you're not, I'd like to see you again—with no kids around."

She paused a moment. She wasn't ready for complications, and the Parker family—father and sons—might present many. "Thanks for the invitation, Matt, but men and relationships aren't really in my plans right now. I'm on a working vacation. You know, deadlines and stuff."

He nodded, his complexion turning ruddy. "Maybe my kid has the right idea." He pulled something out of his pocket. "Here's my business card. If you ever need anything—plumbing services or otherwise—just pick up the phone. No strings attached for old friends. In fact, I'll check on you in a day or two."

"Thanks for the offer, but that won't be necessary," she said calmly. "I'm sure I'll be able to manage."

She saw his eyes narrow, his expression harden. He'd gotten her message.

He nodded, then turned to his son. "Come on, Brian. We're finished here."

She watched father and son walk away, her eyes on Matt's broad back. Regret filled her. She hadn't wanted to hurt him, had just needed to set her own boundaries. She wasn't the type for a one-night stand, and anything else involved too much emotional risk for all parties. Not even Bart Quinn was aware of her medical history and no one in Pilgrim

Cove would ever know about it; there was no reason to share it.

But still, she'd hated the look on Matt's face when he left.

THE NEXT MORNING, Laura awoke early, earlier than she'd planned. She shrugged off the lingering image of Matt Parker and focused on her breakfast date with Bart at The Diner on the Dunes, located off Main Street, nowhere near to any dunes. She glanced at her clock radio sitting on the night table and jumped out of bed. Her feet were protected from the cold plank floor by a large oval rag rug. The multicolored rug added a warmth and vibrancy to the wood-beamed master bedroom as did the tufted colonial quilt and curtains on the double hung windows.

Laura looked around the room, feeling better than she had for a long time. As Bart had mentioned, Sea View House had two separate apartments. The entire first-floor apartment, known as The Captain's Quarters, was hers, and the colonial decor throughout was as pleasing to her eye as the decor in this room. Or perhaps it was the peaceful silence, or the strong, solid structure of the house itself that imbued her with a calmness she hadn't experienced in a long time— not since her mom's diagnosis and then her own. Could the stress she always carried with her have dissipated so quickly?

She inhaled deeply, then exhaled, using the relaxation techniques she'd learned in recent years. She closed her eyes. In several breaths, the image of the sea filled her, the waves coming into shore and retreating, over and over again. When she opened her eyes, her sense of calm had gotten stronger and she began to laugh at herself. She didn't have to imagine the ocean anymore. It was right outside her back door!

She went to that door now, opened it and stepped onto the porch. She promptly shivered. But the morning sun was rising over the horizon, its rays stretching across the waves, across the sand to Sea View House and to Laura. The chilled air smelled of the sea. Salty, distinctive. Good. Clean. So unlike the city air she breathed every day at home.

She brought her hand to her cheek and pinched it. "I am really here," she whispered. "I made a good decision." Then she ran inside to get dressed. The day was too precious to waste. The sooner she had breakfast with Bart, the sooner she could return to her haven.

LAURA HAD NO TROUBLE finding The Diner on the Dunes, on Dunes Boulevard just east of Main Street. Exactly where it had been years ago. Bigger than she remembered. A one-story clapboard affair, still painted white, its nautical motif included a row of porthole-like windows near the roofline.

She pulled into the parking lot, which already held a dozen cars, opened her door and smelled the aroma of fresh coffee. Her stomach grumbled. Another change. Her appetite had returned. She slammed the door behind her and approached the entryway. Above the door frame was a bold red-and-white wooden sign proclaiming Home Of The ROMEOs. Who were the ROMEOs? Maybe the owners lived behind the place? Laura shrugged. She'd find out soon enough.

She stepped inside. The interior seemed more spacious than the diner of her childhood. The furnishings had been changed, and the lighting. The place was brighter. Booths lined two walls with a counter along the third, but there were also several tables in the center of the floor. She had no time for further observations before she heard her named being called. She turned and saw a thatch of white hair and a big smile. Bart waved her over to the large round corner booth in the back of the restaurant.

He wasn't alone. Laura counted seven men in addition to Bart as she walked to the table. All his contemporaries, she guessed.

"Good morning, Laura McCloud." Bart beamed at her before turning to his friends. "This is Bridget and Connor's daughter. The McClouds who used to vacation here."

And then the men all spoke at once. Smiles and nods and a chorus of welcome.

"Your dad and I spent a morning or two fishing off the pier," said one.

"We stood side by side in the park, pushing our little girls in the swings," said another. "My daughter is all grown-up now, just like you."

Laura felt a lump in her throat as the unexpected remembrances slammed her in the gut. She studied the men slowly. Sure, her dad would have been their age by now.

"I'm so glad to meet you," she said. And she *would* be glad after she got used to the idea that her sanctuary in Pilgrim Cove wouldn't be so private after all.

"Let's introduce you properly to the ROMEOs," said Bart.

"The ROMEOs?" echoed Laura, remembering the words over the diner's doorway.

Bart nodded at the Reserved sign in the middle of the table. The word *ROMEOs* was printed clearly on it. And below that…Laura laughed. A big full laugh.

"*Retired Old Men Eating Out? R-O-M-E-O.* That's what you call yourselves?" She looked around the table. Not a dull eye among them. "But you're not old!" she protested.

"The smart girl speaks the truth," said Bart with a twinkle. "We're still young enough to take care of this town."

"And you're not retired," Laura pointed out again as she slipped into a seat.

"Some of us are and the rest of us keep cockeyed schedules," explained another one, shaking her hand. "I'm Joe Cavelli and I still help out at our garage which my son runs now. My son, Charlie, is married to one of Bart's daughters, so that makes me and Bart—' He turned to the man next to him. "Hey, Lou, what's that word you use to describe me and Bart?"

"*Mach-a-tunim.* You and Bart are *machatunim.*"

The man who used to swing his daughter in the park turned to Laura. "It's Yiddish. There's no English equivalent to describe the relationship between the parents of married children." He extended his hand. "I'm Lou Goodman, retired librarian. Pleased to know you, Laura."

She shook his hand, and one by one, the remaining men introduced themselves: Ralph Bigelow, retired from the local utility company and now doing electric repairs for Bart's properties; Rick "Chief" O'Brien, retired from the Pilgrim Cove Police Department, but still keeping watch on the town he loved; Mike Lyons, retired environmental engineer, now studying sea-coast habitat as an avocation; and Max "Doc" Rosen, retired Boston physician now living in Pilgrim Cove all year round instead of summers only.

"And I'm Sam Parker," said the last man at the table.

Laura recognized the features. Had to be Matt's father. Same jet-black eyes and long sooty lashes, same well-defined mouth. But the hair was strictly salt-and-pepper, heavy on the salt. "Happy to meet you," she replied. And that's all she said.

"Heads up," called a female voice. "Here comes fresh coffee, steaming hot for my guys. Just the way they like it."

Laura looked up. A petite older woman winked at her, mascara intact, then turned to fill the mugs on the table. "Our French toast is the best in town. Made from challah bread with a dash of vanilla. Our omelettes are the most delicious with fresh veggies and fresh eggs we get every day…''

''Do you grow the chickens in the backyard also, Dee?'' Chief O'Brien asked. ''You work too damn hard. Sit down and take a load off.''

''Oh, pipe down, Rick. I love managing this diner, being with folks.'' The blonde turned to Laura as she set the coffeepot on the table. ''Don't pay attention to him. The Chief always says I work too hard, but I think he's jealous. Too much time on his hands. My name is Dee Barnes, by the way.''

''It wasn't my choice to retire,'' said the cop, his eyes never leaving the woman standing near him.

Dee Barnes patted his shoulder, her expression changing to concern. ''I know, Rick, I know. Mandatory retirement issues. But you're too darn young to have nothing to do,'' she said, exasperation once more in her voice.

''And you're too damn young to have aching feet all the time!''

Laura looked from one to the other, feeling the zap of electricity in the air, and smiling as the other ROMEOs at the table started whistling and clapping.

''Okay,'' said Bart, tapping a spoon against his cup. ''The day can officially begin now. Dee and the Chief are at it again.''

''Whoa,'' said Laura. ''I thought Pilgrim Cove was a quiet, peaceful town.''

''Oh, sweetie, you'll have a great time here,'' Dee reassured her. ''You're at Sea View House, so not to worry." She turned toward the table in general. "Now, who's having what?"

Laura watched the woman memorize the orders. All nine of them, including hers. She took the Chief's order last, querying him only with a raised eyebrow, and then she disappeared in a flash.

Laura sipped her coffee, trying to digest everyone and everything.

Then Doc Rosen said to Bart, "Don't forget to give Laura our special business card." The rest of the men nodded and murmured agreement.

"Sure, she'll get a card. I wouldn't forget such a thing," said Bart, reaching into his shirt pocket and presenting Laura with a larger than normal size business card. Laura examined it. On one side in bright red ink was the word *ROMEOs*. On the other was a list of every man's name, phone number and special skill printed in blue.

"We all take a particular interest in the tenants of Sea View House," said Bart. "I've been handling the rentals for twenty-five years, and some of us are on the board of the William Adams Trust. It's been a happy place for most people, and we want you to start your visit knowing you've got friends to call on if you need us."

"Hear, hear." The ROMEOs raised their coffee cups in unison.

Either she'd fallen through the Rabbit Hole or she was surrounded by the most wonderful group of men on earth. Laura wasn't sure. And she wasn't asking for clarification.

"Thanks," she said. "That's quite a welcome."

"It's easy to welcome a blue-eyed, fair-haired angel," replied Bart with a wink and an exaggerated brogue.

Why, the gent was flirting with her! "Angel, is it?" said Laura, in the lilt of the Irish. "I believe you've been kissing the Blarney stone again, Bartholomew Quinn."

Chuckles came from everyone, even from Dee who was deftly serving breakfast platters without interrupting the conversation.

"She's got your number, Bart," said Sam Parker. "I haven't enjoyed such a good laugh in the morning for a long time."

Laura felt herself grin like a jack-o'-lantern. She couldn't remember the last time she had gently teased anyone or cracked a joke. It felt good to make people laugh. Very, very good. She took a deep breath, then exhaled. At that moment, she was stress-free. Her body felt like a relaxed rubber band, and she had no desire to be anywhere else.

Until she heard the deep masculine voice above her.

"Good morning, gentlemen...and ladies."

Laura looked up into Matthew Parker's strong face. He nodded at her, but his smile was for the waitress and the men.

Sam and Bart began to speak simultaneously.

LINDA BARRETT 35

"Have you met Laura McCloud?"

"Did you meet Laura yesterday at Sea View House?"

Matt paused, then smoothly replied, "Briefly, just as I was leaving."

"Then take a moment to join us," suggested his dad, waving him toward a chair.

Matt shook his head. "Sorry, no time. And you have no time either, Pop. Our guys are out on other jobs, the ladies are both out sick, and I need coverage at the store while I go to the middle school. Every boy's bathroom is stuffed...those kids...." He shook his head. "The janitor can't handle it."

Sam stood up at once. "I used to do it all," he said to Laura, "the emergency calls as well as the business management, but this darn arthritis...can't turn those wrenches anymore. And even Doc can't cure it."

"But I can help you at the store," said Doc Rosen, getting to his feet.

Matt looked at his dad, deep affection in his eyes. "Someone else can deal with the wrenches, Pop, as long as you still play a mean piano and keep your fingers nimble enough to ring the cash register."

Everyone laughed, and Laura found herself joining them until she felt a pair of ebony eyes studying her. Assessing her. No words spoken. No smile for her. Then Matt turned to leave, the two ROMEOs with him.

And Laura wished he had smiled. She focused on Bart once more, concentrating on what he was saying.

"Everyone in that Parker family can play a mean piano. Without any lessons. Matthew, himself, is the Pilgrim Cove version of Billy Joel. A real piano man."

"And his kid brothers were even better...."

Bart nodded. "True, true. But Jared's gone, rest his poor soul, and who knows where Jason is now...."

Laura stood up. Fascinated as she was, she couldn't afford to get involved in anyone else's life. Her curiosity about one thing, however, had been satisfied. She'd discovered how a plumber knew so much about voice. Apparently Matt had told the truth when he'd told her that he had a good ear.

She should have told him the truth about her mom. He would have understood her need for privacy. Not that she'd lied—but she'd avoided the heart of the matter. The next time she saw him, she'd explain.

No she wouldn't! Too complicated. Sometimes, the less said, the better. She'd nod politely if they crossed paths again.

By three o'clock that afternoon, Laura needed a nap. She explored the town, noted the location of Parker Plumbing three blocks from Quinn Real Estate, went grocery shopping for perishables, unpacked them, set up her computer and audio attachments in one of the spare bedrooms, and had taken a three-mile walk on the beach. A brisk walk. It was amazing how completely at home she felt when she let herself into Sea View House after the walk. She'd been in

Pilgrim Cove only twenty-four hours and already felt as if she'd been there forever.

And now she couldn't stop yawning. She plopped onto her queen-size bed and closed her eyes. It was wonderful having no schedule. She could sleep whenever she wanted.

IN A WEEK, she'd established a routine. A long walk on the beach each morning, then chores and professional work. She slept every afternoon and woke up famished. And she ate as if she were rediscovering food. Even her own plain cooking tasted good.

On the evening of her one-week anniversary in Pilgrim Cove, she decided to celebrate with a meal at The Lobster Pot, the restaurant recommended by everyone she'd met in town while doing her errands.

After her nap, she showered, shampooed and towel-dried, catching sight of herself in the full-length bathroom mirror hanging on the back of the door. She didn't pause to look at her reflection. She knew only too well the effect the surgeries and the chemotherapy had had on her body.

Besides, she didn't want to think about all that now. It was behind her, and as Dr. Berger had said, "In your particular case, the ten-year survival rate is ninety-six percent. Go, have a good life!"

And she was trying to do just that. But...she couldn't pretend it had never happened. At least not until she'd survived five years.

Most of the time, however, she felt great. She

looked better now, too. Her walks on the beach had added some color to her winter-pale face. Pressing against the sand had provided resistance for her leg muscles, so she was toning up. Maybe she'd join a gym when she got back to Boston.

And her hair? A woman's crowning glory? Laura grinned as she combed her tangled locks. She'd stop complaining. So what if her curls rivaled Little Orphan Annie's. Didn't women pay for permanents? At least she had hair! She'd donated her wig five months ago to the special program at her hospital and then tried to learn how to handle ringlets.

This evening she chose a soft merino wool navy-blue turtleneck and navy blue slacks topped with a brick-red wool blazer. On her feet were her favorite black leather low boots, comfortable in every way and still stylish. A little makeup, some lipstick and she was out the door.

The parking lot was crowded. She'd expected it to be on a Friday night. She drove carefully around the building and got a space in the back. She walked up two shallow steps to a wide wraparound porch, probably filled with outdoor tables when the weather was milder, and continued to the front of the building, inhaling delicious aromas with every step she took. Her stomach growled, her salivary glands went into action, and she geared herself up for a long wait. After being tempted by The Lobster Pot's savory fragrances, she wasn't interested in eating anywhere else that evening. Until she opened the door and literally bumped into Matt Parker as he stood, broad back to the entryway, talking to the hostess, his two boys and father surrounding him.

He caught her before she completely lost her balance, his hand strong and sure on her arm.

"Sorry," she said quickly. "Thanks. I'm fine." She wasn't usually clumsy. Why did she have to start now? She looked down and saw the tear in the carpet that she'd tripped on.

"You need to inform Maggie and Thea," said Matt to the hostess. Then he looked at Laura. "Bart's daughters own the place. Maggie Sullivan and Thea Cavelli. You met Joe Cavelli last week at The Diner. He's Thea's father-in-law. Charlie's father."

"Slow down," said Laura with a laugh. "I don't think I'll ever keep all of this straight. It sounds like everyone's related to everyone else."

"Not quite, but we all feel like family around here," said Sam, joining the conversation. "It's good to see you again, Laura McCloud. Enjoying Sea View House?"

"Absolutely. All I do is eat and sleep! It was the right choice for me."

"Well, how about joining us for dinner and eating some more?" asked Sam, his voice as warm as his words.

"She might have other plans, Pop," said Matt.

The hostess intervened. "I can get another seat at a round table now, or she'll have a thirty-minute wait. You guys know how Friday nights are around here."

Laura groaned inwardly. She didn't want to go where she wasn't wanted, and it was clear Matt wasn't thrilled about her sitting with them. Not that she blamed him. "I don't mind waiting."

"Ridiculous," said Sam.

Just then, Matt's younger son—skinny with golden-brown eyes—stepped toward his father. "Who—who—who's the la-a-a-dy?"

Matt sighed with a sound of capitulation and tousled the boy's light brown hair, before turning to Laura. "Would you like to join my family and me for dinner, Ms. McCloud?"

CHAPTER THREE

"JUST A MOMENT." Laura held up a warning finger to Matt and squatted until she was eye level with his son. "My name is Laura," she said in a slow, relaxed manner, her diction precise. "And your name is…?"

"C-Casey!"

"I'm happy to meet you," said Laura, keeping the same rhythm of speech and giving him a high-five.

The kid slapped her hand and grinned.

Laura straightened to her full five feet seven inches, and glanced at Matt, who was a picture of confusion as he looked from her to his son. "I'd be happy to join you, Mr. Parker, but not as a guest. I'll pay my own share."

His eyes darkened, if that was possible. He stepped behind her and she felt his warm breath against her ear as he whispered, "Afraid I'll want my wicked way with you?"

She shivered. Right down to her toes. Whether it was due to the exquisite sensitivity of her earlobe or to the instant visual she had of making love with Matt, she didn't know. All she knew was that she'd shivered. And that Matt must have felt it. A correct conclusion, she surmised, when she heard his contented chuckle.

"The table's ready," said the hostess, holding several menus in her hand. "Follow me."

"You heard the lady," said Matt, still smiling. "Follow her."

Laura would rather have walked out the door, but she held her head high as she made her way toward their table sensing, rather than seeing, Matt right behind her. The restaurant boasted three separate eating areas, she noticed, each accessed by the wide central aisle they were walking down.

When they reached their table in the main dining room, she felt Matt gently massage her shoulders as he helped remove her jacket. "Relax," he whispered, and held her chair until she was seated. All the while, three pairs of Parker eyes watched every move Matt made.

"Thank you," Laura said, wondering if this was the first time the youngsters had seen their dad in the company of a woman other than their mother.

"Did you eat here earlier in the week, or is this your maiden voyage on the good ship Lobster Pot?" asked Matt conversationally, indicating the nautically themed interior.

"Maiden voyage," replied Laura, glancing at the informal surroundings. The wood-paneled room was dotted with framed, colorful fishing and boating posters, each with a caption beneath the picture. She took a moment to study them. One showed a chubby baby in a pastel-blue-and-white sailor suit facing the audience with the caption: "It's a buoy!" And down the wall from that one were two young teens in a sailboat with the caption: "Wouldn't you rudder be fishing?"

"Oh, my! Who thinks of this stuff?" Laura wasn't sure whether to laugh or groan.

"How about that one?" Sam indicated a poster that proclaimed Pilgrim Cove to be "A hull of a place to live."

Laura acknowledged that pun with a chuckle and a shake of her head.

"Dad, Dad. Wha—Wha—what's so f-f-funny?"

But it was Brian who answered his brother. "You're too young, Casey. They're spelling jokes and—" he paused "—and definition jokes. Like *b-o-y* and *b-u-o-y*." He turned to the rest of the table. "Anyone got a pencil? I'll show him."

Impressed at the older boy's concern for his brother, Laura reached for her purse. "I do," she said, handing him a refillable lead model and a piece of scrap paper. Was this the same kid who'd wanted to vaporize her last week when he'd seen her with his dad?

She watched Brian print the words and listened to him explain. He repeated the procedure with "rather" and "rudder," speaking slowly and smoothly. She looked at Matt. "He is remarkable," she whispered.

"I'm glad you think so," he replied. "No hard feelings?"

"Of course not. He's only a child."

"An eleven-year-old miniature adult—unfortunately."

Laura studied the two children again. "You're a lucky boy, Casey, to have such a terrific big brother." Casey grinned, but Brian turned red. Shoot! Preteens got embarrassed so easily.

She looked at the walls for another colorful distraction. Either corny or funny would do. "Hey, guys. There's a good one." She pointed to an impressively large sign in the center of the wall. "The Lobster Pot—Where No Lobster Is A Shrimp!"

Now *that* was funny. Laura grinned and sat back in her chair, totally relaxed as everyone started to laugh.

Then Casey said, "I—I—I don't get it." And everyone cracked up. Including Casey, who evidently just wanted to be part of the fun.

Matt winked at his son. "Don't worry about it, sport. It's vocabulary for another day." He looked around the table, his gaze settling on Laura. "Are we ready to order?"

"Lobster," she replied without hesitation.

"Lobster." "Lobster." "Lobster." Each one replied consecutively, barely glancing at the menus.

"Well, that's easy enough," said Matt. "Five lobster specials."

"And what a great choice that is! And so rare in a seafood restaurant!" An auburn-haired woman approached Matt, patted his shoulder and Sam's, but walked directly to Laura. "Hi, and welcome to Pilgrim Cove and to The Lobster Pot, the best fish house on the East Coast, or at least in Massachusetts." The woman extended her hand but never stopped talking. "I'm Maggie Quinn Sullivan, daughter of the one and only Bartholomew Quinn and partner in this restaurant. Since I'm not a modest woman, I'll tell you right out I'm a darn good cook, better than my sister, but don't mention that to her."

"Not a word. But I bet she says the same thing!" Laura laughed and shook the woman's hand. "I can't wait to put you both to the test. I'm famished!"

Maggie called to one of the wait staff. "Get a round of clam chowder over here before we lose a customer to starvation. It's on the house."

"Your sister is Thea Cavelli, right?" asked Laura. "I feel like I've been studying for a Pilgrim Cove exam."

"Not to worry," replied Maggie. "You'll know everyone soon enough." She looked up. "Good, here comes the chowder." She stood aside and waited as the waitress served the steaming thick soup.

Laura sipped her first spoonful and allowed the flavor to saturate her taste buds—delicious! Perfect texture. She savored another spoonful, then looked up at Maggie, who was obviously watching for Laura's reaction. Food was serious business here! Laura chuckled silently. Bart's daughter didn't have to lose sleep over the chowder.

"Better than in Boston, and I'm not kidding,"

Laura said, dipping her spoon again. "It's perfect in every way."

"And the Quinn sisters win over another loyal patron," joked Matthew.

"And proud of it," said Maggie, rapping him on the head with her knuckles. "Behave yourself."

Matt saluted as the woman waved and took herself to another table, greeting and chatting up her customers.

"She's a whirlwind," said Laura.

"If that's true, then her sister, Thea, is a tornado," replied Matt.

"They both take after their dad," said Sam. "You should have seen Bart in his prime. No one could keep up with him. And believe me, I tried." Sam Parker stared into the distance. "We were all full of piss and vinegar then."

"Grandpa!" Casey's voice combined astonishment and horror. "Wh-wh-what you said! L-L-Laura's here." And he covered Laura's hand with his small one and patted it as though to comfort her.

GREAT. Matt groaned inwardly. Just what he needed. His vulnerable son was taken with the woman who wanted to be left alone. If circumstances hadn't interfered when they'd all arrived at The Lobster Pot, Laura would have eaten by herself without thinking about it twice. She seemed to be an independent sort of woman.

But she had made an impression on Casey. She'd

picked up on his stutter without missing a beat and without making a big deal about it. Knowing about speech must be part of her business.

Even now, she and Casey were having a conversation next to him. Matt tuned in.

"S-s-sometimes, my—my—my words get stuck."

Matt's heart filled with pride. His son had to deal with his disfluency every single day, and meeting new people often produced extra stress. But this time, Casey seemed eager. Matt glanced at Brian to see if he'd noticed, but he and his grandfather were conducting their own conversation. Matt listened to that one, too. Baseball. Tryouts for Little League were a week away, and Brian's eyes glowed with anticipation. This year Casey would play, too.

Matt refocused on Laura and Casey.

"Sometimes the words sound bumpy." Laura spoke in an unhurried manner, reiterating Casey's statement, her attention never leaving the boy's face.

"Yeah!" replied Casey. "B-b-bumpy."

"Well," Laura continued, "talking is a skill. It takes time to learn, like sewing…"

Matt winced.

"…or throwing a basketball. Skills take practice, and sometimes we make mistakes."

"R-r-right," said Casey. "And ba-ba-baseball." The word exploded out of his mouth.

Time to join the conversation. "Casey and Brian

are going to Little League tryouts next week. It'll be Casey's first time.''

He watched a frown spread across Laura's forehead. "What exactly does that mean? Tryouts? No one's going to be left behind, are they?" Her eyes flashed, and she actually leaned toward Matt's son as if to protect him.

Whoa! She was a tigress. He wondered whether she knew how her indignation lit up her eyes. Too bad she had no interest in him. A light love affair would have suited him just fine. She was a pretty woman, her face as pleasing to the eye as her voice was to the ear. More important, she was also intelligent and kind. She laughed at the corny puns in The Lobster Pot. But she wasn't looking for anything more than a safe harbor in Pilgrim Cove. She'd made that perfectly clear the first day in Sea View House, although…she had shivered—a full-body shiver—when he'd whispered in her ear earlier this evening.

He sighed and erased any thoughts of pursuit. He wouldn't cross her boundaries, not when she brought smiles to his son's face and encouraged the little boy to speak to her. The value of confidence-building for the child could not be overestimated.

"Nah," piped up Brian, looking at Laura. "Nobody is left out. Everybody gets on a team. The coaches just try to spread the talent so there's good competition all season.

"Oh. That's all right then. Very fair.''

Typical girl attitude. But life, as Matt had learned, was not always fair.

His thoughts were interrupted by a high-pitched squeal followed by a tiny spinning female plopping on his lap.

"Hi, Uncle Matt!"

"Hi, sweet Katie. How's my best girl?"

"Fine. I just came from ballet. I was practicing my pirouettes. How'd you like 'em?"

"Is that what they were? I'm glad you landed on me. The floor would have been a little harder."

She wrinkled her nose, and Matt kissed it. "Where's your mom? Where's Papa Bart?"

"Her mom's right here." Lila's voice came from behind him and he turned around. At first glance, she looked as lovely as always, until Matt looked closer. Her face seemed thinner.

"You working too hard?" he asked.

"No Matt, I'm not." Lila gave his arm a squeeze. "How are you?" She surveyed the group at the table. "How's everyone? Hi again, Laura. Enjoying your meal?"

"You've already met?" Matt asked.

"Yes," Laura replied. "In Bart's office, when I spoke to him about renting Sea View House."

"In Pilgrim Cove, you run into people over and over again," Lila said, "so you might as well get used to it." She paused a moment. "By the way, how's the house working out for you? Anything wonderful happen to you yet?"

"Aha," Matt said. "Sea View House's reputation is on the line again!"

"Actually, the answer's yes," Laura replied. "I'm sleeping like a baby. The soundest sleep I've had in years."

Matt studied her. "I guess you really do need a vacation. Even a working one."

"Sea View House is different for everyone." Lila's eyes rested on Katie. "Some people find a night's sleep, and some find a night of love."

Matt knew immediately who she was thinking of. His brother, Jason. Katie's father. Sea View House must've been their special place. He squeezed her hand. "Are you okay, hon?"

"I'll be just fine, Matt. As my mom keeps telling me, it's time to move on." She scooped Katie from Matt's lap. "Come on, child of mine. We'll go visit Grandma and get some chowder."

"Can't I play with Casey?" the girl protested, squirming from her mother's arms.

"Maybe tomorrow."

"Dad's playing catch with us tomorrow morning," offered Brian. "He promised. We're practicing for tryouts next week."

"Good. I'm trying out, so I need to practice, too!" Katie replied with a grin. "What time should I come to your house?" She looked up at Matt with exaggeratedly innocent blue eyes, and all he could do was laugh.

He glanced at Lila. She nodded. "Nine o'clock,"

he said. "Let's hope it warms up outside, or it'll be the shortest practice in history."

Katie reached up and kissed him again, then walked around the table high-fiving everyone. When she got to Sam, she planted a kiss on each cheek. "Hi, Grandpa. See you tomorrow."

Matt watched Laura's focus move from Katie to Sam and back again, curiosity in her eyes, then understanding. But she didn't ask questions. He'd fill her in at some point, if she wanted to know. It's just that there wasn't much to tell. No one knew where Katie's father was. Not even Matt. And he'd gone searching for his brother through the years. Jason Parker did not want to be found.

"Seems to me," said Laura quietly, "that there's another pair of parents of married children among the ROMEOs."

"Not quite," said Matt, "on two counts. Bart's the grandfather. Lila's dad is Tom Sullivan—a teacher and coach at the high school and not yet a ROMEO— so the relationship would be between Tom Sullivan and my dad."

He paused, watching her expressive face as she processed the information. "And two," he continued, "Lila and Jason are not married."

LAURA CHECKED her rearview mirror a block from the restaurant. The Parker clan was following her home. She'd told Matt it wasn't necessary. At least three times. "No problem," he'd replied—three

times. She'd come to the conclusion that "no problem" was his favorite slogan, and that he'd do whatever he wanted. And as for paying her own way—at
least they'd allowed her to leave the tip. She'd started
to protest their generosity, but the look on the elder
Parker had stopped her. Sam was from another gen-
eration and a lovely man. She couldn't argue with
him. So she'd left the tip and shut her mouth.

And now she was driving along very dark streets,
the only light coming from lampposts along the way.
No moon to help out. Everything did look a little
different at night, but she had no problem finding her
way back to Beach Street. The only problem she en-
countered was misjudging the driveway in the darkness. She clipped the edge, but the car righted itself
quickly.

By the time she'd unlocked her door and climbed
out, Matt was striding toward her.

"Next time, make sure your porch light and the
pole lamp are on before you leave the house at
night." He pointed to the black pole with the glass
chimney on top located on the front lawn near the
sidewalk. "It makes a difference, since you're on a
corner and have no immediate neighbors at this time
of year. Most of the other houses are occupied only
in the summer."

"I understand. But I do have a couple of neighbors
on the next block across the street."

"Too far for illumination," Matt responded. "Let
me walk you in and show you where the switch is.

I'm surprised Ralph Bigelow hasn't dropped by to point out the circuit breakers and such.''

"Oh. He may have,'' said Laura. "But if he came around any afternoon this week, I wouldn't have heard him. I was sound asleep.''

He stared at her. "You really are suffering from burnout, aren't you?''

"Mmm. Something like that.'' She opened the front door, reached along the wall for the switch, then turned on the light. She stepped inside and waited for Matt to follow her. When she tilted her head back to look at him, his features were half in shadow, half in light. The planes of his face stood out in sharp relief, providing an overall impression of mystery.

She wished there was brighter lighting in the foyer. She didn't like mystery.

"Laura.''

She turned quickly at his serious tone. "Yes?''

"Are you ill?'' he asked gently. "Is that why you're sleeping so much? Is that why you came back to Pilgrim Cove?''

"No!'' She responded before taking a deep breath. He was hitting close to a nerve. "I'm not sick at all. Except for heartache and grief. My mom was ill for a long time. She just passed away. I took care of her for the most part—and, well, we had happy times here in Pilgrim Cove. So, I wanted…I thought…''

Good Lord! What had she really hoped to accomplish by returning? Could Pilgrim Cove provide her with happiness? Or even the hope of happiness? She felt her eyes fill as the truth hit with the delicacy of a sledgehammer. She'd wanted to be a carefree child again, and she'd run to Pilgrim Cove, to the memory of ten perfect summers. She must have been out of her mind to think she could recapture the past. No one could reverse the clock. A lucky childhood only happened once.

She breathed deeply, blinked back her tears and looked around her. Matt stepped closer and reached for her hands. "I'm very sorry about your mom, Laura. I know you want your privacy, but if there's anything you need, please call." He stared over her shoulder, shaking his head. "Somehow, life doesn't turn out the way it's supposed to, does it?"

"You're so right about that," she whispered.

His fingers pressed hers and she felt strangely comforted. Connected. For a brief moment.

And then Matt shifted gears. "The outside pole lamp is lit by the hall switch. Make sure it's on every time you go out at night. Leave a couple of lights burning inside, too. You could kill yourself in the dark."

"I hear you."

"Good. Lecture's over." But he continued to stare at her, without making a move to leave.

"Thanks for your concern," she said. "Hadn't you better go now? Your family's waiting."

He nodded. "I'll be back tomorrow afternoon to check out the apartment above yours. No one's renting it now, but summer's not so far off and I might as well inspect the pipes before the busy season gets here.''

Laura nodded. ''Upstairs is called The Crow's Nest, right?''

''Right,'' he said with a smile. ''But the pipes between the apartments are aligned, and I might have to get inside your place.''

''No problem.'' Her smile came naturally as she adopted his favorite phrase.

His eyes twinkled. ''Then, good night.''

But he paused, studying her again before opening the front door. He closed it behind him, and then shouted at her to lock up.

Bossy, wasn't he? She never forgot to lock up, and she turned the tumblers now. ''I'm all set,'' she called.

''Good.''

She pushed the curtain of the sidelight and watched him walk toward his van. He had an energetic stride even at the end of the day, and carried with him an air of confidence. He seemed comfortable with himself. Comfortable with his kids, with his business, with giving her orders about lights and locks.

Matt was an attractive, generous, what-you-see-is-what-you-get, uncomplicated guy who was great with children. He was either a lucky catch for some woman or simply too good to be true. Laura shrugged her shoulders. She wouldn't be around long enough to figure it out.

MATT GOT BEHIND the wheel of his vehicle, his mind spinning. Laura was going through an understandably hard time. Losing a parent was tough, and grieving was normal. Matt, himself, had gone through it when his mom had died. Not to mention Valerie, his wife. So Laura wasn't as complicated or mysterious as she'd seemed the first time they'd met.

"You could have spent longer saying your goodnights," said Sam. "I wouldn't have minded. Casey's fast asleep and Brian's yawning."

"And why would I have wanted to do that?" baited Matt as he pulled away from the curb. He knew full well what his matchmaking father was getting at. Any time a new woman appeared in town, usually during the summer, his dad always took notice...on Matt's behalf. Sam had lucked out this year. A new woman had shown up in early spring.

"Laura's a nice girl, son. Very lovely. I knew her parents. They were good people. Family people."

"I'm not looking, Pop. And you know it," Matt said quietly but firmly. Then he lowered his voice even further and nodded at the sleeping Casey. "Look how Valerie's death affected him. He feels deserted. I can't risk that happening again. So, no way am I getting involved."

Sam Parker sighed heavily. "Most young women don't get sick, Matt. You know that."

Matt patted his dad on the arm, ready to tease him. "I could be interested in Laura for a—shall we say—short-term arrangement on the side while she's here—"

"No, you won't," Sam interrupted in a flash, as Matt had known he would. "She's not *that* type of girl. And this is a small town. Leave her alone!"

Matt hooted quietly as he turned onto Bay Road, on the other side of the peninsula, about a mile and a half from Sea View House. "That's just what I had in mind to begin with, Pop. Leaving her alone."

"Joke around all you want, but I'll tell you what's not a joke," said Sam.

Matt glanced at his dad. "What's that?"

"That woman knows how to talk to Casey. Never saw anybody relate to him like she did."

"Grandpa's right," piped up a sleepy Brian from the back seat. "Laura was nice to Casey. She let him take his time. So it was okay that she ate with us."

Did his family think he hadn't noticed?

"So you liked Laura?" Sam asked his grandson, his voice encouraging.

"Yeah. Uh…as Casey's…uh…friend," replied Brian. "Like Dad always says, we don't need any ladies in our house. Right, Dad? We're fine the way we are."

BUT WERE THEY? Matt repositioned his pillow six different ways trying to get comfortable later that night. The outside temperature had dropped to almost freezing since they'd gone to the restaurant, cold enough to awaken Casey when Matt carried him inside. But now everyone was asleep under warm comforters except him. He was kicking his covers off! Because of Laura.

He sighed. The woman had been on his mind since he'd first seen her a week ago. Of course, that day at Sea View House wasn't actually the first time he'd met her. He could still remember kissing her soft lips all those years ago.

Their paths hadn't crossed much until that particular summer, her last one in Pilgrim Cove. At sixteen, Laura had seemed to blossom. She'd hung around with the other kids at Neptune's Park. All the teenagers held daytime jobs, so evenings reconnected them.

Laura had worked as a counselor at a day camp, Matt recalled. So maybe that's why she'd been so good with Casey tonight. She obviously liked children. As for Matt, he'd worked with his dad. It was as natural as breathing that he and Sam work together. And they'd continued to do so while Matt attended the regional community college. By then, Laura's family had stopped coming to Pilgrim Cove, and Matt had picked up with Valerie, a local girl.

He and Valerie had been casual school friends. Then they'd grown up and fallen in love. They'd had almost ten years together before she'd gotten sick.

Ovarian cancer. By the time she saw a doctor, the disease had spread. The best Boston hospitals couldn't save her, so Matt brought her home and took care of her. They'd clung to each other and cried at first, then Matt had moved beyond tears. Often he'd simply watch her breathe, not quite believing he was going to lose her. Later—much later—his tears flowed again.

And now he had to protect his children. He couldn't put them at risk again by allowing another woman into their lives. Brian had become quiet and withdrawn after his mother died, shadowing Matt's every step, afraid to let his father out of his sight. Normal behavior, according to the experts, but so unlike his elder son that Matt had never forgotten it.

And at three-and-a-half years old, Casey's speech development had begun to deteriorate. Starting in kindergarten, the public school had provided speech therapy twice a week, and it had helped. But the stuttering remained a challenge his little boy had to handle. The youngster had already had his share of teasing, but more was sure to come. And no one could protect him twenty-four/seven. Not even Matthew Parker, devoted dad.

Matt finally sat up against his pillows, hit the clock-radio button tuned to his favorite R & B station, and turned on the bedside lamp. He scanned the choices on his night table and automatically reached for the big Sunday crossword puzzle he kept there all week. No mystery or suspense fiction tonight. Real life was puzzling enough.

Had he done too good a job in persuading his kids women were not important, or even worse, that women were to be feared? Looking for reassurance,

Brian had asked, "We're fine the way we are. Right, Dad?"

In recent years, Matt had thought they were fine. In fact, more than fine. But tonight, he wasn't sure. Laura McCloud had returned to Pilgrim Cove. Laura McCloud had affected each member of the Parker family. And now Matt wondered if his solid male bastion had been built without a foundation.

CHAPTER FOUR

LATE THE NEXT MORNING, Laura opened the kitchen door, stepped onto her back porch to sample the air temperature, then quickly returned inside and shut the door behind her. Whew! Winter was hanging on. Couldn't be more than forty degrees outside. Her terry bathrobe was no protection.

She wondered if Matt would be able to have that promised baseball practice with the kids. Surely they'd have to postpone it. But then she pictured the eagerness in Casey's face, and Brian's, and Katie's...and knew that Matt wouldn't want to disappoint them. Somehow they'd manage to play ball.

She chuckled to herself while getting dressed. If she wouldn't let the weather cancel her walk, why should it cancel their practice? A red turtleneck shirt, black tights and leggings topped with her made-for-the-cold ski jacket, woolen hat and gloves were her basic armor against the cold. On her feet were a pair of wool-and-silk socks and fur-lined boots with thick rubber soles. Living in Boston had prepared her well.

Exiting Sea View House through the back porch, Laura walked directly down to the beach. The ocean surged, whitecaps topping every restless wave, and the horizon was invisible, lost in a blurry mist of gray water and equally gray sky. Laura paused to absorb the scene as she always did before walking. At the water's edge, every day was unique.

She turned north, bending into a light but steady wind, knowing she'd appreciate the push at her back on the way home. Despite the outdoor temperature, she warmed up as she strode, and her thoughts turned to last night's dinner at the Lobster Pot.

So many personalities. So many new sights. New people. And for the most part, a lot of fun. Fun! A pleasure she certainly hadn't expected to experience any time soon. Amazing how human nature seemed to discard expectations and rules. Her grief for her mom accompanied her everywhere, and yet she'd been able to laugh and joke last night. Maybe she needed more than solitary walks, as satisfying as they were. Maybe what she really needed was to enjoy the company of others. It was something to think about.

Almost an hour later, the house was in sight again. As Laura approached, she saw a familiar masculine figure, hands on the porch railing, his head turning one way and then another scanning the entire beach. No hat prevented his dark, wavy hair from blowing in the wind.

She called and waved to him, and could swear she saw his body relax as he turned and waited, his hip leaning against the wooden barrier.

"Good morning," he greeted, then checked his watch. "Or afternoon."

"Hi. You always seem to show up when I'm not home, don't you? Come on in. I've been outside long enough. Did you check the pipes yet?" She knew she was babbling, something she never did unless it was scripted into a commercial. She clamped her lips together and led him into the kitchen, pulling her hat and gloves off along the way, then her jacket, and hanging them all on a coat tree in the corner of the hallway.

"I have checked the upstairs—went in through the side entrance," Matt replied, following her into the house. "But that's not why I came over today."

His words and tone stopped her mid-stride, and she turned around to question him. Nothing came out of her mouth. His warm, dark eyes were fixed on her, barely blinking, as though memorizing her.

"You look…great," he said, sounding surprised. His hand lifted and his fingers stretched toward her. "Your skin is beautiful, rosy, your hair is wonderful." He touched a strand. "Maybe a walk on the beach is worth more than it seems."

"Or maybe I looked pretty awful when I showed up last Friday," she said with a smile.

He winced. "Oops. I didn't say that! Don't put words in my mouth."

But she continued to tease. "The difference in one short week seems to have been impressive. And in a month you'll be saying you don't recognize me!" A month? Suddenly she didn't feel like joking. A month seemed like a long time off. She'd been living her life day by day and couldn't think in terms of months yet.

She took a teakettle from the stove and filled it with water, then pointed to a seat and waited until Matt lowered himself into it. "So, what's on your mind, Matt?"

"On my mind?"

"Am I hearing imaginary voices, or did you say the plumbing was not your real purpose in visiting me today?"

"Yeah, I did. You're not crazy, but it is your fault that I've gotten distracted." He closed his eyes.

"It's Casey," he finally said. "I wanted—no, I needed—to talk to you about him."

Laura poured them each a cup of tea and sat across from Matt, waiting for him to continue.

"You handled Casey so well last night when he chatted with you," Matt said. "Lots of people are uncomfortable, and he picks up on their vibes very quickly. Adults often ignore him or finish his sentences for him or ask him to try harder." He leaned toward her. "Try harder! Can you imagine telling that child to try harder? Their so-called encouragement makes him feel worse. And I can't go around punching these idiots in the nose every time one of them hurts Casey's feelings—as much as I'd like to. Especially when I'm trying to teach Brian that fighting with kids who tease his brother doesn't help."

Laura saw the pain flash across his face. She reached toward him and gathered his fisted hand into both of hers. "I'm so sorry about the bad experiences you've had," she began. "Casey's such a sweet child. I'm not a therapist, but many of my courses did involve speech pathology and communication. That's why I can relate to Casey." She felt the tension slowly leave his fingers, and suddenly her two hands became engulfed in his much larger one. He squeezed gently.

"Thanks for listening," he said. "I wish I could educate the entire population of Pilgrim Cove." A crooked smile crossed his face.

"The entire town's not necessary," Laura said. "Casey's world is what's necessary. And from what I've seen, the most important people in his world are already doing the right things."

He exhaled audibly, pressed her hands again and sat back in his chair. "You don't realize how much I appreciate your words. I'm in touch with the school therapist regularly…it's just that the whole process takes so long. It's hard to measure results. And in the meantime, Casey's growing up and the events in his childhood will stay as memories. He's had enough lousy experiences. I want him to have good ones."

"I'm not a parent, Matt, but I'm sure you're underestimating yourself and the home you've provided. Casey's a happy kid."

But Matt shook his head. "Not always. He's come home crying more than once. He's sensitive, although for a seven-and-a-half-year-old, he's got grit. He participates in everything at school. His second-grade teacher is young and understanding. And that helps.''

Laura continued to listen while Matt described Casey's situation. The positives, the negatives. She offered no more than an occasional nod or ''Mmm-hmm.''

''…and we've all learned to speak more slowly in the family, to take turns talking and listening so there are few interruptions.'' Matt finally paused and glanced at the wall clock. ''My God, I've talked your ear off!''

Laura immediately pulled her earlobe. ''Nope. It's still here. I didn't mind listening at all. My pleasure.'' And it was a pleasure to see him more relaxed about Casey. Not that she could take much credit. He'd talked himself around. But now she wanted to discuss the real challenges Casey had ahead of him.

''Think for a moment about what Casey needs to master,'' she began. ''You and I take speaking for granted, but it's really a very complex, coordinated process from the brain to the muscles in the mouth, face, neck, tongue and throat. So when there's a problem, it takes a long time to fix it.''

''I know, I know,'' Matt admitted. ''I get so frustrated sometimes.''

''Imagine how Casey feels! Life's about communication, and he's got seventeen vowel and twenty-four consonant sounds in the English language to master. That's several hundred sound combinations. Give him a break!''

Matt started to laugh, a rich, deep, almost happy sound.

''And give yourself a break while you're at it.'' Laura rested against the back of her chair. ''I'm glad you felt comfortable enough to stop by, Matt. If I can do anything to help with Casey, just ask.''

''I'll hold you to that,'' he replied. ''But now, tell me about your work. What exactly does it involve?''

''Okay,'' said Laura, ''but it will be easier if I show you.''

She led him into the spare bedroom, furnished like a study, where her computer was set up on a table. ''This is how I prepare for a taping and why I say speech is my business. I'm actually part announcer, part narrator, part actress, part listener, part computer tech, part voice coach and I'm always conscious of my diction and modulation.''

''All I see is a computer,'' said Matt.

''That's almost all I need,'' Laura replied, sitting in front of the machine and turning it on. ''It's programmed with a timer, so I can pace myself as I practice. I can also set the timer, like an alarm clock. The script is on the screen, of course, and the clock runs in its own window in the corner. I also use a mike and record myself, then listen to the playback.''

''Neat,'' said Matt. ''You've got a portable skill you can take anywhere. Have voice, will travel. And don't forget the computer.''

"The bad part is that I haven't done any work at all since I arrived at Sea View House," Laura said. "And there are two scripts I need to work on. My agent will be on my case soon. Norman's got high hopes for rebuilding my career."

"That's great! I bet you're excited."

"I am, but…I guess I'm still tired. The spark's gone out of my engine."

"You've only been here a week." Matt stepped closer to her and gently put his hands on her arms. "You need time, Laura. Grieving's a hard process."

His words were as warm as his touch, his voice tender. She could have melted into him had she allowed herself. "Right," she whispered, moving out of his reach just as the phone rang.

Laura dashed back to the kitchen, grateful to focus on someone other than Matthew Parker. Until she heard Norman Cohen's cheerful voice. And he was cheerful. Full of news about upcoming projects. He'd been busy.

"A week from Monday?" she squealed.

She listened while he explained the assignment, an opportunity she couldn't refuse. "Okay," she said. "I'll see you next Monday."

She had to get back in gear within nine days. Norman was right. She had a career to regrow.

"Who was that?" asked Matt.

Laura looked up, startled to see that he was still there. "That was my agent." She nodded to the spare bedroom they'd just vacated. "I'm taping those two scripts a week from Monday. And then Filene's Department Store wants three voice-overs for Memorial Day television ads for big summer sales. Thirty seconds each. I've done work for them before and they asked for me! So I've got to get back on the ball.''

''Does that mean back to Boston?'' asked Matt, a frown forming on his forehead. ''You just got here.''

She stared at him. ''Do you think I dragged all that equipment for nothing? I'll take the ferry into Boston. But it seems,'' she added, ''that my time to hide is over. I can't afford to turn these opportunities down. Besides, working hard will also help me get back to myself. It's called therapy.''

Matt didn't say anything, but his dark eyes shone with approval. After a few moments, he turned to leave. ''I've got to get back to the shop. The boys are there with my dad and the staff, and Saturdays are usually busy.''

She walked with him toward the front door. ''By the way, did you and the kids have that practice this morning?''

He rolled his eyes in answer. ''The Butterfingers Team made out just fine in my garage. Unfortunately, the walls took a few hits.''

Laura smiled. ''I'm glad,'' she said, ''that you all had a good time.''

''Three out of four isn't bad,'' replied Matt with a wink.

MATT OPENED Laura's front door and stepped outside, immediately noticing the drop in temperature. The gray sky had darkened while he'd been inside. He turned back, intending to knock again, but Laura was still standing where he'd left her, the door ajar.

He pointed to the sky. "See those clouds? They're blacker than they were earlier and full of rain. The temperature is dropping, and the wind is out of the northeast."

"Shoot! Isn't it too late in the season for a nor'easter?"

"Not too late for freezing rain," Matt replied. "With all the ice that can form, it's often worse than a snowstorm."

Laura nodded, at first looking glum, then resigned. "Thanks for the warning."

"Here's another one," said Matt. "The electricity can go when the power lines get caked with ice, or more likely, when a motorist hits a pole. Do you have flashlights? Can you light a fire in the fireplace and keep it going? Is there any wood in the wood box?"

Her eyes widened, her jaw dropped and he had his answers. No, no and no.

"I'll go to the store right now," she said, "and get flashlights."

"Forget it," he replied, his tone sharp. "I've got spares in the truck. Take down some extra blankets because you've got to stay warm if the heat goes. The house will get cold quickly."

He stomped to the curb, annoyed by his reaction. Or was he annoyed by his attraction to her?

She seemed so fragile, as if she needed to be taken care of. But not by him! Damn! How could she have all kinds of special software for the computer and not one basic flashlight! Clueless. The lady was clueless.

He shook his head. Earlier, he'd wanted to ask her out to dinner. Dinner by themselves someplace. A man and a woman on a date, if that was what two adults going out alone for pleasure was still called. Now he was glad he hadn't asked.

The small dart of fear that had stung him two seconds ago was a reminder. Not fear of the storm, but fear of getting too involved.

Matt jerked the truck door open. He was better off alone with his boys. And that was a fact. That way his heart wouldn't get broken again. Six years ago, his mother had died. Some said her illness prevailed because a woman with a broken heart couldn't fight back. Those had been hard times, with one brother dead and one gone away, but Matt didn't agree with the theory. He knew cancer was a matter of early detection and medical treatment. Both his mom and his wife had gotten too little too late and lost the battle. They'd passed away within two years of each other. Casey had been almost four and Brian almost eight years old when their mother had died and Sam had moved in.

Matt walked back to the house, still shaking his head. Getting involved with Laura would only mean trouble, and he and his boys didn't need any more of that. They'd make out fine without a woman in the house.

Laura still stood in the doorway, a bulky sweater wrapped around her. He handed her the flashlights.

"The batteries are good," he said abruptly. "But call me if you need anything else."

"I'll be fine," she replied, her chin raised. "Thanks for your help." She closed the door and locked it.

Obviously she'd picked up on his critical tone— and he wasn't sorry. For Casey's sake, he'd promote only a professional friendship with Laura. He walked back to the van, got behind the wheel and gunned the engine. After executing the sloppiest U-turn in the history of Pilgrim Cove, he headed back to the store.

MATT KNEW ABOUT WEATHER. Laura had to give him credit for that much. Standing at the living room window, she was barely able to see the tree branches turning in the wind and rain. The stygian darkness indicated a cloud-covered sky. No moon to illuminate the outside, and only Matt's flashlights to brighten the inside.

This was a storm for the ears, not the eyes. Ice pebbles beat against the house, an unending staccato of sound. Small tree branches snapped and whirled down the street while the larger branches stayed bowed to the ground. Coated in thick ice, every tree looked like a weeping willow frozen in place. But these trees were noisy, emitting the loud creaking sounds of changing ice formations.

The rain had started about two hours ago at five o'clock, but had quickly turned to sleet and hadn't let up. The house had gone dark within the past half hour. Laura wasn't worried and wasn't cold—yet. She'd coped with winter weather all her life. She knew to choose the insulated warmth that layers of clothing provided rather than the weight of one heavy garment, so she'd donned long johns and wool socks, flannel shirt and leg warmers, sweater and a down vest. And to think, she almost hadn't brought any of them! Her image of Pilgrim Beach had been a sunny summertime visual, but her practical side had prevailed when she'd finally packed her bags.

She turned from the window with the thought of making a sandwich of some kind—no tea, of course—when she heard a cry, a sound different from the sounds of the storm. She bent down, head to the windowsill, shut her eyes and listened hard.

A baby's cry. Her hands prickled, her breath shortened. Her whole body tensed, but she forced herself to focus on the sound. Again the cry reached her. Through the window. But from where? Now Laura didn't wait. She clutched her flashlight with one hand and pulled open the front door with the other while her mind raced. How could a baby…

The windblown, icy rain slashed against her, the roofed porch providing no protection. She pointed the flashlight on the ground near the window and saw nothing. She walked the length of the porch and back to where she'd started. The cry came again, soft and difficult to place. Laura headed down the steps hugging the banister with one arm. Her hair was plastered against her head; ice crystals pelted her face. The flashlight's beam was like a vapor against the elements.

"Hello," she called, squinting against the rain. A pathetic bleat answered her. She twirled around and searched the ground beside the steps. And there, huddled in the corner, was a kitten. A kitten as dark as the night.

Laura snatched it up and made her way back inside. She was relieved at the success of her search, but astonished that baby felines could sound so human. The house was a quiet refuge after being outdoors in the wind and freezing rain, and both the kitten and she were soaked. The poor little thing shivered uncontrollably. Flashlight in hand, Laura headed for the bathroom, grabbed some towels and wrapped the kitten in one. Then she made her way into the bedroom.

The phone rang. "Of all the times…if Alison was calling with stories of wonderful Atlanta weather…." Although she was grateful that so far the regular phone lines hadn't been affected by the storm, Laura kept muttering as she stumbled her way to the phone, kitten in one arm.

"Hello," she snapped.

"What's wrong?" Matt's voice.

"Not a thing."

"Good. I'm coming to get you. The electricity will be out for hours yet. Your house will be as cold as a tomb."

"I appreciate the thought, Matt, but I can get along just fine. Unlike what some people may think, I'm not an idiot who can't take care of herself."

Silence on the other end. She wasn't surprised at his reaction, only surprised at herself. She didn't usually snap at unintentional insults, but he'd made her feel stupid when he'd left her house earlier and she hadn't liked it.

"I've got a wood-burning stove. A big one." Matt's voice was soft and coaxing. "With a lot more brightness and heat than those flashlights can give you. My living room is warm and dry. Any clear-headed, intelligent woman such as yourself would recognize the advantages on a night like this."

Laura grinned, suddenly happier. On a night like this, she could think of other warm activities. She looked at the kitten who was rubbing against her non-stop. "Hold on," she said, putting the receiver down and wrapping the cat in another dry towel. She picked up the phone again. "Okay. We'll come. But I need some time. I'm soaking wet."

"Wet? What's going on? And who's 'we'?" The softness was gone. He sounded like a man who wanted answers.

"I have a kitten. Do you have any milk?"

"Good Lord! You were out in this nightmare rescuing animals? Laura, you need to wipe down right now. Down to the skin, you hear? Dry clothes next to your body, and dry your hair as best you can. I'll be there as soon as possible.''

CHAPTER FIVE

DESPITE HAVING A FLASHLIGHT, Laura could barely see into her dresser drawers as she scavenged for fresh clothes and grabbed anything that promised warmth. She'd be able to start her own line of winter wear and call it "hodgepodge." The kitten watched her from the middle of the queen-size bed, where it was wrapped in an extra wool blanket Laura had hauled down from the closet shelf.

"Sure glad one of us can see in the dark," she murmured, struggling into the dry clothing. She looked at the kitten. "But you're no help to me at all."

A pitiful meow answered her, and Laura chuckled as she again rummaged through the closet, this time to find a tote bag in which to carry the cat. "Come on, sweetie. You'll be protected in here when we leave." She gently placed the still-swaddled kitten in the bag and carried it with her to the bathroom, where she wrapped her own head in a bath towel, turban-style. It was the best she could do; her woolen hat was soaking wet and unusable. She gathered her comb and brush, tossed them into her purse, and then threw in her cosmetics case.

Carefully making her way to the front of the house, she paused only to take her winter coat from the closet and put it on. With the tote bag on one arm and her purse on the other, she was ready. She aimed a beam of light on her watch. Matt would probably arrive at any moment, although she couldn't imagine how any vehicle could grip the road now. Almost four hours had passed since the storm started. Much sleet and hard ice had accumulated on the streets.

She stood at the sidelight, peering into the dark night on Beach Street. Freezing rain still pelted the ground. The tote bag jiggled on her arm, and she spoke softly to the kitten but didn't lift it out.

The house was chilly, the residual heat dissipating rapidly, and Laura shivered first from the plummeting temperature and then from concern. Where was Matt? Visions of his van sliding into a telephone pole flashed through her mind, and another shiver ran through her.

A moment later, however, a pair of headlights pierced the darkness, but the vehicle wasn't familiar. Disappointment hit her, until the car pulled to a stop in front of the house. The driver's door opened and all Laura could see was a big black umbrella and then a pair of long legs and work boots walking toward her. Definitely Matt. Moving through the ice and slush almost as though they didn't exist.

"New car?" she asked, stepping aside when he reached the door.

"The family car," he corrected, walking inside. "An SUV with all-wheel drive. Good in slippery conditions." He looked at her. "We'll be all right, Laura. Don't worry. You'll be safe."

His quiet reassurance calmed a last nerve, and his sincerity warmed her. A ringing phone shattered her thoughts for the second time that evening, and Laura startled. She walked to the kitchen, Matt following her. "At least the phone still works," she said.

"For now."

She picked up the receiver and Bart Quinn's familiar voice came to her over the cables. "I'm concerned about you, Laura McCloud. Have you any heat or light out there at Sea View House?"

Out there? Laura grinned. The house was part of the town, wasn't it? "No, Mr. Quinn, but I'm fine."

"Is that Bart?" asked Matt.

Laura nodded in the dark, then spoke. "Yes, it's Bart."

"Do you mind?" Matt asked softly, reaching for the phone. "Hello, Bart. It's Matt Parker. I just got here and I'm taking Laura home with me now. She won't be alone in this freezing mess." He was quiet a moment. "Sure, I'm prepared. I've got chains on the rear wheels. We'll be fine." He handed the phone back to Laura.

"You're in good hands, my dear," came the Irishman's voice. "Matt's got a sensible head on his shoulders. I always say it's a lucky house, that Sea View House! Always believed in it myself.''

Laura could imagine the old gent rubbing his hands together in glee. "Thanks for…'' She hung up. "The line's gone dead.'' She looked at Matt. "Bart Quinn's just a mischievous leprechaun!''

Matt chuckled. "I've heard his Rosemary call him that more than a few times in my life! But he loves looking after this property, and he's collected a lot of terrific stories about past tenants. Maybe he'll show you the latest volume of the Sea View House Journal. Who knows? You might be writing in it yourself one day. Now, let's get going.''

She had no quarrel with that directive and followed him to the front porch. Then she carefully locked the door, more out of habit than to prevent vandalism. Not a soul would be out on such a night. The big golf umbrella protected her a bit as they crept down the stairs, hanging on to the railing and trying to keep their footing on the ice. Finally they reached the SUV, and Laura almost fell into the front passenger seat.

Hot air blew against her face. Delicious. Matt handed her the tote bag with the kitten, which was crying again. She scooped it out and started petting the dark fur. She felt the ridges of backbone and ribs. The poor thing needed food.

Matt got into the car, threw the umbrella in the back and watched Laura whisper baby noises to the cat as she dried his coat. "Come here,'' he said, switching on the interior light.

Puzzled, Laura turned to him. He reached over and suddenly her turban was gone and her damp hair was jumbled everywhere. "What are you doing?"

He nodded at the vents. "Might as well dry you, too. Give me the cat and get to work on yourself."

"You *are* bossy," Laura said, nonetheless complying with his suggestion. She knew that without her gel and spray and other guck, her curls would definitely resemble a bird's nest. Maybe Matt's kids had a baseball cap she could borrow. The thought made her feel better and she leaned over to get the most of the air flow.

It took a minute before she realized that Matt hadn't started to drive, nor had he made any move to pull away from the curb. "Do you think it's too dangerous?" Laura asked, sitting straight in her seat again, still finger-combing her hair.

"No, I'm just waiting until you're done and buckled up. No hurry." His voice was rich and calm, lingering.

She glanced up at him. His dark eyes glowed with warmth as he leaned back against the door, looking as though he could sit there forever.

She felt herself blush at his undivided attention, at his admiration and interest. Needing a distraction, she snatched her hairbrush from her bag and tugged it through her strands, or tried to. "I may look like a wild woman, but at least it's getting dry."

"Wild and wonderful," he said softly. "I like it.

Your hair's the color of honey right from the hive. You're a golden girl.''

Totally unexpected, his words were sweeter than the honey he'd mentioned, a balm to her bruised self-image. She'd tried hard to bury all her feminine yearnings and desires as she'd gone through her treatments and afterward, but Matt's one little compliment reminded her that she was still a woman. In every sense.

She blinked rapidly to hold back unexpected tears, then took a deep breath. To what end were his compliments? To what end his admiration? She couldn't allow a serious relationship to grow. Not with her medical background, not with her body. And not with someone she wanted as a friend for the long haul. As a friend to look forward to seeing whenever she returned to Pilgrim Cove. For she would come back. She already loved the town, the people and the memories it held for her.

She needed a friend. Not a lover.

DID SHE THINK she could hide her loveliness behind chatter and a mop of wild curls? Did she think he wouldn't notice the beauty behind the despair in her big blue eyes? She'd been touched by his words— he'd seen her reaction—but it didn't make sense to him. He turned off the inside light, then stretched and squared his shoulders as if for battle. He shifted the car into drive.

Time was on his side. On his side for what?

The rotten weather prompted extra concentration, a good excuse for Matt to shift his thoughts. Bay Road loomed just ahead, and he eased into a right turn. "Almost home," he said. "I left the garage door open so we could drive right in. No use getting wet again."

"Thanks," she replied. "And thanks for thinking of me."

The challenge was in *not* thinking of her! But she didn't know that.

"No problem."

For some reason, she started to giggle, and he was reminded of bubbles in a glass of champagne. Delicious. "What's so funny?" he asked, feeling a smile stretch across his own face.

"You."

"Huh?"

"Matthew 'No Problem' Parker."

He made the connection. "I have a limited vocabulary," he deadpanned, while mentally noting the irony. No problem? Laura McCloud was turning out to be the biggest problem on his horizon since Valerie had died and Casey had begun to stutter.

"Right," Laura said. "Now tell me something I'll believe."

He didn't have to think about that one. "How about, 'I'm glad you're here.'" He pulled into the open garage and shut the motor.

"I'm glad we're both here," Laura replied, "in one piece. So thanks again."

"No pro…" Matt began, but then changed to, "my

pleasure,'' and took pleasure in hearing her laugh once more.

A minute later, holding the squirming tote bag and a flashlight, Matt led Laura into his house. It was after ten o'clock, and he hoped the boys were already asleep. No such luck. His dad's scary storytelling voice carried through the halls.

''...give me back my golden arm....''

Ghost stories. Just what they needed for the kids to stay up all night. And probably the only thing that could have distracted them from his and Laura's arrival. He led Laura to the living room and paused, appreciating the live portrait of his father and sons, wrapped in blankets and sitting around the wood-burning stove as though it were a campfire out on the open range. The doors of the stove were open, and the firelight cast a warm glow on all their faces. The boys' eyes were glued to their grandpa.

Matt looked at Laura, and she smiled back. ''You've got a beautiful family,'' she said. And instantly, the portrait disassembled. Two young boys in flannel pajamas jumped up and ran to him. Sam got out of his rocking chair and walked over, greeting Laura with words of welcome, urging her to warm up by the stove.

''Laura, L-L-Lau-ra. You c-can hear the s-s-story, too.''

''I think the story's going to wait, sport,'' Matt said, slipping off his jacket and holding the tote bag toward Laura. "Take a look at what Laura brought with her."

He watched as Laura removed the kitten from the bag and unwrapped the blanket. He watched as the boys crowded around her.

"O-o-oh...a kitten."

"It's awfully small," said Brian.

"It's a b-b-ba-by! It's go-gonna grow." Casey looked at Matt as if to say, "right?" And Matt nodded, basking in his son's grin, knowing he should appreciate the moment. In a few years, Casey would realize that his dad didn't know everything.

"I'm afraid it won't grow if we don't feed it," said Laura. "I don't know the last time it ate."

"How come?" asked Brian.

"She found it outside in the freezing cold rain and got soaked rescuing it," explained Matt.

"Oh-h-h," replied the boys in unison.

"Did you hafta cli-i-mb a t-t-tree?" Casey's eyes were two golden saucers, and even Brian looked impressed.

For a moment, Laura wished she *had* climbed a tree! The children's admiration felt unexpectedly wonderful. "No trees," she said. "Just down some steps."

Matt leaned into Laura and whispered, "They're your friends for life now."

Five minutes later, three adults and two children stared at the kitten while it ate a portion of tuna and dry cereal and lapped up a saucer of milk.

"We-e-e never had a kitten before," Casey said.

"And you still don't," replied Matt. "The cat belongs to Laura."

"I know," Casey said, his smile fading. "But m-m-may-be I can help you t-t-take care of it." He turned to Laura, his eyes beseeching.

Matt watched Laura speak to Casey, heard her voice calm and soft and relaxed. "I'd like that. But first, I'll need to take him or her to the vet for a checkup. We've got to make sure it's healthy."

"Her," said Matt. "Definitely a female feline. Miss Puss-In-Boots." He grabbed a section of newspaper and gave it to the boys. "First chore...tear it up in strips and make a litter box. And then we'll toast some marshmallows."

"Yes!" said Brian.

With the kitten curled in her blanket and the boys busy, Matt turned his attention to Laura. "You're wearing your coat and you've been near the stove for a while. Are you still feeling chilled?"

She shook her head and smiled at him. "On the contrary, I'm feeling toasty." Then she nodded at the children, her expression soft and tender. "Your family is wonderful. And you, Matthew Parker, are a very lucky man." Her sincerity rang clear, but her voice, that beautiful voice, trailed away on a note of... sadness.

He was shaken by her tone. Shaken by the yearning

on her face when she looked at his children. Had her mother's death put the sadness in her eyes? Or was there something else?

LAURA'S LIMBS FELT like rubber, so comfortable was she sitting on a floor cushion, leaning against the couch and staring into the open fire. The boys were still tossing in their sleeping bags, somewhere between asleep and awake.

"Dad, sing something." Brian's voice.

"Yeah," whispered Casey. "Sing s-something nice."

Closer to awake, she thought, her eyes traveling from Casey to Matt, who was feeding chunks of wood into the stove. He glanced at her, then at the fire, then back to her and winked. Then she heard the quietly sung words, "'Oh, give me a home, where the buffalo roam…'"

She smiled at his choice of song, but there was nothing funny about his voice. The man could carry a tune! A beautiful tenor. She'd heard Bart mention that the Parker family all played the piano, but hadn't heard they could sing, too.

"'And the deer and the antelope play,'" Casey sang in a clear boyish soprano.

Laura swiveled toward the child. He was leaning back on his elbows, staring at his father. Watching.

"'Where seldom is heard…'" Three voices as Brian joined in.

"'A discouraging word,'" continued the trio.

"'And the skies are not cloudy all day.'" Sam Parker added his baritone at the end.

Laura listened to the boys and their grandpa carry the tune while Matt harmonized. Casey didn't miss a note. Not once did he struggle with his words. She knew that during choral recitations or group singing, stuttering almost always disappeared. There was something about speaking or singing in unison that helped, and there was a phrase for it in the literature. She put her fingertips to her forehead and concentrated on remembering everything she'd ever learned about disfluency. "Delayed auditory feedback," she exclaimed softly to herself. "That's it." She'd do a little research. See if anything new was going on in the field.

She refocused her attention on the men's chorus and started to hum along. Casey looked at her, and she gave him a thumbs-up. His grin was worth everything.

The last chorus faded away. Matt walked to Brian, then to Casey, tucking them into their sleeping bags again, reestablishing contact, speaking quietly to each. Then he looked at Sam. "You all set, Pop? Want another pillow?"

"I'm fine, Matt. Going to close my eyes. You take care of Laura now. Make sure she's warm enough."

"I'll do that."

And then the only noise in the room was the crackling of the fire. Laura watched as Matt added another split log to the stove, then walked across and lowered himself beside her on the floor, legs stretched in front of him. "Ready to go to sleep yet?" He patted the couch behind them. "It's all yours…unless…you want some company."

His dark eyes twinkled. She knew he was teasing but felt herself blush at the thought.

"You need to feed the fire all night," she replied.

"Exactly." Now her face burned at her ingenuous remark, and she turned away from him for a moment. Having fair skin was a strong disadvantage at times.

Then she pointed at the stove. "*That* fire!"

"Oh," he said with an air of such mock disappointment that she had to chuckle.

"If you behave yourself," she said, "I'll turn a loaf of bread into the most delicious French toast you ever ate—provided the electricity is on tomorrow morning."

"Wow. Serious competition for Dee Barnes at The Diner, huh? I'll be good," he promised. "Can't deprive my family of a home-cooked meal."

She didn't reply, but the silence between them was comfortable as they sat next to each other, staring into the bright orange flames. Matt's arm was still resting on the couch behind her, and she wanted to lean back and feel the weight of it around her. She'd seen the interest in his eyes, the curiosity and admiration. He'd wrap himself around her with the slightest encouragement.

So she did nothing except watch the fire. And dream.

Her eyes closed, her head nodded, and a moment later she was enveloped in a cocoon of warmth beyond the scope of a wood-burning stove. A cocoon of human warmth. She leaned into it and heard a satisfied sigh.

"Stubborn lady."

Whispered words floated in the air around her and then into her semiconscious mind. *Tomorrow. I'll be stubborn tomorrow. But right now, I need...this. I need Matt.*

Matt looked down at the woman in his arms, the woman who, in her sleep, cuddled next to him with the same trust as the kitten had shown her. He'd lined the floor with almost all the blankets in the house, but their makeshift bed still wasn't the softest place to sleep. He placed a pillow between her back and the couch, and shifted her farther across his chest. Hmm. His arm tightened. Felt good having her there.

A sudden image of Laura as a teenager flashed through his mind. Long legs, trim body and laughing face. Always in motion. She'd caught his attention that summer, and he remembered his disappointment when her family hadn't returned the following year. He remembered the kiss they'd shared half his lifetime ago. Sweet, natural, trusting. After he initiated the first light contact, she'd responded and he'd followed her lead, not wanting to rush her, not wanting to scare her away.

She'd been a happy, outgoing girl. Now she was a quiet, self-contained woman. Intelligent. Articulate.

Reserved. He missed her spontaneity. Her laughter. But at least, she had returned.

He stared at the blond curls, helpless to resist touching them. Stroking them. Then he stared at her profile—creamy skin, short straight nose and long lashes feathering her cheek. He could have studied her for hours.

Instead, his gaze swept across the room, resting first on his sons, then on his dad, then at the room itself, with the mementos of family living. In his mind's eye, he pictured the rest of the house. The eat-in kitchen, the dining room with its chronically home-work-strewn table, the three bedrooms upstairs. The boys shared the master bedroom while he and his dad had smaller rooms. A sensible arrangement after Sam had moved in. And if Sam's arthritis got much worse, Matt would build out a bedroom on the first floor. His thoughts moved to the basement, where he'd paneled the walls and laid industrial carpeting on the floor. Instant playroom for his sons. Handy for his own sanity when they were cooped up in the winter.

He felt good about the house. It was strong and well-built. More important, it was well used. He had turned a house into a home. For the sake of his boys. For his dad. For himself.

And now it wasn't enough.

The thought hit him with the velocity of a fastball to the gut. He looked at the beautiful woman in his arms and was suddenly afraid. Somehow, Laura McCloud had gotten past the armor he'd worn since

Valerie's death. Somehow, she'd managed to crack it open.

Laura murmured in her sleep and threw her arm across his chest, igniting a band of fire.

He sucked in air. "Holy Toledo," he muttered as he shakily exhaled while tucking a blanket more snugly around them both, "It's going to be one hell of a night."

THE SUN'S GLARE WOKE Laura the next morning. She opened her eyes and promptly closed them again, burrowing back into…into what? She groped her immediate surroundings…felt a strong heartbeat under her palm; her leg seemed plastered against a tree trunk. Blankets lay half on and half off, tangled around. She yawned and, little by little, her memory returned. The ice storm. The kitten. Matt's house. Fully conscious now, she took inventory of her limbs. His limbs. The tree trunk was Matt's leg. She tried to sit up but was off balance and fell back to where she'd started, her head on Matt's shoulder.

"What's your hurry?" Matt's low voice sounded like a rumbling locomotive. "Look around. Everyone's still sleeping."

She couldn't respond immediately. She was using all her energy to pretend that waking up on top of a man was no big deal. *Be cool, Laura. Matt's fully dressed and so are you. You haven't been sleeping together in the real sense. You've been camping out indoors. That's all.* Talking to herself wasn't a bad thing, was it?

She felt his arm come around her back, lightly holding her next to him, and God help her, she didn't want to budge. *Get a grip, girl!*

She looked over at the boys. They were still in their sleeping bags.

"And besides," Matt continued, squeezing her closer, "I like you next to me like this."

"You're just looking for creature comfort." She gave voice to her thoughts with a touch of desperation.

He was silent for a moment. "You must be right," he conceded, matching her quiet diction. "I was scared stiff of the storm and desperately needed your comfort." But his eyes were twinkling, revealing the truth.

Of course, he hadn't been frightened of the storm, of the ice, of the driving! He hadn't been frightened of anything.

"I haven't had any kind of relationship with a woman in four years, Laura, other than occasionally...well, never mind that." No humor laced his words now, and Laura was startled at the complete change of mood.

"Haven't wanted a relationship," he continued. "Haven't looked for one. But with you...there's something about you. I like having you here. In my home. With my family." He stared at the ceiling as he spoke, not meeting her eyes.

If she didn't know better, she would have thought he was either embarrassed about his feelings or afraid of her. But he didn't have to be. She had no intention of threatening his way of life.

"Thank you for making me feel welcome here, Matt. Your friendship means a lot to me, but you can relax. I'm not looking for an intimate relationship, either. I actually prefer my privacy." She tried to laugh. "As the great old-time actress said, 'I vant to be alone.'"

He looked down at her then, straight into her eyes. She couldn't turn away. "When did you start lying to yourself?" asked Matt.

"Lying? What are you talking about?"

"You no more want to live the rest of your life alone than the birds and the bees do," Matt replied.

This time she managed to sit up. "How can you say that? You don't know me!"

"I just spent a night with you, Laura. You're the cuddler type."

She felt the heat travel from her chest to her neck and face. He had a way of disconcerting her without trying very hard.

"Laura," he whispered, tenderly stroking her cheek. "Don't be distressed. We *both* slept well last night. Very well."

That wasn't what she wanted to hear.

"I know you're grieving for your mom, Laura, and that your energies have been used up in recent times. In fact, you've probably been exhausted lately. But, honey, I'm here to tell you that you're alive and healthy. You're just a little off course about life right now. Trust me, your needs and emotions are as normal as anyone's.''

She knew that, but she also knew she couldn't give in to them. She couldn't expect him to understand; he didn't know everything about her. And he never would. But for now, she'd allow him to believe whatever he wanted to.

She smiled and rose from the floor. ''I treasure my friends, Matt. Can we leave it at that?''

He got up in one fluid motion. ''I'll be here for you.''

Maybe. Maybe not. Her old boyfriend, Donald Crawford, had said the same thing during her mom's illness. She mentally shrugged. Matt's actions didn't matter in the long run. She'd be gone in another two months anyway.

''Is the electricity back yet?'' she asked, changing the subject. ''And the kitten! Where's the kitten?'' She began a frantic search.

''Yup, it's back. Haven't fed the fire in three hours. And look over there.'' Matt nodded at the black tail sticking out from Casey's partially zipped sleeping bag.

''Well, what do you know about that?''

''A good dad deserves a good breakfast. I promised French toast and I'm going to deliver.''

He smiled, his black eyes glittering. ''I have no doubt. No doubt at all.''

AN HOUR LATER, all Laura was worried about was having enough bread to satisfy the appetites of the four Parker men. Brian polished off six slices of the fried bread after drenching his plate in maple syrup, while Casey ate four.

"Good Lord," she said. "I can't remember Alison and I ever eating more than two slices at a time."

"That's cause you're girls. Girls don't eat a lot. They want to be skinny." That was Brian's pronouncement.

"Ka-Ka-a-tie eats a lot and she's s-s-skinny," replied Casey, wrinkling his face.

"That's cause she's still a kid," said Brian. "Just like you."

"I w-w-wish I—I—I was big-ger," said Casey.

"You will be, sport," Matt said. "Growing just takes time."

"Yeah," he sighed. "Too long."

Laura remembered feeling the very same way when she was young. "What's the hurry?" she asked. "Anything in particular?"

Casey glanced at Brian, then down. "No. Nothing." He turned to Laura. "What you going to name the kitten? Are you going to keep it?" He stuttered on and off as he spoke.

Laura sat down and placed her coffee cup on the table. She began cutting her food. "Good questions, Casey. And the answer to both is the same—I don't know."

"How come?" Brian asked, his curiosity tinged with concern. "The kitten's cute."

"First, I need to make sure she's healthy. Is there a veterinarian in town?" She aimed her question at the group in general, and this time Sam Parker answered.

"We've got a new one. Name of Fielding. Opened a practice near the neck."

"The neck?"

"That's where the peninsula starts giving way to the mainland," Matt spoke up. "Not too far from Sea View House. I'll show you later."

"Thanks."

"No problem."

She raised her eyebrows.

He grinned.

She leaned back in her chair, comfortable with this family, glad she was able to prepare the simple meal and make it seem festive. She noted the magnets on the refrigerator holding a variety of papers, the simple Cape Cod curtains on the windows through which she could see the sun sparkling on the melting ice. "Amazing change," she murmured, nodding at the outdoor scene.

"Just Old Man Winter drawing his last breath is all," said Matt. "I'm betting on spring making a showing by next week."

"Optimist," Sam said, before insisting that he and the boys take on the cleanup chores and shooing Laura and Matt away.

"You're so obvious, Pop," Matt said with a grin, leading Laura back to the living room.

Blankets still littered the place, which Laura started to pick up and fold. Matt did the same. She paused to examine the room in more detail than she had been able to the night before in the dim light of the fire.

There was a large upright piano in rich mahogany at the opposite end of the long room. A handsome wall-to-wall bookcase unit encompassed an entertainment center. Books and a variety of framed photos displayed on every shelf. She stepped closer and recognized Matt and the boys in several. Saw Sam and a woman standing close together probably not too many years ago. Saw them each holding a small child—Brian and Casey. But one picture in particular captivated her.

Two identical teenage boys with identical irreverent expressions beamed up at her. Dark hair, ebony eyes—their resemblance to Matt was unmistakable. "What a great shot!"

The pain that settled on Matt's face stole her breath away. Grief lingered in his eyes, refusing to move on.

She wished she hadn't said anything.

CHAPTER SIX

"THOSE ARE...were...my kid brothers. The twins—Jason and Jared." He could barely get the words out. Unusual for him after all this time. Of course, he didn't often discuss the twins anymore. The accident was old news in Pilgrim Cove. Old news that could still take him by surprise, the hurt as fresh as if it had happened yesterday.

Laura looked sympathetic and slightly confused. She already knew some of the history but none of the details of the sad story. He'd give her the short version—clean and quick. Better for him, too.

"Eight years ago, on the night of their senior prom, my brothers were in a car accident. Jared was driving. Didn't survive. Jason and Lila were in the car. They both escaped serious injury. Jason disappeared a month later. But Lila stayed in Pilgrim Cove and had Katie. Katie's my niece, Jason's daughter."

"Yes," said Laura. "I sort of figured that out at The Lobster Pot. But surely he comes to see her...?"

Matt looked at the lovely woman in front of him, loath to remove the hope that shone in her eyes. The hope for a happy ending. But she'd eventually hear the truth from someone else, so it would be better if it came from him. At least she'd get a firsthand account.

"He doesn't know about Katie. And we don't know where he is."

Laura's mouth rounded into a perfect *O,* and she was silent.

"We had an APB out for him in all the northeastern states. I hired a private investigator. But the kid was smart. Left no trace. No social security number anywhere on any paycheck. He wanted to disappear and he did." Matt paused for breath, his eyes still watching Laura. "He sends us a card at Christmas just to tell us he's alive. No return address of course. A different postmark every year, and who knows if he's actually even in that city."

He looked off into space. His throat felt tight. "I always tell Lila when I hear from him. The way I figure it, she has a right to know. Three years ago, Jason's message to Lila was to forget about him."

He needed air. Badly. He took three deep breaths before going on. "So I told her to get on with her life." He pictured Lila in his mind when he'd uttered those words and amazingly started to smile. "You know what she said?" he asked, then continued without giving Laura a chance to answer. "She said, 'Stop sounding like my mother! One of you is more than enough.'"

He turned to Laura then, smile fading, arms folded across his chest. "A lousy melodrama, wouldn't you

say? Right out of a bad script.'' He knew his voice
was as defensive as his posture.

But when she looked up at him, he forgot about
his own discomfort. Tears were rolling down her face,
and she was shaking her head back and forth.

''Don't say that,'' she whispered. ''It's not a bad
script. And not a melodrama. Not when there's so
much pain. Sometimes bad things happen, and we
struggle…and sometimes we find our way, and sometimes we need help, and sometimes we just can't do
it.''

She stepped close to him now, raised her hands to
his face and stroked his cheek. Stunned, he clasped
her wrist and lowered her palm to his mouth. And
kissed it. Once, twice, three times, wishing he never
had to let go.

''I'm so sorry about Jared,'' she said, her lips trembling. ''A parent's worst nightmare. Teens and driv-
ers' licenses. And now I understand why Katie throws
herself at you, and why Lila's so comfortable with
you. They're your family, too.''

He nodded, still holding her hand.

''And they're lucky to have you,'' Laura continued. ''Children need all the loving adults they can
find.''

He shrugged. ''I didn't think about that,'' he said.
''It just seemed to me that the cousins should know
each other. Casey and Katie are the same age and in
the same class. And Lila needs a friend.''

His mind wandered back to those years. A terrible,

mixed-up time for everyone. The Sullivans, the Parkers, and Bart Quinn, who'd always adored Lila, his only granddaughter, and still did. Yeah, Lila had needed a friend, and Matt was Jason's big brother, already married with one child and one on the way. His own parents had been devastated by their losses and could barely function. So Matt had done what he could.

"And despite everything," said Laura, "here you are, raising two beautiful boys, watching out for your dad, keeping an eye on Katie and Lila, running a successful business and making it all happen."

His ears started burning at her compliment. But she wasn't finished.

"I wouldn't call that a soap opera at all, Matthew Parker. I'd call that being responsible." She dimpled up at him, her blue eyes twinkling. "It's like baseball—stepping up to the plate when it's your turn."

He wasn't sure her analogy really fit, but he'd follow her lead and keep the conversation light. "Do you women always have to analyze everything?" he teased, as he retrieved her coat from the closet.

She held up her hand. "Okay. I won't say another word, except to say…I think you did everything right."

His ears definitely were on fire now. "Get into the car," he growled, "and change the subject."

"Yes, sir!" she answered with a mock salute, scooping up the kitten and placing it in the tote bag for the trip home. She went back to the kitchen to say her goodbyes, her face animated, her voice sincere, and Matt was once again surprised at how easily his family accepted her. Including Brian. He was more surprised at how comfortable *he* felt having a woman in the house again. Maybe it was because that woman was Laura McCloud.

LATER THAT AFTERNOON, Laura deposited two large shopping bags on the kitchen table. "How could one little kitten need so much stuff and cost so much money when I got her for free?" She turned to the guilty party. "If you weren't so cute…"

Perhaps she was losing her mind talking to a kitten who, according to Dr. Fielding, wasn't even old enough to get her shots yet. Good of the vet to see her on a Sunday. Maybe because he was just starting the practice or maybe because she'd begged him so nicely. Anyway, he pronounced the kitten healthy and spent time teaching Laura about the care and feeding of cats.

And now she had two large bags of stuff! And a roommate whose life and welfare depended on her.

She started emptying the bags. New litter box with unscented paper—didn't want to encourage allergies. Food bowl that she'd keep full of dried food at all times. Better for teeth and digestion than canned. Toys. Not too small or too big. A scratching post.

Laura shook her head in amazement. A week ago, her life was quiet and insular. She'd wanted to retreat and regroup and restart herself. At her own pace. In her own time. Following her instincts.

So much for Plan A.

And now she was headfirst into Plan B. Which was no plan at all. But flexibility would work for now. She was feeling stronger emotionally and physically.

"Is it all due to you, my soft, furry friend?" she asked, scooping the kitten into her arms. A contented purr was the answer as the kitten snuggled against her.

But Laura knew her sense of well-being wasn't solely because of the cat. Being outdoors, running miles each day along the Atlantic coastline was part of it. And if she were honest with herself, she'd admit that Matt Parker was a key element. He could easily become dangerous to her peace of mind. The better she got to know him, the better she liked him. Not good in the long run.

"So, kitty, maybe I'll be one of those eccentric spinster ladies who talks to her cat all the time." Somehow, this joke fell flat and Laura felt her smile disappear.

"Shoot!" she rallied as she continued to sort out the purchases. "You need a name, and I need to get to work on my commercials."

She picked up the phone and called Matt's house.

The phone rang three times before she heard it being picked up. No hello greeted her. Only breathing came through the wires, and she made the connection.

"Hi, Casey," she said slowly. "It's Laura."

"H-hi."

"I have a favor to ask you and Brian." In the background she heard Brian ask for the phone.

"No-o-o. It's L-Laura. I'm talking."

Laura grinned. "Can you and Brian think of a name for the kitten? We can't just keep calling her 'cat' all the time. Right?"

"Right."

"If you guys come up with a list, then we'll vote on it. What do you say?"

"I—I—I say yes!"

"Great. And thanks a lot, Casey. Tell Brian thanks, also. Okay?"

"Yes. Bye." Dial tone.

She replaced the receiver in its cradle, knowing she'd go with whatever name they suggested, happy about Casey's enthusiasm for her little project. Heck. She couldn't take any credit. Casey was enthusiastic about everything in his life!

She'd give the kitten to Casey next week when she went to Boston to record the two commercials. She'd be staying at her own home in the city overnight, and the cat was too young to be left alone at Sea View House for that length of time. So, one problem was solved. A win-win for everyone, including the kitten! Hmm. Maybe she'd give it to the boy for keeps when she left Pilgrim Cove at the end of May.

LAURA STOOD at the ferryboat rail watching the big city loom toward her and delighting in the novelty of a boat ride to work! The thirty-minute commute was exhilarating in the fresh air and bright sunlight. She opened the buttons of her coat, thinking that Matt had been on target. Spring was just out of sight. Another week, and she'd need only a sweater.

The boat would dock at Rowes Wharf, and then she'd hop a bus to the recording studio. A lot better than spending almost two hours on the road, fighting for a parking spot, and then feeling half-drained before starting to record.

From the moment she walked into the studio, she knew she'd be on her mark. The familiarity of the environment—both the larger area where the technical staff worked and her sound isolation room—was like slipping into a favorite old bathrobe. The quiet chatter of the production team was familiar to her ears. She also knew one of the techs at the controls, had worked with him before. She felt confident. She had the talent to develop. And just as important, she now had the energy. Her depression was lifting.

She owed her agent a big thanks for not abandoning her during the past two years when she'd only accepted assignments on a limited basis. He'd proved his loyalty and his friendship. And he'd never lost faith in her ability.

The two tapings went well. The rep from the ad agency who was monitoring the travel service account was happy with Laura's effort.

"Great job, Laura," he said, shaking her hand

when it was over. "We'll be in touch if anything has to be reworked, but I doubt it."

"Thanks," said Laura, happy to hear praise from the client.

As she sat in the cab taking her to Norman Cohen's office, she realized that the whole week preceding her trip to Boston had gone well.

Her regimen hadn't changed because winter had stayed longer than usual. As soon as the slush of the ice storm melted, Laura had returned to her walking schedule. Matt had made a habit of stopping by when he was in her neighborhood. Most of the time she was on the beach a mile or more from the house. But if he saw her car in the driveway, he'd walk around the back and wait on her porch. She found herself scanning the distance to see if he was there. If he was, she'd make them both a cup of tea, and then he'd be off again. Yesterday, he'd taken the kitten with him.

Their relationship was strictly platonic, she reassured herself. The way it was supposed to be. The way each of them wanted it to be.

Norman was waiting for her when she reached his office, and greeted her like a long lost daughter before getting down to business. "You have an appointment tomorrow morning with the voice-over director of the Filene's commercials. I'm going to take you there. Tell me again, why don't you have a car?"

"Like you don't know!" The man's memory was phenomenal, and she'd already clued him in. "The ferry, Norman. The ferry." She leaned forward over his desk. "I love it. Maybe I'm a seashore girl at heart, but never knew it before. Maybe I enjoy living at the water's edge."

He leaned back and smiled. "Maybe you do. You look damn good, Laura. A hell of a lot better than when I last saw you. So how are you doing? Really?"

A kaleidoscope of images flipped through her mind like a slide show. The beach, Matt, the kitten, Sea View House, Matt, The Diner, Casey, The Lobster Pot, Matt, the ocean, Sam, the ROMEOs, Matt, Brian, the van, the ice storm, Matt.

"I'm doing fine, Norman. Better than I expected." Memories of her mom were constant companions—tears welled at odd times throughout the day—but new memories were being born, too, giving relief to the loss.

"Glad to hear it. Even gladder to see it with my own eyes." The agent paused, studying her, and the silence that followed took on a mysterious quality. Laura's spine straightened.

"What's on your mind, Norman?"

He rolled his chair closer to his desk, closer to Laura. "A new opportunity." He held his hands wide apart, palms facing each other. "Big." He didn't say more.

"Breakthrough?" Laura asked.

He continued to stare at her. "Definitely. You'd have to audition."

She could handle that. She'd gone on plenty of auditions when she was just starting out, and she understood that they were normal for new projects, particularly for clients she hadn't worked with before.

"And it's very competitive," added the agent. "A really hot project."

She sat straighter if that were possible. "Tell me."

"If you win this assignment and perform successfully, big doors will open, Laura. Let's just say, any money worries you have will be over."

Why was he holding back? She asked him.

"Because this is a huge commitment," said Norman. "Full-time work. Long recording sessions. Total concentration. A challenge to your vocal and physical stamina. I didn't know if you were up to it, or frankly, if you even wanted so much work." He was silent again, this time his voice trailing off in question.

A moment of decision, but it wasn't hard. She had to move forward with her life.

"Tell me," she repeated.

Norman Cohen folded his hands over his stomach, leaned back, his demeanor relaxed now, and quietly said, "A series of audio books."

She whistled under her breath. Books on tape had become big business, and the number of books available was increasing exponentially. Contemporary lifestyles had contributed to this explosion. People now listened to books while commuting to work because they had less time to read at home. Opportunities for narrators like herself, also called readers, had exploded in this field. But only the most talented were hired. The listening public had quite an influence on who got the work. They voted with their dollars.

"You're auditioning to narrate the first set of children's fairy tales being published by Sunrise Books, a division of..." The agent quietly named one of the New York publishing giants.

Laura's heart started to thump hard, and once again she recognized why she'd never changed agents. Norman Cohen not only knew the business and had his fingers in many pies, he also knew his clients and how to make successful matches. She trusted his instincts, maybe more than her own, and now she wanted to hear more.

"You'd be starting with the second book," Norman continued, "and you'd be in exalted company. Julia Roberts has agreed to read the first one. Sunrise wants to make a splash, but they can't afford Ms. Roberts for all twelve releases."

Laura gulped, trying to temper her excitement. "Frankly," she said, "the children won't know the difference, or at least won't care as long as the narration's good."

"Exactly," said Norman. "But their mothers will. So you'll have to be good. You'll be vocalizing all dialogue with unique characters' voices as well as the narrative." The man looked her full in the face. "You can do this, Laura. It's an opportunity to use everything you've got—acting skills, speech arts, creativity—and to derive satisfaction from your work. Not to mention a decent paycheck."

"There must be a lot of voice-over actors who would jump at this. The competition *will* be stiff."

Norman shrugged. "Maybe. But I'm not concerned about it."

"Why not?"

"Because Sunrise is looking for a verbal performance—voice and talent—accompanied by intelligence," replied the agent, pointing a finger at Laura. "And that's you."

Whoosh. She collapsed against the back of the chair.

"And then," continued Norman, "the publisher has plans for children's classics on tape. For elementary school level as well as the older kids. Who knows? You might wind up reading your own favorites from childhood...if Sunrise goes through with the second phase of the project."

"Could we just take one step at a time, Norman?" Laura could barely manage a whisper.

"Absolutely." The agent got up and walked to a big file cabinet. He reached in and pulled out an accordion-type folder.

"Here's your homework," he said, giving the folder to Laura.

She looked inside. Three scripts for the Filene's ads. And an unbound copy of *Snow White*.

"They're not making the audition easy, are they? Seven dwarfs! Seven voices! Just for starters."

"Six," Norman offered. "I think Dopey's silent."

"And I think," Laura said between gulps, "that

maybe I should practice reading to real children before I audition."

"Great idea, Laura! Excellent. Do they have a library in that place you're living?"

She almost whacked him with the file. "As a matter of fact, one of my friends is a retired school librarian." An image of Lou Goodman and the ROMEOs flashed through her mind. "The residents of Pilgrim Cove have a multitude of skills and talents. It's a wonderful town."

He eyed her with interest. "Maybe it is. Seems to be doing you good." Then he winked. "Just make sure the boat doesn't sink. I need you in Boston."

"I'll be here whenever I'm needed, but I'm not cutting back on my time in Pilgrim Cove."

"That's fine. As long as we're on the same business page." He paused. "You're sure about the commitment, Laura? Is it too soon for you?"

"I'm sure, Norman, and even if I weren't…well, I have to pay bills. Hard work can be therapy, too." Repeating this philosophy was becoming second nature to her.

He looked at her with avuncular affection. "Smart girl. So call me after your meeting tomorrow morning with the Filene's people, and let me know when the department store tapings are scheduled." He stood up behind his desk. "And now I'm taking you to dinner," he pronounced. "The best food in the city." His eyes twinkled. "Phyllis cooked up a storm. In fact, when she knew you were coming to town, she gave me orders to bring you back with me. And then we'll drive you home.''

A sweet gesture, and Laura was touched. ''If you were a little older, Norman, you could qualify for ROMEO status.''

''Huh?''

She chose not to enlighten him.

LAURA WAVED GOOD-NIGHT to Norman and his wife, and let herself into the home she'd shared with her mom. Instantly she was transported to her other life. She walked slowly through each room, expecting to see her mom rise up from a chair, expecting to hear Bridget McCloud's voice in greeting. She leaned against the wall between the kitchen and dining room and tried to catch her breath.

Why hadn't she anticipated this reaction? Why was she so surprised? Two and a half weeks in Pilgrim Cove couldn't erase a lifetime of love and memories. The heavy silence, however, reinforced her new reality. She was alone. A feeling that seemed much stronger here than at Sea View House. And not because of the kitten.

Laura walked slowly to her bedroom and automatically began to undress. During her time in Pilgrim Cove, she'd gotten involved with people. Funny, how she seemed so connected to the town after such a short stay. Her own illness and her responsibilities of the past few years had put limits on her time and energy for fostering friendships.

A layer of dust covered her bureau and she retrieved a cloth and bottle of furniture polish. She started polishing in her room and then rubbed every piece of furniture in the house, leaving her mom's bedroom for last. When she finally walked in, she inhaled the faint aroma of Bridget's favorite cologne, which lingered in the air. One whiff and she was deluged with memories and surrounded with love. She grabbed a handful of tissues and let her tears fall.

Until the phone rang.

Laura rubbed her tears away as she picked up her mother's extension. Maybe her sister had beaten her to the punch. Calling Alison had been on Laura's agenda that evening.

"Hello." She barely managed the greeting after blowing her nose again.

"Laura? Is that you?" Matt's deep voice resonated in her ear. Her spirits picked up.

"Yeah, it's me."

"You sound funny."

"I'm in my mom's bedroom."

"Oh…" A world of understanding came across in the one syllable. "I can be there in two hours." He hadn't hesitated. His caring voice, his warm tone…right in character for the honorable man she knew so well now.

For the man with whom she was falling in love.

The thought left her breathless. Falling in love? More like catapulting! Despite her best intentions.

Pain slashed through her. New tears erupted at the

admission. Men, as Laura had learned, do not stay with women who've had breast cancer. She'd absolutely have to find a way to fall out of love.

"No, no," she finally replied, glad her words sounded strong. "I'll be all right. I've got a business appointment tomorrow morning. In fact, I'll be going back and forth to the city a lot from now on."

Silence. "I see," said Matt, his tone a bit cooler. "Your career must be taking off again." It was a statement, not a question.

"No guarantees, but you knew that was my goal."

"Are you…thinking about leaving Sea View House, about cutting short your stay with us?"

"No!" Her response exploded from her heart first, then from her mouth.

"Good." Matt sounded more relaxed. "And if you change your mind about wanting company…just call."

"Thanks, but I'll be fine."

"I'm sure you will," he replied. "And I'll see you when you get home. Good night."

Home! A loaded word. She could only whisper her good-night before gently replacing the receiver into its cradle. Then she dropped her head into her hands. Pilgrim Cove and Matthew Parker were pulling her back. The two had become one. At least in her mind. It seemed that forging on with life was a repetitive dance pattern—two steps forward and one step back. She took a deep breath and stood up. A quick call to

Alison, followed by a hot shower and she'd feel better.

But not as good as she felt after a run on Pilgrim Beach. The thought stopped her in her tracks. She'd gotten stronger every day since arriving at Sea View House. If the rest of her stay proved to be as satisfying as the first part, why couldn't she sell the city house, settle in Pilgrim Cove and live near the beach all year round?

Excitement flared then fizzled to ash. There was no reason her brilliant plan couldn't work.

Except one.

Matthew Parker.

He cared about her. She could sense it. But he'd run like hell if he discovered the truth. She wasn't a masochist. A one-sided love would negate any other joy she could find in Pilgrim Cove. She'd keep her brilliant idea to herself.

CHAPTER SEVEN

LAURA ENJOYED the boat ride back to Pilgrim Cove even more than the ride into Boston. The late-afternoon air was a tad warmer than the day before and the sun sparkled off the water as if reflecting the facets of perfect diamonds—millions of them. She reached for her sunglasses.

When the ferry approached the Pilgrim Cove harbor, Laura drank in the sight. Had it been only twenty-four hours since she'd left? True, her time had been filled with a variety of people, locations, a host of raw feelings, new information, new discoveries and new commitments to her work. She'd been on the go from the moment she'd stepped ashore in the city yesterday until thirty minutes ago when she'd stepped onto the ferry.

On the phone last night, her sister, Alison, had chatted nonstop about possible condos for Laura in Atlanta. Laura had explained about the potential blossoming of her career, but Alison wasn't giving up. Laura hadn't wanted to quash her sister's enthusiasm, so she'd simply told her to slow down. After all, who knew what the future held?

Laura's car was parked in the lot adjacent to the harbor, and she waved to the attendant before climbing in. She put her "homework" in the passenger seat and headed toward Matt's house to retrieve the kitten. The naked trees planted along the street were starting to bud—perhaps some maple and birch. She was curious to see what developed in this seaside environment.

At Matt's house, she rang the front doorbell and immediately heard the sound of raised voices and the soft thuds of sneakered feet running on carpeting.

"Hi-i-i, Laura." The greeting was appropriate, but the voice was flat.

"Hi, yourself, Casey. What's going on?"

He opened the door wider, and Laura walked inside. Brian was holding the kitten.

"We thought of a name," said the older boy.

"Great. A name that you both like?" Laura looked from one boy to the other.

Two heads nodded.

"Then I'm going to love it." Whatever they'd come up with would be fine.

"It's Midnight!" yelled Casey.

"'Cause you found her in the middle of the night," said Brian. "And besides, she's almost all black. So it fits."

Laura looked at the boys, surprised at the pride she felt. "You guys are the greatest. How clever of you. It's a purr-fect name." She trilled her pronunciation.

The kids grinned, but to her astonishment, hung their heads, their cheeks turning pink.

"Give me five, kids," she said, her palms out, wanting to make them feel more comfortable.

Matt's sons straightened and slapped her hand.

"So why don't you look happy, Case?" she asked.

Silence.

She looked at Brian and raised a brow.

"Uh—he wants to keep Midnight, but he knows he can't." Brian stepped closer to his brother and put his free arm around him.

Darn! She should have seen this coming. She squatted in front of Casey.

"I'll be going into Boston often from now on and I'd love for you to be the official kitten sitter every time I'm away. It'll be a load off my mind."

The child nodded.

"And you can come with me to the vet when I take Midnight for her shots."

Casey wrinkled his nose.

"Only if you want to…"

There was an interesting struggle on the child's face as he looked from the cat to Laura. "Yes," he finally said. The word aspirated on a big breath as though matching the big decision.

"Good boy." Matt's deep voice came from behind Laura, startling her.

She stood quickly and twirled around, observing his guarded expression as he examined her from head to toe. His intensity silenced her greeting.

"So, you came back," he said with a trace of surprise in his voice.

Matt's words were so far removed from everything she'd been thinking and feeling, she could barely answer. "What do you mean?"

He hesitated. "I wasn't sure you would."

Laura put her hand to her forehead. "Wait a minute. Didn't we speak on the phone last night? Didn't I say I'd be back today?"

"You did, but women have been known to change their minds."

He stared at her, and she met his gaze. "In my experience, it's the men who do."

"Ahh," Matt replied, his brow clearing. "You're an interesting woman, Laura, and now I understand you a little better. But I wonder how long it will take me to know you well. To know the real Laura McCloud."

She bit her lip. The real Laura McCloud was none of his business. And if her feelings were bubbling to the surface too easily, she'd clamp down on them.

"There's not much more to know." She forced a chuckle into her voice and reached for the kitten.

But Matt wasn't letting her off that easily. "Who was he, Laura?" he whispered as he accompanied her to the door. "Who walked out on you?"

IT WASN'T THE WHO as much as the why that bothered Laura. She recognized that later in the evening as she prepared a simple meal for herself in Sea View

House. She'd made a quick getaway after his loaded question. And hadn't stopped thinking about his damn question since.

Donald Crawford was not the love of her life. She saw that now, so her heart wasn't broken. But he'd managed to do more than reject her growing affection. He'd destroyed her hope. Worse than the look of horror on his face had been his words. Immediate. Devastating.

"I'm not cut out for this, Laura. First, your mother gets sick. Then you. I'm sorry for you, being stalked with bad luck, but I can't take it. I'm young. I want a life!"

She hadn't said a word. Couldn't. Just walked to her front door and opened it wide. Slammed it when he was barely over the threshold. Damn it! She was as young as he. She wanted a life, too! And she didn't want pity. Anger had overridden fear at that moment, and she viewed it as a gift to get her through that hard time.

But now there was Matt. Another man, but so different from Donald. At least in her mind. Caring and sensitive, he was occupying a bigger place in her heart every day. If their relationship grew and he walked out, her heart *would* be broken. And this time there'd be no recovery.

So, despite her delight with the town and its citizens, it was time for Laura to get out of Dodge.

Maybe she'd be doing Matt a favor. He was a widower. Already lost the major love of his life. Laura didn't know the details, only that his wife had died, leaving him with two boys. Matt seemed, however, to be ready to move on with his life. He was interested in Laura. He'd been ready to run to her in Boston last night. Of course, he was being encouraged by every ROMEO in town! Including Sam. So maybe Laura was the first woman he'd pursued since Valerie. Maybe they'd actually be good for each other.

Her head ached. Too much thinking. Well, she'd fix that right now. She grabbed a can of soda and raised it in a mock salute. "To life," she said. "And to whatever it brings."

THE NEXT MORNING, she received a call from Norman Cohen with the audition date for the audio books. She had a two-week window, but she also had Filene's three commercials to prepare.

"Don't worry, Norman. It's the best thing that could have happened." She tried to reassure him, when he—despite having recently been pushing her to do more—was now concerned that the total prep would be too much in too short a time. "Weren't you the one who said I had to jump into the deep end of the pool?" she asked.

She listened and laughed. "I have no intention of drowning. Sure, try to move the date, but don't sweat it. I can meet the deadline."

After another minute of conversation, she replaced the receiver. Work would occupy her mind from day to night. She would attack it with the singlemindedness of a mountain climber traveling one step at a time but with his mind on the summit. And she'd have no time for thoughts of Matt.

Now she created duplicate calendars for the kitchen table and den, penciling in each day's work goal and appointments. No chance of messing up her schedule or forgetting her appointments in Boston. Both recording and medical. She glanced at her precise entries when she was finished and added critical phone numbers on top of the calendar. Everything she needed was now right at hand.

Dr. Berger was scheduled the week after the audio books audition. Three weeks to go—it would be mid-April by then—and she'd be through another four-month checkup. Maybe the one after this would be in six months. The interval between checkups increased as time passed.

She pulled out the scripts for the department store and went to work. Sitting, standing, walking and talking. Taping and replaying. Until she finally heard the loud knocking at the kitchen door and ran to answer it.

Matt. Scruffy, sexy, and frowning.

"I got worried, Laura. I've been on the porch looking up and down the beach for almost half an hour, until I realized you might actually be inside. You're always outdoors at this time."

"Just what time is it?" She suddenly noticed that shadows were forming, the light was going.

He glanced at his watch. "Almost five o'clock."

"You're kidding! I've been working."

His eyes narrowed. "You look pale again. No long walk today?"

She shook her head.

"Let's do it." He held out his hand.

"What?"

"Put on a jacket and let's go for a walk." He started looking around.

On the beach alone with Matt Parker? Dangerous to her heart. "I can skip a day, Matt. You don't have to waste more time because of me."

He stopped in his tracks and turned to her. "Put that idea out of your head. Spending time with you is not a waste." Then his eyes started to twinkle. "But I'm not letting you get away with being lazy. First it'll be one day, then it'll be two. Then you'll never get out of the house. Isn't the beach the main reason you're here? Come on. Let's go."

The beach may have been the main reason—once, but she was discovering more to hold her in Pilgrim Cove now. Laura looked at Matt again. His twinkle was gone, replaced with a hunger that was unmistakable.

"You have no idea how beautiful you look after an hour's walk. You're all smiles, your cheeks are rosy and your eyes sparkle." He paused, then added, "I love seeing you that way."

Her breath hitched. Why did he use that _L_ word so easily? She should tell him to go back to work and leave her alone. But his eyes shone with warmth, and he held out his hand to her again. This time she accepted it. And felt his fingers clasp hers with firmness.

She took a breath. A deep one. Maybe it was time to take a chance.

But did the heavens have to twinkle with millions of stars? Did all of nature have to conspire to create a perfect world that evening? Moonlight. Starlight. Whispering waves.

Laura was acutely aware of her surroundings as she and Matt walked side by side. His hand reached for hers regularly, his attention rested on her constantly. She ignored the small warning voice in her head.

She peeked up at Matt and jabbed him with her elbow. "C'mon, old man. Let's pick up the tempo."

If he could see the expression on his face!

"Old man? I'll show you old!"

And they were off at a jog. She matched his stamina but not his stride, so he slowed down almost immediately and paced himself despite his mock protestations of being old. When he smiled at her, it was easy to respond.

But all too soon, their three-mile loop brought them around to where they'd started—on the back porch of Sea View House.

"Sorry, I can't come inside," Matt said, checking his watch in the porch light. "The family will be wondering."

But he wanted to. She could see it in his eyes, and that was enough for her. For tonight.

"And there's homework to be done, and dinner to

be made," she added. "I understand, Matt. It's okay." She put her hands on her hips and teased, "Besides, I don't remember inviting you in!"

He leaned forward, his fingers stroking her cheek, her jawline. "You talk too much," he whispered, before brushing her mouth with his, effectively silencing her, and then disappearing up the driveway toward the street.

TALK TOO MUCH? Laura was still shaking her head the next morning as she made her bed. Matt had the wrong sister. Although Laura earned her living by talking, Alison was the one who never shut up!

She looked out the window at the new day, feeling just as sunny inside as the world looked outside. Her fingers stroked her bottom lip where Matt's touch still lingered, whether in her memory or in reality, she didn't care. What mattered was that he'd contributed to her feeling of well-being. Sure, a sound night's sleep had helped, but the reaffirmation of her looks, her femininity, her desirability—well, what price could she put on that?

She hummed as she straightened up the room, happy with yesterday but also looking forward to the day ahead. She'd put her library idea into motion. The thought intrigued her because she'd never actually done any reading to children. Children were not part of her everyday world. As much as she loved her niece and nephew, they lived in Atlanta, so their visits were short and intense, not leisurely sojourns dotted with visits to the library.

Wearing only a lightweight navy-blue sweatsuit, Laura got into her car and headed west. The William Adams Library sat in the middle of Sloop Street, a major east-west thoroughfare parallel to Main and one block south, not far from Bart Quinn's office. The two-story brick building, set back from the street, was dark red—typical of New England. It looked like a large Tudor-style home. An American flag waved in the breeze from a pole in the center of its circular driveway. Laura ignored that driveway option and pulled into the adjacent parking lot, then walked on the connecting sidewalk to the front door and opened it.

Had she been blindfolded, she would have still recognized her surroundings immediately. The sounds of soft murmurs and the occasional "hush," the acrid smell of paper mixed with a bit of dust, the atmosphere of quiet work, of expectation. Of being in a special place.

And then she looked around. Some memories about libraries were instantly vanquished. Bright colors were everywhere—red, yellow, green and blue—painted walls, large posters, big signs. A parents' corner, a teachers' space, a young-adult section. A generous computer area. And above the staircase, huge murals indicating the Children's Section on the second floor. Laura headed for the steps and almost crashed into Lou Goodman.

"Wow. Sorry," she whispered, grabbing his arm. "Maybe I need glasses. Your next breakfast is on me."

"I'm fine," said the retired librarian. "So why the rush to get upstairs?"

She glanced at the mural. "I want to volunteer to read at a children's story hour if possible—if story hours are on the agenda here."

Lou Goodman's eyes opened wide. "That's wonderful. You're really becoming part of the community now, my dear. Maybe you'll like us so much, you'll want to stay on."

She swallowed hard as a wave of guilt passed through her. Her motivation for offering her services was strictly selfish. She wanted to land that narrator job. "Can't I be part of the community on a temporary basis?" she asked in a small voice. Lou Goodman was one of the good guys in her life here. She just couldn't deceive him.

"Of course you can." Lou leaned closer to her. "In fact," he whispered, "most volunteers start out enthusiastic and after a month, the excitement wanes and they appear less often. So we'll gratefully accept whatever time you can give us."

She looked into the gentle man's warm brown eyes and knew that Lou wasn't that type of volunteer.

"How often do you help out?" she asked as they climbed the stairs together.

"Oh, I get involved with special projects," he said.

"Like the annual book sale that raises extra funds, or the homework-help service."

"I bet you never back down from a commitment here," she said.

He didn't reply, but he didn't have to. Laura knew the answer. Lou Goodman loved books; retirement hadn't changed that.

Five minutes later, Laura was being introduced to the children's staff and learned that a story hour was offered every morning at ten o'clock.

"We're in the middle of one right now. Some children attend daily, some attend weekly and some only occasionally. It all depends on their moms," said Barbara Rayvid, Head of Children's Services. "Frankly, I wish they'd all come as often as possible. The earlier we can foster a love of books in them, the better off they'll be."

Laura nodded and looked from Barbara to Lou. "Are all librarians like you guys?"

"You mean a little nuts?" Barbara asked. She paused in thought, then winked at Lou. "Do you think she'll call the men in white coats to take us away?"

"She'll understand as soon as she works with the kids." Lou turned to Laura then. "So, when do you want to start?"

"The sooner the better."

"Tomorrow morning at ten," said Barbara, walking to the shelves of picture books. "Here are a couple of good ones if you want to look them over before you read. In fact, check them out and take them with you.''

''I will. Thanks very much.''

The librarian suddenly put her finger to her lips and pointed downstairs. ''Listen,'' she whispered. ''The hoards are approaching.''

Laura heard the faint hustle and bustle of a crowd of youngsters. Several requests for quiet. Sibilant whispers, ''Shush, shush. No pushing.''

And suddenly the second floor was filled with children, boys and girls. Among them, Brian Parker.

Barbara turned to Laura. ''Welcome to the fifth grade.''

Laura nodded and smiled. She stepped toward the class. ''Hi, Brian,'' she called softly.

The boy spun around, as did the classmate next to him.

''Who's the lady?'' the friend whispered loudly to Brian. ''She your dad's girlfriend?''

''What lady?'' asked another boy, swiveling to see her.

Brian's ears turned red as he recognized Laura. He slunk to the other side of the line and turned to his friends. ''Nah. She's new to town. We hardly know her.''

Laura was hurt by his words but held her tongue. Matt's son was embarrassed in front of his friends because of her. Well, what did she know about little boys? Nothing! Of course, there was always the possibility that Brian just didn't like her after all.

Lou hadn't heard Brian's remark, and Laura was glad. The librarian now was explaining what the fifth-graders were up to. "They're going to write and perform an original play set in colonial America on the eve of revolution. Every student is focusing on one historical person and they're going to argue the pros and cons of independence. It'll be like a court drama, except," he chuckled, "we already know the ending."

"And I bet they all want to be John Adams," said Laura, "because of the William Adams connection."

"You're not far off, but their teacher has it all sorted out."

"So when are they putting on this spectacular event?"

"At the end of May," Lou replied. "Their play will be part of the school-wide Memorial Day program."

The end of May! Exactly when Laura would be leaving Pilgrim Cove. A sharp wave of regret struck her so unexpectedly she almost lost her breath.

After saying quick goodbyes to everyone, she left the building.

BRIAN LOOKED OUT the window of the school bus on the trip home that day and saw nothing except the shocked look on Laura's face when he'd turned away from her. The way he figured it, he had two choices. One was to forget he'd ever seen Laura McCloud at the library. He kind of liked that option, but the downside was that Laura might call his dad and tell him that Brian had been rude toward her. Very rude. And then he'd be in big trouble.

The second choice was to tell his dad about seeing Laura before she had a chance to, and make it sound not so bad. Then if Laura called, his dad would be prepared and not think too much about the whole thing.

Shoot! Who knew he was going to run into her in front of all his friends? He didn't even know what to tell them. And now, of course, all his buddies wanted to find out who she was, because in Pilgrim Cove, everybody knew everything about everybody else. So, saying, "This is Laura McCloud from Boston," wasn't enough. The truth was, he didn't know what to say.

His dad liked her. But that was private stuff.

He'd heard Matt tell Grandpa Sam that he'd stopped at Sea View House on his way home the other day to check up on Laura. He'd never, ever done that with anyone else who rented from Bart Quinn. And there had been other ladies living in the house last year and the year before.

And there was more evidence, like the night she'd slept over during the storm, when his dad and she had slept next to each other on the floor, close like. That had to mean something.

"C'mon, Bri. You go first." Casey's voice interrupted his thoughts, and Brian followed his brother off the bus, automatically glancing up and down the street as he descended the steps. Looking out for a little brother like Casey was a big job. Casey was a good kid, but Brian wished he'd grow up faster so he could take care of himself. Or at least figure out how to talk right. Older kids made fun of him in the halls when the teachers weren't looking, and sometimes they picked on him when he got off the bus. But not today, no one was around today. One day, Brian knew he'd get into trouble defending the kid. It was only a matter of time. With the new zero-tolerance policy for fighting in his school, Brian could just feel bad luck coming his way.

Next year would be worse. Brian clenched his teeth at the thought. In the fall, Brian would be in middle school. Who would watch out for Casey then?

Life in the fifth grade was complicated.

Life at home was complicated.

Getting older was complicated. He wished he were still a kid.

He and Casey stomped up the driveway, activated the garage door and went through the garage to the kitchen. Their grandpa was just hanging up the phone, and Brian's stomach plopped. Laura must have called.

But his grandpa's eyes were twinkling. "Coach just left you a message, big boy. Extra practice today for Saturday's game."

"Yes!" He raised a fisted hand in the air and ran upstairs to change clothes and get his glove. Baseball! The best game in the world. When he was standing on second base studying the player at bat, nothing else mattered. Life was great.

AT EIGHT O'CLOCK that evening, Laura sat on a kitchen chair facing the middle of the room, as she read aloud one of the children's stories she'd taken from the library. Normally she'd mark up a script in her own style of shorthand indicating stresses, pace, tone and any other cues she thought she needed to make the narration as effective as possible. But tonight she wrote brief notes on a separate sheet.

The phone rang when she was halfway through the story and she sighed. The narration had been flowing and she hated to be interrupted, but she reached for the receiver.

"Hello."

"It's Matt," came the voice on the other end, the voice that set her mouth to smiling. "I wanted to give you a heads-up. Brian and I are on our way over from his baseball practice. If it's not too late for you."

"Late? At eight o'clock? I'm thirty-three, not ninety-three. I think I can handle a visit."

She heard his chuckle and started to laugh herself. He had the kind of timbre that pulled others along even if they didn't know what the joke was about. He had laughter that was catchy.

"We'll be there in five," said Matt.

"That's fine."

Laura heard the van pull into her driveway exactly five minutes later. Her kettle was already warming on the stove. It seemed that sharing a cup of hot tea had become a ritual for them whenever Matt stopped by.

She heard a clattering up the back steps and she opened the kitchen door. On the porch stood one unhappy-looking boy and one serious-looking man.

"What's wrong? What happened?" Laura couldn't keep the alarm from her voice. "You were at a baseball practice. Brian, did you get hurt?" She moved toward him. "Let me see."

If anything, the boy looked more miserable and confused. He took a step back.

Laura stilled. "Well, at least come on in."

Matt's arm was around his son, urging him inside, before he turned to her. "Brian's not hurt, Laura, but he's got something to say to you."

"All right." She faced the boy. "Did you get my message from your grandpa?"

"Huh?"

Matt stared at her. "Please, Laura. Just let him talk."

She nodded, but really, the kid looked miserable.

"Today at the library," he began, "when I saw you…I should've said hello instead of…you know… saying I didn't know you."

"You were embarrassed, Brian. I understand that. So I was thinking, that perhaps I should *not* have said hello in front of all your friends."

The kid started to breathe normally. "You thought that?"

"Only afterward, unfortunately. So, I'm sorry if you had your hands full with your buddies."

"I didn't know what to tell them. They all asked me who you were." His eyes focused everywhere but on her.

"Hey, pal," she said, lightly brushing his hair with her fingers. "Just stick to the truth and you'll be okay."

His expression was intense. "Like what?"

"Tell them I'm the lady who lives at Sea View House now. Tell them that you and your dad fixed some plumbing problems out here, and now we're all friends. In fact, tell them I'm a friend of the family."

"Okay," said Brian after a moment. "Plumbing problems. Family friend. I can do that."

"Of course you can," she said, giving him her full attention again. "But I'll try not to be there next Thursday morning, so you won't have any problems."

He blushed again and started to smile. "That's okay. No problem." He turned, searching the area with his eyes. "Where's Midnight?"

"Try the middle of my bed," Laura said, indicating the back of the house. It seemed the library incident was over.

Brian's grin got bigger as he looked at his dad. Matt nodded his approval, and Brian disappeared through the center hall moving toward Laura's bedroom.

She and Matt were alone. "Let me pour—"

"Wait, Laura."

She turned toward him. The glow of his smile transferred that warmth to her.

"Thanks, Laura. Thanks very much. Brian was wrong. But you were terrific with him. Growing from boy to man is not an easy thing."

His voice carried such conviction, Laura had no doubt he was speaking from experience. "I should have known better," she whispered.

He waved her words away, instead stepping forward and stroking her cheek, then leaning in close.

She tilted her head back, lips parting slightly.

He kissed her gently on the forehead.

CHAPTER EIGHT

LAURA PUNCHED the steering wheel as she drove to The Diner on the Dunes two mornings later. Matt had given her a kiss on the forehead. After their romantic walk on the beach, she'd expected more. She blinked back tears of disappointment.

It's better this way. She'd be gone at the end of May and wouldn't have to face telling him about the cancer. But her self-directed pep talk fell flat. She'd allowed herself to fall for Matt and she'd hoped he felt the same way.

She pulled into a parking spot, shut the ignition and checked her face in the mirror. Her eyes looked a little red, so did her nose. She reached for her compact and performed some touch-up work, then added bright pink lipstick. Somehow, lipstick always made a woman look good and feel better. Of course, a smile would help! She tried one out in the mirror, but viewed a grimace instead. She exited the car and slammed the door behind her.

She walked to the entrance of the diner, glanced at the ROMEOs sign and felt a natural smile cross her face. She'd be fine. She went directly to the men's reserved corner and was swept into the conversation before she had a chance to sit down.

"You've given us good news, you have, Laura McCloud!"

She tilted her head at Bart Quinn's sudden Irish brogue and caught his eye. "And what news would that be, Bartholomew Quinn?"

The Chief laughed, Ralph Bigelow slapped his hands on the table top, while Lou and Doc Rosen wore identical happy expressions. Laura winked at them. They loved watching and listening to her matching wits and lilt with their unofficial leader.

"The library, lass, the library. Lou says you've volunteered. I knew this would happen. Sea View House is already claiming your heart."

Joe Cavelli, whose son was married to Bart's younger daughter, eyed Laura and said quietly, "They're making book on you."

"What!" She stood in front of her chair and searched each face. "What could you possibly be betting on?" Her speech reverted to normal American, all traces of the Irish gone.

"Now, now. Don't worry yourself." That was Bart, trying to smooth things over. "We've only just begun the pool."

"Well, you can just end it. Whatever it is."

But the Irishman was stubborn. "No, no. I've got the feeling about this."

"I'm lost," said Laura, finally sitting down. "Where's Dee with her wonderful coffee?"

"Taking the day off," said the Chief, avoiding her eye.

"Well, good for her!" said Laura. "I never thought she'd allow herself."

"She didn't have much choice," said Doc, winking at Laura. "The Chief, here, kept her dancing last night until she begged for a break."

"Oh-h-h." Interesting. She looked at the Chief, whose complexion was turning ruddy. "Dancing? All night?"

"Don't stare at me that way! Look at him, instead," replied Rick O'Brien, pointing at Doc. "He and Marsha closed the place down."

"I had no choice, either, no choice at all," Doc explained without flinching. "My wife loves to dance." The doctor's quiet demeanor was at odds with the mirth in his eyes.

"Fred and Ginger times two," murmured Laura. She looked around the table, not knowing what to think. The Pilgrim Cove senior set was full of surprises.

Her coffee cup was filled by a part-timer. Laura smiled her thanks and tuned into the conversation going on around her.

"Any more going into the kitty on Laura? Remember, it's not a question of 'if,' it's a question of 'when.' One bundle is for the end of June. The other is for the end of the summer."

Laura placed her mug carefully in front of her, took

her spoon and tapped the cup's rim. Finally silence prevailed, and everyone turned their attention to her.

"What pool on Laura?" she asked in a quiet, authoritative voice.

In unison, all the men looked at Bart.

"Why, it's as obvious as the nose on your face, my dear. You're donating hours at the library to the children. You've made friends. You're part of the community now." He beamed at her.

"And?" she prodded.

"And you'll be buying your own house here and settling in." He smiled encouragingly. "It'll be a happy day when I show you some properties. But will it be by the end of June or by the end of the summer? That's what we're deciding."

Stunned, Laura needed a moment to figure out an appropriate reply for a bunch of charming rascals old enough to be her father and more. "Haven't I mentioned that my sister wants me to move to Atlanta?"

Every face fell. What she'd give to have a camera!

"However," she continued, stretching out the word, "I'm not sure yet."

Grins all around again. And a babble of voices. All urging her to stay in Pilgrim Cove. Her heart filled as she acknowledged the genuine affection they felt for her.

"You've got the pink color in your cheeks," said Bart. "Sea View House will do it every time." He turned to Doc Rosen. "Has she not gained a pound or two since she's arrived?"

Only the expression in Doc's eyes changed as he focused on her. His keen appraisal made Laura feel as if he could see through her, that his visual exam would reveal her secrets as clearly as an MRI would. Her nerves tingled; her hands felt clammy. How could he possibly know about her? She'd told no one.

Finally Doc nodded. "She'll do." He faced Laura then. "Grief destroys appetite. Another couple of pounds wouldn't hurt."

She exhaled and relaxed, until she heard the Chief say, "Here's a man who'll have an opinion. Morning, Matthew."

Laura swiveled in her seat, and sure enough Matt Parker was walking toward their table, all six feet of him, broad shoulders outlined by the fabric of his jersey, long legs encased in snug jeans and his eyes fixed only on her.

"Morning, all," said Matt. "My opinion about what?" he asked as he joined the group but remained standing.

"How do you think Laura looks now that she's been in Pilgrim Cove almost a month?" It was the Chief's voice, and from the corner of her eye, Laura saw the retired cop elbow Lou, who was seated next to him.

"How does she look?" Matt repeated the question as he continued to stare at her. "She looks good. Too damn good!"

Pinned to her seat by the force of his gaze, Laura couldn't breathe, her heart almost leaped from her chest. She focused on Matt, oblivious to everyone else at the table. Oblivious to the whole diner.

When he jerked his head toward the door, she rose without saying a word and followed him outside. He led her toward the rear of the building, away from the busy main entrance, then stopped and faced her. Her back was to the diner; she saw only Matt and gasped at the intensity of his expression.

"You're driving me crazy," he said. It should have been a compliment, but he didn't sound happy. His hoarse voice revealed strong emotions held in check.

"What…?"

He placed his forefinger gently over her mouth and silenced her. "I think about you all the time." The words came out one by one, reluctantly but in a softer tone.

Interesting but still confusing. "All the time?" she asked, standing very still.

"And I'm not used to being distracted like that. It's not a way for a man to live!" He paced in front of her now. "You may not know this, Laura, but after Valerie died, I decided not to allow myself to become involved with a woman."

She hadn't known, but now understood his mixed signals a little better.

"But you," he whispered, coming to a halt, "you're different." His hand quivered as he raised it to stroke her cheek. "You're kind. Intelligent. Brave. Honest. And you're always on my mind. Damn it!"

Should she laugh or cry? She waited.

"And the other night, when I kissed you…"

She remembered all too well. "On the forehead," she reminded him.

He winced. "I wanted to do this." He tilted her face toward him and captured her lips, covering her mouth with a hunger that belied any doubts.

Instantly her arms locked around his neck, and she answered him with a hunger of her own. Like nothing she'd ever felt before. Like nothing she'd ever imagined. As though from a distance, she heard Matt whisper her name.

"Yes, I'm here." She returned his kisses until she had no oxygen left at all.

And then suddenly, she could breathe again. Matt was staring straight ahead, over her shoulder, a look of horror on his face.

"You won't believe this," he said.

She felt herself being turned around by Matt's strong hands. And through the rear windows of the diner, she saw five grown men on their feet looking back at her, arms raised in victory, cheering.

Heat traveled from her toes to her forehead in three seconds. She felt the burn in her cheeks. "The price you pay for living in a small town."

"They're going to call my dad in no time flat. Let's give them a real story to tell." He reached for her again.

HE'D NEVER HAVE TO KNOW.

In her kitchen, Laura slathered some cream cheese

onto a bagel two hours after she and Matt left The Diner's parking lot. Each had gone their own way, he to a job and she to the grocery store. She'd absolutely refused to return to the ROMEOs' table after their group display and now she was starving.

Surely they'd make love soon, and then he'd know.

She'd see Matt later that evening—early if she wanted to attend Brian's game at five o'clock and join the family for pizza afterward. Seemed pizza was a ritual for any evening game.

A temporary love affair would work for her. Almost two months left on her lease.

She had a lot of preparation to do for the audition in two weeks. The baseball game would take up too much of her time anyway.

Temporary? Liar! Her feelings for Matt ran deep. Temporary would not be her choice. Although things might wind up that way…once Matt learned about her illness. Would he stick around?

The bagel was gone. She hadn't tasted a bit of it, which was a shame because she'd used regular cream cheese instead of light. Doc Rosen said a few more pounds, hadn't he?

So maybe Matt would be okay with a temporary love affair. Not likely. Not based on the way he'd devoured her earlier. His eyes had shone with more than heat. If it wasn't love, it was close to it.

Laura slumped in her chair, her lids closing. The two halves of her brain made her head ache with their silent duel of words and rationalizations. There was a

chance, of course, that she was concerned about nothing. That Matt would simply take her situation in
stride. He was a grown, mature man.

And maybe cows really did jump over the moon.

Shoot! There was only one thing to do now. She
stood up, changed into running shoes and headed out
the back door. She might hit her longest distance yet.

MATT WAS BACK at Parker Plumbing and Hardware
by noon, amazed at how quickly the morning had
fled. Or maybe he'd daydreamed the time away as he
unstuffed two kitchen sinks and consulted with a
home owner about adding a bathroom to his house.

Daydreaming. Very unlike him. Matt Parker was
definitely *not* a dreamer, day or otherwise. Dreams
had been knocked out of him years ago. But this
morning, when he turned a wrench, he remembered
Laura's first day at Sea View House when she'd
handed him one. The image of her beautiful face and
her mass of curls floated in his head as he worked.
So what else could he have been doing except daydreaming?

He parked the van in the lot and spotted the SUV.
Good. His dad and sons were already here. Although
the family didn't open the store with him in the early
morning, they usually reconnected there at lunchtime.
On his way to the shop, he'd picked up a gallon of
fish chowder and a dozen sandwiches—food for
everyone on his Saturday staff, including his family.

He was darn lucky that his dad helped with the

kids. Their living arrangement worked well for all of them. As he often told Sam, "The kids keep you young, Pop." To which Sam always replied, "Then why is my hair grayer every day?" But he'd wink and grab whichever boy was closest and give him a hug. Yeah, the Parker men all stood strong together. But with that thought, Matt's mind suddenly flashed to his younger brother, Jason, and he sighed. Almost all.

Hands full, he pushed the door open with his shoulder. Business was brisk. Customers were standing in front of both registers, and his two part-time staff who were ringing up sales waved to him without speaking.

"Hi, ladies." He raised the lunch bag, and they nodded, eyes brightening. The "Golden" girls, as Blanche and Ethel Gold liked to call themselves, were easy to please. Fresh fish from the cold north Atlantic waters would make their day. In fact, they used to have their own fishing boat, often supplying catch to local restaurants until one day, a storm surprised them. They survived, but their boat didn't. In deference to their husbands' howls of anguish, they never replaced the boat.

Interesting family—the sisters were married to two brothers so they still shared the same last name. Matt didn't know if they needed the money they earned working for him, or if they just wanted to remain active. He never asked and never would. They were jewels and they'd have a job with him for as long as they wanted.

Matt moved to the back of the store and into the break room, where Brian and Casey were watching television. Instant noise followed his appearance, and Matt wondered if his kids were excited to see him or if they were simply clamoring for lunch.

He set the purchases on the table and took out bowls from the closet. This was one lounge that offered real kitchen conveniences—sink, microwave, refrigerator, coffeepot—as well as a couch, perfect for catnaps. Sam had used it more than once and Casey had slept on it many times in the past.

"Practice starts at four, Dad. You won't forget to pick me up at the house, will you?" asked Brian.

"Four?" Matt looked into his son's earnest face and hated to disappoint him. "I'm sorry. I can't leave that early. But Grandpa can drive you."

Brian shook his head. "Nope. Grandpa and Aunt Ethel and Aunt Blanche are going to close up tonight," he explained, using courtesy titles for the women who'd known him since he was born. "We figured it out already."

"You did?"

"Yup. Grandpa asked them," Brian explained. "Because tonight's special."

"It is?"

"Yeah, Dad. It's baseball! At night...maybe lights..."

"And y-y-you have t-t-to pick up Laura!" Casey grinned at him. "Grandpa said so."

"He did, did he?" Matt was beginning to see where the conversation was going.

"Yeah. And Aunt Ethel and Aunt Blanche said so, too." That was Brian, trying to add weight to the argument.

Holy Toledo. "We'll see." Matt was deliberately noncommittal as he filled their soup bowls. "I'll have to check it out. Meanwhile, eat up and don't make a mess. They need me out front."

And he needed to speak to Sam.

But his dad was with a customer, and a moment later so was Matt. Spring always brought out people with home-improvement projects on their mind. This was the season for the retail side of his business to make numbers. He carried a full line of tools and home supplies from lightbulbs to mailboxes to table saws.

It took an hour to get private time with his dad. And not in the break room where the people in his life had ears as big as satellite dishes.

Sam seemed as delighted with the privacy as Matt and started talking before Matt could say a word.

"I got a phone call this morning," began Sam, "from Bart Quinn. He called me from The Diner." A grin slowly crossed Sam's face. "Darn! Wish I'd been there."

Oh boy. Matt knew exactly what was coming next. And then was shocked to see the grin fade and a tear roll down his dad's face.

"What, Pop? What's upsetting you?" Matt grabbed his father's arms.

But Sam just shook his head. "I'd almost given up hope. In four years, you've never brought a woman home. Valerie was a wonderful woman, but you can't mourn forever. You're still young. You've got a life ahead of you. And the boys... Well, a mom would be great for them."

"But we're all right, Pop."

Sam nodded. "We survive. Parents and children together. But there's more out there for you. And you've got to reach for it."

Now his dad grabbed Matt's arms. "Listen to me, son. I know you're afraid, but if Laura's the right one, take the chance!" Sam's grip remained strong. "Because if she is the right one, you'll have a second chance for a wonderful life. And this time, hopefully, a long one together. Filled with passion and trust. Like your mom and I had. The kind Bart Quinn had with his Rosemary. The kind Lou Goodman still has with Pearl. Grab the chance, Matthew. This is what I've been praying for."

Matt froze, stunned at Sam's fervor. Seemed his quiet dad could hide his feelings very well. Until his son was affected. Until he thought his child needed him. Would Matt feel any less emotion about the welfare of his own sons? He pictured Brian in his mind's eye. He pictured Casey. And his heart swelled with love and pride and wonder. He'd protect them with his life.

"I hear you, Pop," he whispered, and felt Sam's hold relax. Then he added, "I can't get her out of my mind."

"That's the way it starts," said Sam, a faraway look in his eyes.

"She's…she's…wonderful! And this morning at The Diner…"

"I heard it was the parking lot, to be exact," Sam interrupted with a twinkle.

"The ROMEOs and their cell phones," groaned Matt. "Did they call the whole town?"

"Now, now," Sam soothed as though comforting a child. "They've got your best interests at heart."

Matt's imagination soared. The image of his dad's cohorts at The Diner that morning cheering in the window…the mental picture of Bart Quinn's big fingers trying to punch numbers on a cell phone "no bigger than a leprechaun's toe"…the tactile memory of holding Laura in his arms…her shock and blush when she saw the "boys"…

He started to chuckle. The movie reel running in his mind played over and over. His chuckles grew into waves of laughter emanating from deep inside his belly.

"I'm sure you're right, Dad," he finally replied when he could speak again. "My best interests. Just make sure they've got Laura's best interests at heart, too."

BY THE END of the first inning, Laura was enjoying herself immensely. A perfect evening for baseball.

The setting sun was a bright orange ball in the darkening sky, and an evening breeze carried the fragrance of new grass, the promise of spring. At the end of March, it also held a chill. She was glad she'd worn a jacket.

She could have been sitting in the bleachers of Anytown, U.S.A., for a typical family night of Little League baseball. Loads of parents, friends, and little brothers and sisters roamed the sidelines or sat and watched. Some adults had brought their own, more comfortable, lawn chairs. Laura shifted on the hard bench. Next time, so would she. Next time…

Of course, sitting beside Matt and watching Brian catch a fly ball made the experience more special. She cheered with the rest of the team's supporters whenever any of the kids did something right. And her heart tugged whenever a child dropped the ball. The poor kids' faces were masks of disappointment for every error they made. They took it so seriously that Laura started to call, "Next time, honey. Next time, sweetheart."

Matt turned to her, brows raised. "Honey? Sweetheart?"

She jabbed him. "Well, they're so young. And they're trying so hard."

He hugged her in return and started naming the players. She'd never remember them all tonight, but maybe in time…

She surveyed the area for Casey and Katie, and

spotted them behind the dugout, noses pressed against the fence. "Seems your niece is as excited about the game as your sons are."

"She'd never allow herself to be left out," Matt said. "She's a great kid, too."

"Spoken like an unbiased uncle," she teased.

Matt's arm came around her, and he hauled her against him. "You questioning my objectivity?"

She nodded against his chest. "You bet."

"Well, you should!" He leaned down, his lips meeting hers in a quick kiss, causing her heart to ricochet.

She loved feeling his arm around her as though they belonged together, and she was going to enjoy it. She wasn't going to worry anymore. No promises had been made, no vows given. Just as she had acquired her own history, Matt also came with a series of relationships and events from which sprang a myriad of attitudes. If she focused only on the baggage they both had, she'd drive herself crazy and miss the good times.

She and Matt were still at the beginning stages of their relationship. The exploration stage. They could break apart over something totally unrelated to her past illness. From now on, she wasn't going to worry.

She tilted her head back. "Want to kiss me again?"

He obliged immediately, and kept his arm around her, as well. Laura couldn't think of a better way to enjoy the game.

By the end of the evening, her brain was full of

names and images of everyone she'd met during the game and afterward at Three P's Pizza.

All the three *P*'s stood for, Matt had explained, was Polini's Pizza Parlor, but Benny Polini thought the name was a good conversation piece for his restaurant. Got people talking. Privately, Laura thought the place should have just been called "Benny's," because every kid and parent who patronized it after the game said, "Hi, Benny," as soon as they walked in.

"So, who gets to carry the pitchers of free drinks tonight?" Benny asked.

And Laura learned that the teams were provided with unlimited soft drinks while their coaches paid for the pizza.

"Great rewards for coaching," she joked to Matt at their table. "They give their time *and* their money!"

"And you're donating your time to the library," Matt reminded her.

She nodded. "Yesterday was great. I think I got more out of it than the children did."

Matt smiled. "That's the best kind of volunteering. We all do a little. Dad and I donate repair services or materials to low-income folks who are trying to get by. The ROMEOs somehow find out about families slipping through the cracks of government services."

"So Pilgrim Cove has its social problems, too," said Laura. "I was beginning to wonder."

"You haven't been here long enough to know. But

trust me, there aren't any money trees growing in our backyards.''

An hour later, Matt walked her to the front door of Sea View House while his older son remained in the van. Sam had taken Casey with him to drop Katie off at her house.

"Did we wear you out?'' Matt asked as she turned the key in the lock.

Laura laughed. "I had a great time.''

"Not a very glamorous date, though. Not by Boston standards.''

She couldn't miss the question in his voice and tilted her head to see him better under the porch light. "Pilgrim Cove is growing on me.'' A quiet statement.

His eyes warmed. "Good,'' he whispered. "Want to join us for dinner tomorrow night? Probably a barbecue at the house.''

She hesitated.

"Or have you had enough of us?'' he added. "I understand. It's okay.''

Squeezing his hand, she shook her head. "I can handle you. But, Matt, have you considered that maybe your family needs time? Not only time to get used to me being around, but also your undivided time and attention. The kids are used to having you to themselves. Especially on a Sunday.''

She could see him processing her words before he replied. "They're also used to me going out on emergency calls sometimes, but I see your point.'' He sighed. "I just don't want to imagine complications where there aren't any."

"Believe me, Matt, I'm the last person on earth who wants complications. But we're not sixteen and seventeen anymore. And life is more complex. We both know that." She reached up to stroke his cheek. "Let's take it one day at a time," she whispered. "I've found that it works for me."

He grasped her hand and kissed her palm, then leaned down and kissed her on the mouth with a passion that rocked her senses. She lifted to her toes, pressing for more.

"One day at a time, huh?" Matt finally rasped when he raised his head an inch. "Then we're starting on Day Ten." He kissed her short and hard once more and loped back to the van.

She watched him go, then caught a glimpse of Brian pulling back from the side window, a very curious expression on his face.

CHAPTER NINE

CASEY PARKER'S STOMACH HURT. He hated three
o'clock every school day, but Fridays were the worst.
And today was going to be especially bad. Two of
his regular buddies were absent. They were both
throwing up from a virus, which sounded pretty good
to Casey. It was better than throwing up because they
were scared—like he was.

He really liked Ms. Mosely, but she said goodbye
at the classroom door and then the fifth-grade monitors walked the class to the bus. He wished Brian was
one of the monitors. He could always count on his
brother to help him out on the hundred-mile walk.
That's what he called it in his mind. The hundred-
mile walk.

He waved to Ms. Mosely, then scanned the hall-
ways to see who was around today. Everybody. Including the fourth-grade monsters. A group of three
boys who bothered him almost every day. Well, the
best thing for him to do now was hide in the crowd.
Until he could find Brian.

The exit loomed ahead. He wished he could be invisible and ride the bus in secret. From behind him,

he heard a dreaded voice. "Hey, mumbles. Why don't you spit those marbles out of your mouth?" And then the giggling. Several voices. Girls, too.

He didn't turn around, just continued walking. Dad said to ignore it, so he would. He passed through the big double doors and started down the wide flight of steps. This was the hard part.

"Ca-Ca-Casey! D-d-don't f-f-fall!" Someone bumped against him accidentally-on-purpose, and Casey stiffened to keep his balance.

"Y-y-y-yeah, C-C-Casey," mimicked another kid. "Cat got your t-t-tongue?"

He wanted to scream at them, but he couldn't even talk. Maybe the cat really did have his tongue. Nothing in his mouth worked!

"Those boys are mean." He noticed Katie was beside him and he nodded, happy to see her, but knowing she couldn't do anything, either. She was too small, just like him.

Suddenly the fourth-grade monsters cut between him and Katie. He was alone and surrounded.

BRIAN PARKER LED the kindergarten class through the side exit of the school building. The kids were cute and usually listened to him, but he would have felt better if he'd been assigned as monitor to Casey's second-grade class. Especially for the afternoon dismissal when every kid in school was looking for some action after sitting all day. And very few teachers were outside.

He turned the corner with the children in tow. A crowd of kids gathered on the sidewalk in front of the main entrance. His body tensed, his hands curling into fists. The scene looked familiar, and he just knew Casey was involved. When he saw his friend, Steve, running toward him, his suspicions were confirmed.

"They tripped him, and he fell down the steps. But he flung his bookbag at one of the boys and hit him in the gut." Steve looked proud of Casey's accomplishments.

"Walk these kids to the buses, Steve. I gotta go see Casey." He ran without waiting for a response.

A path through the crowd opened for him as he approached. Katie was helping Casey to his feet. But then Casey pulled away from her, his lips tightly pressed together as he gathered himself up.

"Hey, Case," Brian called as he approached.

His brother stared at him, eyes opened wide. No tears fell. His face was pale, except for the bruise on his cheek. He said nothing.

Brian leaned down and put his hands on Casey's shoulders. "Who did it this time?"

But Casey didn't reply. Just continued staring into space. Brian's stomach flip-flopped. This was worse than usual.

Brian scanned the crowd. Some of the kids were walking toward the buses. A few of Casey's friends looked scared. Katie looked furious.

"It was Mike Murphy and those fourth graders."

Then she grinned for a second. "I kicked one of them."

Great. His little girl cousin was fighting his battles. "I've told those guys to leave Casey alone. They think they're safe because they're on a different bus than we are," Brian said. "I'm going to take care of them after we get home."

"Whatcha gonna do, Bri?"

"What I always do to everyone who picks on Casey. I'm gonna beat 'em up."

"It won't help. Nothing can help." Casey's words were barely audible. Brian rolled his shoulders and cracked his knuckles. If he had to, he'd take on the whole fourth grade, one bully at a time.

MATT PULLED his van in front of Sea View House and turned the ignition off. During the week since the ball game, he'd usually managed to visit Laura once during the day between service calls. Today he arrived midafternoon because of her Friday commitment to the library in the morning.

His visits to Sea View House had become the highlight of his day. And Laura's glorious smile, when she opened the door, gave him hope that she felt the same.

He walked down the driveway to the beach side of the house and knocked, hoping today would not be an exception. It wasn't. Her eyes lit up when she saw him, and he drew her to him for a kiss. It was the natural thing to do, and her response was all he could hope for.

But he wouldn't rush her. He wouldn't take the chance of spoiling everything. He cared about Laura. She was a beautiful woman inside and out, and he wanted her so badly his whole body trembled at the thought of making love to her. *Of being loved by her.*

Suddenly needing air, he pulled at the neckline of his shirt and took a small step backward before Laura could feel how ready he was. When the time came, he vowed silently, the wait would be worth it. And when they were finally together, he wouldn't rush her either. Even if it killed him.

"Come on in." She held the door open.

He entered the kitchen. Two mugs, two spoons and a plate of cookies waited on the table. The light under the kettle was glowing. His throat closed for a moment. She'd always been hospitable with a hot drink after he arrived. But today…she'd been waiting for him.

"This is nice," he said, nodding at the table.

"Your three-o'clock snack," she said with a smile, turning her attention to the stove. "Kids aren't the only ones who need an afternoon pick-me-up."

Matt chuckled and sat down. "I guess you're right."

"So, how's Brian doing with his play?"

"You mean Ben Franklin? He wants…" His cell phone rang, cutting off his explanation of how Brian wanted to reenact the discovery of electricity. "This is Matt Parker," he said into the phone.

"You'd better get home," said Sam. "We got problems."

"What kind of problems?"

"Casey came home crying and Brian was threatening to beat the hell out of some kids who'd picked on his brother. And then they both took off on their bikes. Wouldn't listen."

"I'm on my way." Matt stood and walked to the door, phone still in his ear. "Hang on, Pop." He looked at Laura, who had a confused expression on her face. "Gotta go. My kids are looking for trouble."

"Can I help?" Now she looked worried.

"Thanks, but I can't think how." He kissed her quickly and left.

"Phone me later," she called after him.

He nodded, waved, then spoke into the cell as he walked to his vehicle.

"Call the store, Pop. Casey might look for me there. The Golden girls are working today. Tell them to hold him down if he shows up. Brian, too."

"Will do."

"And then track down Lila. Tell her the same thing. Casey might ride to see Katie." No one else immediately came to mind.

"Okay."

"I'll cover the streets," Matt said. "You stay by the phone."

"Got it."

Matt disconnected from his father and scanned the road in front of him, half expecting to get a call back within five minutes. Only about a mile separated the Parker home from the store, and Casey had probably—hopefully—headed straight there. Brian, as he knew from experience, wouldn't show up until he'd accomplished his goal. Matt cursed under his breath. The situation was getting out of hand with both his sons. Casey was miserable, and Brian was earning a reputation as a fighter.

Matt drove slowly from Beach Street along Outlook Drive, stopping at the corner of Oceanside and looking left and right down that broad cross-street. He faced front again, about to drive through the intersection, when he saw movement. Fast, crazy movement along the side of the street. A boy on a bike. Head bent, pedaling as though his life depended on a quick getaway. And staring only at the ground. Jeez! The kid wasn't watching for traffic.

Matt pulled over, shifted into Park and jumped from the vehicle. He ran across Oceanside to intercept Casey before his son reached the intersection.

"Yo! Casey!"

A dirty, tear-filled face looked up. Casey jumped from his moving bike and ran straight into Matt's arms. "I—I—I…"

"Shh. It's all right, Case." Matt's arms tightened around his child, and then he stroked his son's back, hoping to calm him.

It worked for about five seconds.

"I—I want L-L-L...the la-dy!" he finally managed, pulling himself away from his dad.

"You mean Laura?" asked Matt.

Casey nodded with vigor, his forehead crinkled with worry lines.

"Then let's get your bike in the van."

Matt watched his son fetch the bike where it had fallen and bring it to their vehicle. He slid the side panel open and hoisted the two-wheeler inside. Then he lifted Casey into the front passenger seat. "Seat belt."

Casey obliged, then looked at Matt, his lips pressed together. He waved his arms forward and around, indicating Matt should make a U-turn back to Sea View House.

Matt's heart sank. Speech seemed beyond Casey's ability at the moment. So asking the boy about Brian's whereabouts seemed out of the question. Matt couldn't remember the last time Casey had been reduced to absolute silence. His normally cheerful disposition usually helped him to rise above it.

Again Matt parked in front of Sea View House, this time honking the horn. The door opened almost immediately, and Laura stepped out. Matt heard Casey fiddle with the seat belt and watched him race directly toward his target.

"Easy," Matt called, hoping his sturdy young son wouldn't mow Laura down. As he watched Laura scoop Casey up and twirl him around in one smooth motion, he sighed with relief.

He phoned Sam with the update and asked him to start looking for Brian. Then he followed his son and Laura into the house, trying to understand the meaning underneath Casey's garbled verbiage.

LAURA HUGGED Casey tightly, blinking back her own tears, trying to recall everything she'd ever learned about the problems stutterers faced.

She cuddled the child as she walked, leading Matt into the living room. She sat down in the corner of the sofa, her arm around Casey, who sat right next to her. Matt sprawled on the floor in front of them.

Stroking the child's arms, murmuring reassurances, kissing the top of his head, Laura waited for Casey to relax. She glanced at a worried Matt and raised her brow in question. He replied with a slight shrug. Whatever that meant.

Finally Casey squirmed and pushed himself away until he could face her. Laura waited, but Casey said nothing, just looked at her with pleading eyes.

"Tell me, Casey. Start anywhere."

For a minute, she thought he wouldn't or couldn't respond. He looked at his dad, then back at her. She swore Matt was holding his breath, but he managed to smile and nod at his son.

And then broken words tumbled from his mouth. In fits and starts. With anger and pain. With small fists clenched.

The big kids had made fun of him again today. A lot of them. In the hall and on the steps at school. They scared him. They were mean!

"I see," said Laura, glancing at Matt, then back at Casey.

"They're called bullies," said Laura.

Casey nodded. "F-fourth-grade monster b-b-bullies!"

"Bullies make fun of others just to make themselves feel more important. And they pick on smaller kids because," Laura lowered her voice, "they're not brave at all. They're cowards!"

Casey nodded agreement with enthusiasm.

"So, we need a plan."

Hope shone in Casey's eyes for the first time. He sat taller, leaned forward.

"Let's think of some choices."

"B-b-beat 'em up." He punched the air.

A cough from the floor made Laura glance at Matt. He looked less tense. She felt better, too. Not because she advocated fighting, but because Casey's spirit was on the rebound. For that, Laura was grateful. Confidence was the key to this boy's happy childhood.

"Let's think of other ways, Casey," she said. "Those boys are a lot bigger than you."

"Brian helps me," replied Casey. "He's big, too."

"Case?" asked Matt, his eyes narrowing.

The child looked at his dad.

"Just where is Brian now?"

Casey stared at the far wall and shrugged.

"Casey," Matt repeated his son's name in a warning tone. "Where's Brian?"

The child appealed to Laura with a look.

"Oh, no," said Matt, squatting in front of his son. "You're not playing Laura and me against each other."

Laura said nothing. Matt had been in the parenting business for years. She had no experience at all. Casey was silenced, too. And then the doorbell rang.

Laura buried a smile, thinking how they were "saved by the bell," an impatient bell that rang again just before Brian burst into the house, calling for his dad and then stopping in his tracks when he saw all three of them, including Casey.

"I saw the van," he said, and then spoke to his brother. "Don't worry, Case. At least Mike Murphy won't bother you again."

Laura turned from Casey, whose eyes lit up with relief, to Brian, who was flexing his fingers.

"Will I be getting a call from the Murphys, Brian?" Matt asked, getting up from the floor and examining his son's hands. "Go wash these cuts and bruises while I call Grandpa. He's out looking for you."

"But, Dad," protested Brian, "you don't understand what they do to Casey!"

"There are other ways to help." He put his hands on Brian's shoulders. "Did you ever think of next year? You won't be around in the same building. What will Casey do then?"

"I don't know," he admitted.

"And you don't have to know, Brian," said Matt. "What you should have done is told me about it. I'm the dad, remember? And Casey's teacher knows how to get me at any time."

"Yeah. But Ms. Mosely isn't around to see it."

Laura watched Matt lead Brian into the kitchen, and then turned to Casey. "Do you see the problem, Casey?"

Tears started to form in the child's eyes, and Laura felt herself start to panic. "Don't cry, sweetheart. We're going to come up with a plan. Remember? A plan to handle bullies."

She had his attention again. "What?" he asked.

Laura's mind raced to possibilities. "You could start by asking your teacher for more help." She paced her speech and adopted a soothing low tone. "You like Ms. Mosely, and Brian says she doesn't know everything that's going on. I bet she would be very worried about you if she knew, and she'd do something about it."

Laura continued to talk and make suggestions about handling the bullies, like walking away from them or looking them in the eye and saying, "So what?" in regard to his stuttering. "I know it's hard to be brave when facing somebody who acts tough. But sometimes just acting brave is enough to stop a kid from picking on you." She snapped her fingers. "Maybe your school has an anti-bully program you don't know about. We can find out."

She paused as Casey tried to digest what she'd said. His little face was so expressive, nose crinkling, brow furrowing. She reminded Casey that his own classmates in second grade were his buddies. He had a lot of friends on the block where he lived, as well.

"And you are so good at so many things. For example, you're absolutely great at music. You can sing better than lots of people. And you use your voice for that, too."

The child nodded.

"And you play the piano. Not many seven-year-olds can do that, either!"

Now Casey was smiling.

"She's right, you know, Case," said Matt from the threshold as he returned to the living room with Brian. "You're a terrific little musician. You're a Parker!"

The child grinned at his dad, and Laura's heart overflowed as she watched them interact with each other.

Then Casey said, "Row your boat, Dad."

"Okay." Leaning his shoulder casually against the wall, Matt began the old folk round, "'Row, row, row your boat, gently down the stream.' Casey started the song at the beginning of his dad's second line, the precise moment he should have to develop the round.

Laura looked at Brian, who mouthed, *Our turn.* And they jumped in on time to complete the three-part round. To Laura's amazement, no one missed a beat for the entire time they sang. And Casey carried his part alone like a champion.

"That was great," Laura said when they came to the end. "Such fun. And Casey, you're wonderful. Right on time with no problems. Maybe music can help when you want to say something difficult. You could use a tune you already know."

"Like 'Row your Boat'?" His nose crinkled again. And then he sang,

"Go, go, go away,
When I'm in the hall,
Someday I'll be big enough,
To make the bullies fall."

Eyes wide as though he surprised himself, Casey started to giggle.

Laura couldn't say a word. Couldn't stop staring at Casey. It seemed Matt and Brian felt the same. They were totally silent—at least for the first five seconds.

Laura watched Matt scoop up his younger son and bury his face in the boy's neck. "You are something special, Case. I love you. Very, very much."

"Me, too, Daddy."

And then Brian was standing at her side, his head almost reaching her chin. He looked into her face, studying it as though he'd never seen her before.

"What's wrong, sweetie?"

At first, he said nothing. But after a moment, "You made Casey happy." He started to smile.

Laura leaned closer to him. "You've got it wrong, Brian. Your brother made himself happy. He figured out what to do. I didn't do it for him. In fact, I *can't* do it for him. And neither can you. Even though you wanted to, it's not your job. Next time, ask for help. Okay?''

"Okay."

Laura extended her hand. "Shake?"

"Shake." He suited action to words.

"You're a terrific big brother," said Laura. "Casey's lucky to have you."

Matt turned toward her and Brian, and motioned the boy to him. Then Laura watched him carefully slide Casey down his body to the floor. He led the boys to the other side of the room and into the center hall. "Stay here," he said to the children. "I'll be right back." He pivoted, his full attention now solely on her.

Laura watched him approach with sure, deliberate steps, his dark eyes capturing hers and not letting go. Time seemed to slow down as she waited for him, registering his every move. And then he stood before her, studying her, his eyes warm, his fingers stroking the line of her jaw.

She trembled, her breathing reduced to quivering puffs of air. His palm gently cupped her chin, raised it as he leaned down, his lips brushing her mouth…

"You're wonderful, Laura…more wonderful than I could have imagined." Whispered words, heartfelt words…loving words.

She heard them with all their undertones. And when his lips paused on hers, she raised on tiptoe and kissed him with eagerness and joy. Instantly his arms tightened around her, almost crushing her as his mouth answered her call. And when he finally released her, neither of them moved.

She stared at the rugged face looking back at her and knew her life had just changed. Matt Parker would be part of her forever, no matter what the future held.

MATT GLANCED in the rearview mirror at his boys in the back seat. He saw a quick elbow jab, some active pantomime accompanied by facial expressions only a love-blind parent would think cute. As a single dad, he couldn't afford to be that besotted.

His sons were either up to something or worrying about something. They were quiet riding back to the house, for the first half-mile.

"Dad?"

"Yes, Brian?"

"Hmm…Casey, stop poking me!"

Matt heard his younger son's loud whisper. "Just t-tell him."

"Tell me what?" Matt checked his mirror again. Brian was leaning forward, staring at him. He couldn't see Casey.

"About…about Laura," Brian said.

Now Matt really was curious. "What about her?"

"She's nice. I like her."

"Well, good," Matt replied, wondering where the conversation was heading. "I like her, too."

"Me-e, too! I l-o-ve her." The passion in Casey's words made up for the hesitations.

And suddenly, Matt's stomach rolled. His relationship with Laura was only in the discovery stage, not in the I'll-love-you-forever-let's-get-married stage. And now his kids' emotions were involved. Very involved. Casey had given his little heart to Laura.

"She-e-e smells nice. A-and she-e talks-s nice." He began to sing his own words to the "Row Your Boat" song.

Matt drove the van almost in a panic. Good God, what had he done? The more his kids got to know Laura, the more vulnerable they'd be. He should have kept his relationship with her separate. But then he thought about the ice storm. Nah. He'd couldn't have left her in that dark, cold house by herself. Never. And then there was the kitten. And the baseball game. She'd cheered Brian's team along with all the parents. Pilgrim Cove was a small town. It was hard to get lost in it, even for a newcomer.

He pulled into the garage, glad to be home, glad his own dad lived with them. Maybe Sam could give him some perspective.

The kids scrambled out and ran inside. Matt followed them more slowly, but was just in time to hear Brian say, "Grandpa! Dad was kissing Laura big time in her house."

And Casey stood in front of his grandfather, an expression of delight on his face, his head bobbing in agreement as fast as he could manage it.

Sam raised his eyes to Matt, and for a moment, Matt felt like a kid again, breaking curfew. He felt his face heat up and wished he had loitered in the garage for a minute more.

But Sam's smile and twinkle rivaled his grandson's. "Did you say 'kissing'?"

"Yup," replied Brian.

"Well, well, w-e-l-l. Is that right?" His dad actually beamed at him. "My son's finally courting! Does my heart good to hear this."

Whoa. Time to slow everyone down. The way his dad looked and sounded, he'd be announcing Matt and Laura's marriage to the ROMEOs the next morning at The Diner.

"She's only here temporarily, remember? So don't make too much of one kiss. Laura and I are just good friends." A lame excuse, but he'd learned something he should have realized. A single parent needed some privacy. Unfortunately, nothing was private in Pilgrim Cove.

LATER THAT EVENING, Matt closed his bedroom door and stared at the phone on his table. The kids were in bed, Sam was watching television, and Matt had Laura on his mind. He sat on the edge of the mattress, and bent down to untie his boot laces. Somehow he ended up making knots—to match the knots in his stomach. He laughed at himself. He was as bad as a teenager with a crush. Finally he propped himself against the pillows, stretched out and dialed.

"Hello." She answered on the first ring.

The familiar sound of her voice gave him a rush. He took a breath. "Hi." His tongue seemed to tangle around itself. For a grown man, he was pathetic with women. Or was his ineptness only with this woman, the woman he cared about? *Say something. Ask for a date.*

"I can't stop thinking about you," he said.

"Oh?" she replied, her voice soft and warm. "That's nice. I can say the same about you."

His heart beat in double time. "There's a place about forty minutes from here. Dinner and dancing. The food's very good. Would you like to go?" They'd dance slowly; he'd hold her close all evening. He loved the image.

"Go now?" Surprise laced her voice, and brought him back to the moment. "I'm already in my night-gown."

New image. Black silk, tiny straps. Soft skin and those blond curls. Sweat beaded his forehead, his lip… "Nightgown?" His voice squeaked.

Silence. Then "Yes." A throaty whisper. "A nightgown. Very sexy. A lovely shade of pale blue…heavy flannel with bunches of tiny violets."

He heard the laughter in her voice. "You're driving me crazy, Laura!"

"Sorry. I couldn't help it."

He heard the humor lurking underneath her words. "No, you're not sorry, woman. But I forgive you because I'm a great guy." He wiped his face with his sleeve, glad Laura couldn't see him, glad he was able to joke.

"I admit you've got potential," she said. Her tone continued to be light.

"So how about exploring that potential tomorrow night? An evening away from Pilgrim Cove?"

"You mean, an evening of privacy?" The beat of her words slowed.

"Small towns do have their pluses and minuses," Matt replied. "Lack of privacy is definitely on the minus side of the balance sheet."

"I'm beginning to figure that out," she said. "Let's make our escape. Tomorrow night is fine."

In his bedroom, Matt sighed with relief. Laura wanted to be alone with him as much as he wanted to be alone with her. As he hung up the phone, a knock sounded at the door. "Yo," Matt called.

Casey padded across the room to Matt's bed and jumped in. "I figured out what to do, but you need to help me." The stuttering problem marked his speech.

"I'm listening," Matt replied.

"Can you take me to school early on Monday? Before the other k-kids get there?"

"Why?"

"I'm going t-to t-t-talk to Ms. Mosely. She's the best one to help."

"Shake my hand, Case. It's a deal."

"But I-I'm gonna talk. Not you, Dad."

"You've got my word, son. Ms. Mosely is all

yours.'' He pulled the boy over for a kiss and hug. ''Have I told you what a terrific kid you are?''

''D-a-d!''

Matt laughed while tears stung his eyes. ''Come on, I'll tuck you in.''

After returning to his room, Matt stretched on the bed knowing he still had a smile on his face. Not only was Casey's school problem on its way to being solved, but Matt had a date with Laura to look forward to. Tomorrow night couldn't come fast enough.

CHAPTER TEN

"YOU'RE BEAUTIFUL." The words popped out of Matt's mouth as soon as he saw Laura standing in the doorway of Sea View House the next night.

She smiled at him. "Thanks, but it's probably the clothes. You've never seen me dressed up before."

"The clothes?" Matt tore his gaze from her face and looked at the burgundy-colored blouse and matching short wool skirt. "Nice," he murmured perfunctorily. Then stopped speaking. Legs. She had wonderful legs. Long ones. Shapely-at-the-calf ones. They were encased in a sheer version of the same wine color and ended in a pair of black strappy shoes with high heels.

He sucked in air, glad he was still in the doorway. "Like I said before, you're beautiful."

An uncertain expression crossed her face. "Thank you, but…"

Shy? He hadn't noticed an excess of that quality before. "No buts about it. You're beautiful."

She coughed as if embarrassed. Then looked at him. "Hang on, I'll get my coat. I haven't danced the night away in a long time, and I am ready!"

He nodded and hoped like hell she didn't mean *real* dancing. His imagination hadn't gone past slow-in-his-arms dancing. He shrugged. He'd take her in his arms any way he could get her.

An hour later, the maître d' of The Birches escorted them to a table that offered the illusion of privacy. Tall potted plants strategically placed between candlelit tables, nooks along the outside wall, dim romantic lighting and a low noise level all added to the fantasy. It was part of the restaurant's appeal to the couples who patronized it. The music and dancing would come later.

Matt studied the surroundings, more than satisfied with his choice, and noticed Laura's eyes grow large as she did the same.

He waited until she was seated and then took his place across from her at the table. With a flourish, the maître d' gestured for the waiter to approach and, after a few polite words, disappeared. The server immediately greeted them and produced a wine list. He rattled off the house special stock.

Matt eyed him. "Give us a minute."

"Chablis is fine," said Laura at the same time.

The waiter stepped back.

Matt reached for Laura's hand across the table. He stroked her smooth skin, enjoying the texture so different from his own. "We're not on a schedule tonight. We can set our own pace. Let's take it slow. No kids, no Pilgrim Cove. And tomorrow's Sunday.

We can sleep late." *Either alone or together.* He kept that part to himself.

Her eyes warmed, and she smiled. "You're absolutely right. We have no deadlines. But I have to admit, the freedom feels weird."

"We're stealing a night," Matt said. "I hope it's the beginning of many." He waited. She averted her eyes for a moment, then met his gaze.

"So do I," she whispered.

He squeezed her fingers and felt her gentle response. Life was good. "How about the Boston Symphony next Saturday night? I've got tickets."

She eyed him with suspicion. "You work fast."

"Not true," he protested. "We get season's tickets every year. And for each concert, we decide who wants to go. Dad, Brian. Even Casey gets a turn."

"Well, I don't want to take away—"

"Shh. None of them will mind. Trust me on that." He checked the wine list. "What would you like?"

He signaled for the waiter to return and, a few minutes later, cocktail in hand, sat back to enjoy the rest of the evening. And learn more about Laura.

Laura raised her glass in salute. "To beautiful music and a lovely evening."

"To our plan for many more of them," said Matt.

"Yes." A smile rested on her face as she nodded at him before sipping her Chablis. "Nice wine. Nice restaurant."

He watched her lazily scan the room and knew exactly when her expression changed. A combination of horror and disbelief.

"What's going on?"

She continued to stare at the entrance and began to chuckle. "I'm afraid you'll have to postpone that privacy wish. You won't believe who's walking this way."

"If it's anyone from home, I don't want to know."

"No choice. The maître d' is leading them past us."

Matt turned around then. "Chief O'Brien and Dee Barnes. The romance of the senior set."

"And what's so bad about that?" challenged Laura, sparks in her eyes.

"Absolutely nothing. They've been crazy about each other for ages, but she won't marry him." He raised his hands. "Don't ask me."

"I won't ask anybody!"

And then the Chief and Dee were abreast of them, and Matt couldn't miss the surprise and disappointment that flashed across the older man's face. But Rick quickly put a smile on, greeted Laura and shook Matt's hand.

"I didn't expect to see you here tonight," said the Chief.

"Likewise," replied Matt. "We were hoping…" He shook his head. "Forget it. There are no secrets around here."

"Oh, poor boy," said pint-size Dee, looking from

Matt to Laura. "Were you two hoping to get away from everyone?"

"That was the idea," said Laura. "Matt was trying to show me that privacy does exist in a small town."

"Ha!" Matt exclaimed, gesturing toward his watch. "Not counting the ride, the illusion lasted less than an hour."

"Oh, dear," said Dee. She looked at Rick. "Maybe we could go somewhere else?"

Rick looked at Dee with exasperation. "Lady, I'm dancing with you all night right here. And I have a few other things to say, too." Then he turned to Matt and Laura. "I have a better idea." He paused and looked Matt straight in the eye. "We never had this conversation. We never saw you. Will that work?"

"You bet," Matt said without hesitation.

"My lips are sealed," Laura volunteered.

Hands on her hips, Dee looked up at Rick. "My, my. And you, a cop. What kind of example are you setting?" But her eyes twinkled as she teased.

"I'm retired," the Chief replied. "And no one's testifying in court!"

"Well, then, it's settled. Let's leave these two young people alone." She winked at Matt and put her arm through Rick's.

Matt watched them follow the waiter, then sat down again.

"You know," Laura said slowly, "there is something to be said for a large city."

His heart dropped to his stomach. Did she mean it?

Even he had to admit that—for tonight at least—small towns had their disadvantages. "I guess cities and small towns both have good points and bad."

"Touché," she said, raising her glass. "Here's to the ferryboat route."

"I'll drink to that," said Matt, relaxing once more, wondering if his life would ever be calm again.

For a moment, his eyes rested on Dee Barnes and Chief O'Brien as they sat at their table across the room. Except when he was on the job, Rick O'Brien had never been as intense as he looked that evening. And all because of a woman.

Matt understood the feeling. A woman had the power to tie a man up in knots. He looked across the table at Laura and felt a smile grow. However, a woman also had the power to make a man happy to be alive. He reached for Laura's hand. "Let's dance."

"UNBELIEVABLE," Matt said an hour later as he escorted Laura back to their table. They'd danced between courses and, with Laura in his arms, Matt could have forgone the meal entirely. Unfortunately, his dance skills left a question mark in his mind.

"What's unbelievable?"

"That I haven't crushed your toes yet."

"Crushed? You're not bad at all. I'm having a great time."

She sounded sincere! He exhaled, more confident about the evening. Embracing Laura as they drifted to the music was everything his libido had hoped for.

Not to mention his heart. She fit so well. She smelled so good. He had no desire to be anywhere else.

"I'll tell you what's really unbelievable," said Laura, surprise written all over her face before her eyes started twinkling. "Just look across the room." Her hand fluttered in a certain direction.

He looked. Saw nothing. "What?"

"Dee and the Chief."

"We haven't seen them, remember?"

Laura shrugged. "Okay. Have it your way. But there's a big shiny ring on her finger that wasn't there thirty minutes ago."

Matt twisted so fast he almost landed on the floor. "Ho boy! The ROMEOs will be humming tomorrow." He studied the other couple, glimpsed the happiness on Rick's face, the softness in Dee's, their hands intertwined in full view of anyone passing by. At the moment, they didn't seem to give a hoot about who saw them.

He faced Laura, and his heart filled. "I think they have the right idea," he said without a qualm.

"Do you think marriage is better?" Her grin had disappeared. Her question was bottom-line serious.

"Better than what?" he replied.

"The single life."

"I think the right marriage is better. The kind filled with sharing and laughter and…and being there for each other." He reached for her hand and felt alive when her slender fingers tucked around his larger ones.

"I agree. Not just any marriage will do. I'm…I'm regaining my balance."

Matt's antenna went up. How many details of Laura's life did he really know about? He wanted to know more. Wanted to know her better. "Bad breakup?" he asked, gently squeezing her hand.

"Yes," she said. "The timing was rather awful." Her expression darkened. She seemed to wander into her bank of memories. Matt saw a flash of hurt in her expression. "And now I'm here," she continued. "Not merely for a respite, but for a new beginning, too."

He would have toasted new beginnings with expensive champagne if he'd had some. Instead, he said, "Dance with me again. Let's keep going until they throw us out of the place."

Laura's face lit up. "I'd love to dance all night. But I've never been thrown out of anywhere before."

"It's part of your new beginning." He reached for her again and led her to the floor just as the Chief and Dee approached them.

"Congratulate me, Matthew!" Rick said, urging the foursome to the side of the room. "Dee's finally allowing me to make an honest woman of her."

The jocular words couldn't hide the shine in Rick's eyes when he looked at his new fiancé. "And it only took five years!" he added, turning to Laura. "Five years of going back and forth when all we ever wanted was a home. A real home together."

"My best wishes," said Laura. "This is so exciting.'' She kissed Rick on the cheek and hugged Dee, before reaching for Matt. ''And we're the first to know.''

''By tomorrow morning, all of Pilgrim Cove will know,'' said Matt. ''But since it's Sunday, the news will take an hour longer to spread through The Diner.'' He looked at Dee. ''And what about The Diner?''

The petite woman placed her hands on her hips and raised her chin. ''I'm getting married, Matthew, not hiding away. I'm sixty years young and Rick says I've got the stamina of ten cops. I may not own it, but I run that place and will go on running it.''

The Chief leaned in, put his finger over her lips and said, ''She'll do what makes her happy.''

Now Dee's eyes were wet and shiny. She cocked her head toward Rick but looked at Matt. ''He finally got it.''

''Ha!'' said Rick. ''It took *her* five years to understand that I'm nothing like her first husband.''

Matt remembered Frank Barnes and not too favorably. Because of all his get-rich-quick schemes, he'd left Dee with debt and creditors knocking on her door. After he died, Dee had paid off each note. She deserved every bit of happiness she'd receive in this new marriage.

''So, when's the wedding?'' asked Laura. ''Another five years?''

''More like five minutes!'' replied the Chief before

waving goodbye and leaving the restaurant with Dee at his side.

Matt took Laura in his arms. "Five whole years! That's a long time to waste."

"Guess they didn't communicate too well in the past."

"Sometimes," said Matt, nuzzling her neck, "communication doesn't require words." He heard Laura laugh softly and then thought about nothing at all. Just enjoyed holding her.

"AND NOW THE EVENING'S OVER." Laura looked at Matt as they stood on the front porch of Sea View House. "Where did it go?" Her voice sounded wistful, and he had to laugh at her.

"Are you mourning the absence of a dance floor or the end of my scintillating company?" he teased.

She peeped at him from under her lashes. "Ah...you and the floor made a terrific combination."

"I'll go you one better," he replied. "I think you and I make a terrific combination."

In the dim lamplight, he saw her eyes shine, felt her lean toward him. He didn't wait. He wrapped his arms around her and covered her mouth with his own.

Instant sizzle.

Her need matched his. Her desire matched his. His blood sang, then roared. He inhaled the blend of her light perfume and her unique scent, and almost lost control. He pulled away. Stepped back. And just breathed.

Her breathing also matched his. Fast and uneven. She closed her eyes, and when she opened them, she seemed to have regained a sense of calm.

"I want to invite you in," she whispered. "But I'm not ready for that."

He'd known it somehow. "And I'm not going to rush you." He stood quietly, absorbing the picture she made in the dim light. Her curls—tamed somehow at the start of the evening—had returned to their unruly self with the help of a few fast rock numbers. The big blue eyes, irises so large now they looked black. And her tempting mouth, slightly puffy from his kisses.

"Go inside, Laura." He heard the huskiness in his voice.

"Yes, yes, I'm going." She sounded a bit confused, and he felt better. He wasn't the only one off-kilter.

"Thank you, Matt. For everything. I had a fabulous evening."

"Good. More to come next Saturday. Now get inside," he repeated almost in desperation.

Finally she did.

He walked slowly to the car, needing the time to relax again. To calm down. No matter his disappointment, he'd done the right thing. No woman wanted to feel rushed into making love.

As far as Matt was concerned, Laura could take as much time as she needed. She was worth the wait.

LAURA COULDN'T SLEEP after Matt left, so she paced. For hours.

"Like a damn cat on a hot tin roof," she mumbled at Midnight, who watched from the middle of Laura's bed. No question of who was starting to rule the house.

She looked at her watch. Six o'clock. Four hours since Matt had said goodnight. What to do? What to do? Her brain hurt from thinking. Her heart hurt from feeling. She plopped into her rocking chair, closed her eyes and managed to doze for an hour. But by seven, she needed to get outside. She had changed into sweats when Matt had dropped her off, and now all she had to do was lace up her running shoes and make her way to the shoreline.

The rising sun glistened off the water, the air smelled of salt and seaweed. Laura paused to stare at the calm Atlantic. She took a series of deep, measured breaths. Slowly, slowly, the ocean's white noise began to replace the tumult inside her until she'd found her equilibrium once more. Reassured, she began jogging up the beach.

She maintained a steady pace for an hour before reentering Sea View House. Then she picked up the phone and called her sister.

"So, are you ready to move down here and be close to us?" asked Alison after her initial greeting. "I've got a half-dozen condos lined up for you to see."

Laura laughed. "You're a stubborn woman, Alison, and I love you for it, but the answer's still no. In fact…'' She paused, suddenly tongue-tied.

''What?'' prompted Alison

''I…uh…I've met someone.''

Silence. Then, ''What? You have? That's fantastic. In Pilgrim Cove? Who? Tell me.''

Alison's enthusiasm was just what she needed. ''Do you remember a guy—or rather, a boy—named Matthew Parker? He'd have been two years younger than you. His dad ran the plumbing and hardware store?''

''Yes,'' Alison replied slowly. ''I remember him. Tall, skinny, dark and good-looking. Did he turn out as well as I'm now imagining him?''

''Definitely,'' replied Laura. ''He's still tall, dark and handsome. Certainly not skinny. Built the way you'd want a man to be built.'' Laura closed her eyes. ''Broad, strong. I feel so good when I'm with him. Safe. Happy.'' Now that she'd started, Laura couldn't seem to stop talking. ''And he's got the two sweetest little sons. His wife died four years ago. That's almost all I know about her. The kids are delicious. And…I really think they like me a lot.''

''Oh, sweetie!'' said Alison. ''And does he feel the same way about you? Should I be hearing wedding bells soon or what?''

''I think he does feel the same way, but…'' Without warning, tears spouted and ran down Laura's face. Tears from nowhere. She sobbed. ''I don't know. Be-

cause he doesn't know…you know what. And I don't
know what to do.''

No one else could have understood what she was
blabbering about, but Alison did. In a heartbeat, she
responded.

''If he loves you, the breast cancer won't matter.
Especially with your prognosis. And if he walks
away, then you're better off without him.''

Sometimes her sister showed a surprising ability to
get at the basic facts.

''But you've got to tell him,'' she continued. ''At
some point, you've got to tell him, especially with
kids involved. You'll know when the time is right.''

''I will?''

''Yes. Because when you love somebody, secrets
don't work.''

''I know,'' whispered Laura. ''I'll tell him. When
the time is right.''

THE CLOCK SAID NOON. Matt stood next to the kitchen
counter, watching coffee drip into the glass pot. The
house was quiet. A little too quiet, but he wouldn't
complain. Not until after he downed his first cup of
caffeine and regained full consciousness.

Without warning, however, he was suddenly surrounded by noise. The excited voices of his dad and
kids preceded their arrival in the kitchen. When they
spotted him, a cacophony of sound and words ensued.

''Why didn't you tell me?'' asked Sam.

"Dad, we had the best breakfast, and Ms. Dee was sitting at the table this time."

Matt grinned at his dad. "They didn't waste any time announcing it, did they?"

"Son of a gun, we just had a party! And the Chief said you and Laura were there last night."

"He did? After we promised never to tell anyone!"

"Well, now he knows you can keep your mouth shut. But you should have seen them, Matt. Like a couple of kids. They've set a wedding date already."

At the word "wedding," Matt stood straighter. "No kidding? When?"

"End of next month. Memorial Day weekend." Sam shook his head. "All this time lollygagging, and now everything's a rush."

"He's probably afraid she'll change her mind!"

Sam laughed and nodded in agreement.

"But she was sitting on his lap and everything," said Brian. "And he kissed her. In front of everybody. Yuck! So she can't change her mind now."

"Right," chimed in Casey. "She-e can't." Casey pulled at Matt's arm. "Did you k-kiss Lau-ra in f-f-front of e-everybody, too?"

Brian stepped closer to him, right next to Casey. "Or just in front of us when we were at Sea View House?" he added.

"Ho, ho, ho," chuckled Sam, sounding like Santa Claus. "And don't glare at me, son. Just answer the boys' questions."

"Coffee first," said Matt, playing for time. "And

that's not negotiable.'' He reached for a mug and poured. A splash of milk to cool it enough for immediate consumption. One swallow. His world came into better focus. Two swallows. His brain started revving up like a car's engine on a cold winter's morning. Needed a little more time than usual.

After the third gulp, he put his arm around each son. "Here's the deal, boys. Right now, Laura and I are simply friends. If, and I say if, our relationship changes to something more, you'll be the first to know. But that's not happening now, so don't think about it too much.''

Casey looked disappointed, Brian thoughtful.

"But I like Laura,'' said Casey.

"And she likes you,'' Matt said. He turned to Brian. "And you, too. She's a friend and she likes you both very much.'' Then he grinned. "But I don't know why! You guys are so noisy.''

The boys pounced on him, pummeling him, and he grabbed one in each arm and swung them around until they squealed and clung. He slowed down, kissed them and put them back on their feet. "Grab your gloves and we'll toss a ball around outside.''

Sweet silence in a nanosecond. "Amazing,'' Matt said, smiling at his own dad.

"They're crazy about baseball, and they're crazy about their father,'' Sam said in a matter-of-fact tone. "And I know you were playing down your feelings for Laura in front of the boys to protect them. But there's more to your relationship than you've let on.

So, the question is, will they be crazy about having a live-in mother? A twenty-four-hour-a-day mother?''

Good question. He hadn't thought through all the details yet. "Like I told the boys, Laura and I aren't that far along.''

Sam put his hands in his pockets and stared out the window. "You're a grown man, Matthew. And I haven't been such a good parent. God knows, if I had been more aware of what Jason was going through after the accident, maybe he would be here today. Instead, he's wandering the country, maybe the globe—only God knows where.''

Sam paused, sighed, then turned and stared directly at Matt. "I failed him and I failed Jared, too. May my boy rest in peace.'' He blinked rapidly. "So I'm not in a position to give advice.''

Matt put his arm around his dad and squeezed. "You were and are a terrific father and a wonderful grandfather. You were distracted back then. Mom was…was…beside herself because of Jared. Not in her right mind. I don't want to hear any more talk like that.''

But Sam shrugged him off and grabbed Matt by the upper arms. "Listen to me now. It's important. For you and for the boys.''

Matt kept quiet. His dad's outburst was unusual.

"I should have been stronger.'' Sam's voice was softer now. "I should have seen what was happening. And the fact is, we can't take back time! I can't go back and redo any of it.'' His voice cracked.

Matt couldn't remember the last time his dad had talked about the past. Sure, he spoke of Matt's mom and the apple pies she used to make every fall. But he didn't speak often about the twins. And not about blame. There had been more than enough to go around. But today, the pain etched on Sam's face—and in his voice—seemed as raw as it had been eight years ago.

"Are you saying that I should never get involved with a woman because of the chance it won't work out?" Matt asked. The irony was that before Laura arrived, he would have agreed. His grand scheme was to wait until the kids graduated from high school before even thinking about another marriage.

"No, I'm just asking you to think about your kids. Think hard. If you're not serious about Laura, if she's just a fling to you, then don't let her get too involved with the boys. Their love for her is growing. Especially Casey's. We don't need any more upheavals in his life. In Brian's, either." Sam paused again, but he still wasn't finished. "Laura's a nice girl. A good girl. She's worth more than a fling. So, if you're not serious, then you're not being fair to her, either."

His dad looked so sad, Matt wanted to cry. "Son, I guess what I'm saying is—be careful."

CHAPTER ELEVEN

On Monday morning, Laura checked her calendar, which now always rested in full view on the kitchen table. When she'd first arrived at Sea View House, the calendar had few notations. Now it displayed not only routine appointments but also business meetings, auditions and recording schedules as she rebuilt her career. A glow of achievement filled her when she studied all the entries. This calendar was starting to look very similar to the ones she'd kept before her mother's illness and her own. She was back in business!

She hadn't seen Matt since their date Saturday night, but he'd called yesterday and regaled her third-hand about Dee and the Chief's engagement announcement at The Diner. In the afternoon, he'd been committed to two ball games with his children and hadn't suggested she join them. For an instant, she'd almost suggested it herself, but then realized she needed the time for her own work. Both the audition for Sunrise Books and the taping for Filene's spots were set for later in the week. Show time had almost arrived.

Laura reached for her Snow White script and began to work, first focusing on the different voices she'd developed for the dwarfs and for Snow White, and then slipping into her own narrator's voice. At noon, she felt ready to start from the top. She wanted to time her reading to get the feel of her natural speed. If she got the job, she'd adjust to what was needed. She picked up the script and began.

"Once upon a time, long, long ago, there lived a young girl by the name of Snow White," she said, and soon got caught up in her delivery of the familiar tale.

"...and they lived happily ever after." She took a cleansing breath.

"Bravo, bravo," came the familiar voice of Matthew Parker, who strode into the kitchen clapping his hands. "I couldn't stop listening. Had to find out how the story ended!"

Laura spun around and almost landed on his rock-solid chest. Regaining her balance, she tilted her head back to see him better.

He lowered his head and kissed her.

So easy for her to respond. So hard to stop. "Mmm."

His lips brushed against hers as he spoke. "You were great with the reading. Every dwarf was different. Individuals. You're going to get this gig."

She shivered, not knowing if it was from his kisses or his praise. "Thanks. I hope so. It could lead to a lot of work for me."

"And lots of time in Boston," said Matt with a sigh.

"But the ferry runs every day," she replied, patting his shoulder. "And I have a house in the city, too. All the bases are covered for now." That seemed true enough. If only her personal life would fall into place as smoothly as her professional life seemed to be doing.

"Do you have time for lunch?" she asked.

But he was already shaking his head. "Sorry. I've got to get back to the store. I'll call you tonight."

"Sure." She yawned and stretched her arms overhead…and noticed him watching her every move, noticed his eyes heat up, noticed how he rubbed the back of his hand against his mouth. He didn't move for another moment. Then, "we'll talk tonight," he mumbled as he exited the back door.

But he didn't call. He showed up. Late. He clasped her hand and they walked for miles along the beach; they talked for miles, too—of childhood summers, of their families, of Boston, of Pilgrim Cove, of their educations, of careers—the quiet whoosh of the ocean accompanying their conversation.

"A cup of tea?" she asked when they were back on the porch.

He shook his head. "No, thank you," he said, moving toward her. "This is my dessert."

His kiss was slow and intoxicating. His mouth pressed against hers, his lips lingering and persuasive.

She closed her eyes and opened to him, feeling drugged by his touch but wanting more.

"Laura, Laura."

She heard him whisper her name between kisses, and her name sounded like music when he spoke it. She embraced him, tight and close, and almost whimpered. Her hands crept up his chest and locked around his neck.

She felt his arms around her, crushing her to him. Felt herself being rocked in those arms. And kissed again and again. She couldn't think. Could only feel. And she felt wonderful.

Then, unexpectedly, she was free.

They stared at each other and neither of them moved. The only sound in the night was their labored breathing.

Finally Matt spoke, his voice raspy. "I'm leaving now, Laura. Idiot that I am, I'm not prepared tonight."

She turned her head. "What did...? Prepared? Oh. Neither am I." Still in a daze, she entered the house.

Matt walked to his van, his mind in turmoil. She wasn't prepared. In what way? Women were so hard to figure out, much harder than men. Anyone would have understood that Matt had been talking about not having birth control protection with him.

But Laura's "Neither am I" could mean something else entirely. Such as, she wasn't emotionally prepared to make love yet.

He could handle that. If that was what she meant.

But how could he know for sure? She was so responsive to him. Kissing her was as wonderful as listening to a gorgeous symphony. They blended with each other. Everything worked. Making full love to her was going to be…like…like Tchaikovsky's 1812 Overture. Melodic, but powerful. Cymbals clashing, cannon roaring.

He jumped into the car and tried desperately to turn his mind onto something else.

LAURA STOOD at the rail of the ferry on Thursday morning, focusing all her energy on the audition. Matt had picked up the kitten the night before, had kissed Laura hard on the mouth and wished her luck. She'd been a bit distracted, and he'd probably picked up on her vibes. Her concentration had been on Snow White and Sunrise Books.

Laura clasped her tote bag tightly. She wanted her career back and was willing to work for it. She also wanted her relationship with Matthew Parker to keep growing. She wanted it all!

Just for an instant, she pictured Matt in her mind's eye. A moving picture, because he was rarely still. His teasing grin, his powerful legs jogging alongside her on the beach, the way those legs looked inside his faded jeans…

Shoot! Think about Doc, Grumpy and Sneezy.

She forced herself to concentrate on the characters, and in less time than she could imagine, she'd entered the building where the recording studio was located, where she was about to compete with serious talent. No matter. She took a deep breath, raised her chin and smiled at the woman behind the reception desk.

"Good morning," she said. "I'm Laura McCloud."

The woman's eyes sparkled, and she picked up the phone. "Bill, Laura McCloud's here. I hope she's at least as good as her demo." The woman stood up and held out her hand. "I'm Susan Starr from Sunrise Books. I really liked your demo tape. Break a leg in there, will you?"

Laura grinned at the theatrical phrase for "good luck," and her spirits soared. "Thanks. I hope I do."

Almost immediately, she found herself shaking hands with the studio director, conversing with him and the other members of the recording staff. The greetings were more than mere chitchat. She knew they were taking her measure, listening to her voice, her command of the language, even judging her intelligence.

Laura knew that the production of an audio book was a group effort combining art and science, and success depended on all elements coming together. Although the production schedule called for the twelve books by the end of the summer, the publisher would not sacrifice quality of narration. They'd keep auditioning until they found the reader they wanted. This was business. Big business. And Laura was ready to be a player.

Moments later, she was in the comfortable recording booth where the lighting, temperature and humidity were controlled. Three people would be listening to her delivery, including Susan Starr from Sunrise Books. Laura put on her headset, reached into her tote for her marked-up copy of the script and took a sip of water. Upon cue, she began to read. And felt herself change into character again and again. She sneezed. She yawned. She spoke to a mirror.

The director's voice did not come through the headphones to stop her, and she told the entire story without interruption. A good sign. When it was over, he gave her a thumbs-up and then asked her to repeat portions and exaggerate voices. Either she'd missed the mark on some of the characters, or he wanted to see if she could take direction without getting flustered.

"Beautiful performance, Ms. McCloud," he said afterward, walking toward her and extending his hand. "Excellent clarity and flow, great dialogue." He asked her a few questions, then said, "We'll be in touch with your agent as soon as we make a decision. Thanks very much for auditioning."

"You're more than welcome," Laura replied with enthusiasm. "I was delighted with the opportunity. In fact, I had a good time."

She left the studio hoping she had a fair shot at the job. She'd felt comfortable throughout the audition, but the director was the only one to chat with her after the reading. The woman from Sunrise hadn't even said goodbye. Was that a bad sign?

The afternoon sunshine greeted her as she made her way to her brick ranch-style home in Boston. No time to wonder about the audio books. Practicing tomorrow's scripts for the department-store account would consume the rest of her day in town. How ironic to have two big recording dates in a row after having so little for so long. She'd call Norman as soon as she got home. He'd be waiting to hear about the audition.

An hour later, she walked inside her house and immediately started opening windows. The place needed airing. Next time she came in, she'd call a cleaning service. They'd strip all the beds, vacuum the rooms. Dust and polish everything. And Laura would force herself to box up her mom's clothes for donation to charity. Procrastinating would not make the sad chore easier.

She went into her bedroom, kicked off her shoes and lay on the bed, wanting to relax for a moment before she called her agent. She closed her eyes. "Just for a minute," she murmured.

The ringing telephone jarred her awake. She fumbled for the receiver.

"I hear you're back in civilized territory," said Norman Cohen.

"Hi, Norman." She yawned between words. "I must have dozed off. But I think the audition went fairly well. The director seemed to like me."

"I know."

Silence. "How could you know anything? I just

left them a little while ago.'' She glanced at her watch. ''Okay, three hours ago.''

''And I got a call five minutes ago.''

Laura's breath caught in her throat. She wasn't expecting such swift feedback. Wasn't prepared for either victory or defeat.

''Congratulations, my dear. You are now the voice of Sunrise Book's youngest reader division. We've got contract details to work out, but it's yours.''

''It is? Are you sure? My God, Norman! I wasn't expecting…it's so soon. But it's wonderful. Thank you for suggesting it. And now I have to call Matt.''

''Wait a second. Don't you want to know what they said?''

''Of course I do.''

''Think about this, Laura. They said your voice had the lyrical quality they were looking for. You've got the kind of voice children take to.''

Casey's image appeared in her mind. Matt's son had attached himself to her immediately. And she to him. Her heart warmed as she thought of him. ''I love kids, Norman. Maybe reading to them at the library made a difference in my delivery. They gave me immediate feedback just by being themselves.''

''Well, something worked, Laura. Everything worked. Now, don't let success go to your head. Tomorrow's another day that'll help fill your bank account.''

''Yours, too, my friend,'' she teased, knowing he was worth every percentage point she paid him.

"You better believe it. Now, tell me. Who's Matt?"

She chuckled at his question. Norman never hesitated to mix business and personal stuff with her. But how should she explain Matt? "I knew him when I was a kid. He's a nice guy."

"What do you mean, nice? When do I meet him?"

She had to laugh. Norman was doing a fairly good suspicious-father impersonation.

"I'm a big girl now, Norman."

"Not so big, and not so old," he replied quietly. "Not from my perspective. I've got daughters your age. Bring him to dinner…you know Phyllis will be insulted if you don't."

She was touched by his concern, but had to swallow her amusement as Norman tried to bully her by hiding behind his wife. "Dinner. I promise…when the time is right."

"Does this mean you're not moving back to town?"

She didn't know the true answer to that one. At least not yet. "Not a day before my lease is up in Pilgrim Cove."

"I hear you," said the agent.

"Good night, Norman." Laura replaced the receiver and immediately picked it up again and dialed Matt's house. He should have been home by then unless one of the boys had a baseball game.

The phone rang twice before it was picked up. "Hi-i."

"Casey! Hi. It's Laura."

"Laura? G-g-good. C-c-can you c-c-come to my-y game?"

"I'd love to," she replied, her heart stirred by his efforts. "When is it?"

"S-S-Sun-day."

She heard noises in the background. Then Casey's voice as if from a distance. "Dad. It's Lau-ra. She-e's coming t-to my g-game."

"Casey, don't bother her with that. She may have other plans."

Surprised at his words and his clipped tone, Laura prepared to set him straight as soon as he came on the phone.

"Hi, Laura. You beat me to it. How was your day? How was the audition?" His voice was certainly warm with her.

"He wasn't annoying me, Matt," she replied, "so don't scold him. I'd love to go to his game. It's important to him."

"I know that. I just don't want him to assume…to get too used to…too close to…"

Her heart almost stopped at his unexpected words. She could fill in the blanks. "Are you saying, Matt, that you don't want me around your children anymore? You think I would hurt them?" With all her vocal training, she couldn't hide the pain in her voice. She didn't put on acts with people she loved and trusted.

"I didn't mean that," Matt protested. "I just

meant…you've got other things going on. Hell, I don't know what I meant. I don't want to hurt you. It's just that my kids like you a lot.''

''And that's bad? But I like them, too, Matt. Very much. I don't understand.'' This was too important to allow for a misunderstanding.

Silence at the other end. A deep silence. Then, ''Sweetheart, I think my foot got caught in my mouth. The boys and I would be delighted for you to come with us to Casey's game.''

One word. It only took one word to make her relax again. *Sweetheart*. Commonplace, but powerful.

''And I'll be delighted to come and cheer every inning. Oh, my goodness,'' she added as a thought struck her. ''We really do have a Casey at the bat, don't we?''

Matt's laughter came through the wires, loud and clear. ''More like a Bad News Bear, if you ask me.''

''Well, I'm sure they'll try hard. I'm looking forward to Sunday.''

''And I'm looking forward to tomorrow night when you're back and I'm holding you again.'' His voice was soft, low and full of meaning.

''Me, too, Matt. Me, too.''

''Okay then. See you soon. Sleep well.''

She hung up the receiver in a thoughtful mood, replaying the whole conversation in her mind. And then realized she'd never told him her big news. Somehow, Casey had seemed more important.

The sound of the phone startled her. ''Hello.''

"I forgot to ask about the audition," Matt said without preamble. "Has Snow White got a voice yet?"

"She sure does. Compliments of Laura McCloud. I'm still floating."

"Fantastic! You're the best. You know what? They're the lucky ones. Every little kid in America is going to want your stories!" His unabated enthusiasm had her blinking away sudden tears.

"Is that an unbiased opinion?" she managed to tease.

"Absolutely." But he was laughing and she found herself joining in, feeling renewed. Confident. Just like she used to be before the bad times started. The old Laura was back! Ready to handle anything. Ready to take chances.

MATT PACED the dock, a bouquet of long-stemmed red roses in hand. Where the hell was the ferry? He glanced at his watch and groaned. Six-fifteen. Another fifteen minutes to go. The rest of the world seemed to be on schedule. It was he who was topsy-turvy.

"Hey, Matt."

Matt pivoted to see Chief O'Brien walking his way. Rick's smile got broader as his glance moved between the roses and Matt's face.

Just what he needed. More food for the ROMEOs to chew on. Matt transferred the bouquet to one hand and held up the other with a policeman's stop motion.

"This meeting is a figment of your imagination," Matt declared. "You never saw me. I figure one good turn deserves another." He held the cop's glance as best he could while the Chief began to laugh.

"Red roses, huh? Does this mean you're in the doghouse or just in love?"

"I seem to remember a few hangdog looks on your face over time, Chief."

"Not anymore." Chief O'Brien nodded at the approaching boat. "She's a lovely woman. Good luck, son." He started walking away, then turned. "By the way…this conversation never happened."

Now Matt grinned and nodded his head before casting his eyes on the incoming ferry and the woman waving to him from the rail. The Chief, his dad, the rest of the world faded from his mind. All he wanted to focus on was standing twenty-five yards in front of him. Then she walked down the ramp onto the dock and straight into his arms.

"Funny," he whispered, as she leaned against him, "how you were the one on the boat, but it's me who feels like I've just come home."

She peeped up at him, tears welling in her blue eyes, her arms still wrapped around his waist. "Maybe home is wherever the right person is."

"Then we're both home," he said softly.

He kissed her lightly on the lips, and finally presented the roses. "In honor of your success and in apology for my concerns yesterday. I'm very glad you're in my life."

"Thanks, Matthew," said Laura bending her head to sniff the fragrance of the flowers. "They're absolutely beautiful."

Not as beautiful as you are. He couldn't remember the last time he'd given flowers to anyone. But looking at the glowing picture Laura made with the roses, he vowed to shower her with bouquets for no other reason than the pleasure of watching her delight.

"Can you have dinner with me now?" he said as they walked to the parking lot. "I'll follow you back to Sea View House, and we can go from there."

"Just you and I?" she asked. "No surprise guests?"

He nodded. "No kids, no parents, no friends. At least not at our table. Total privacy can be elusive at The Lobster Pot."

"This is Pilgrim Cove, Matt. It can't be any other way!"

"You don't mind?" he asked.

"Not at all. Part of the charm of a small town."

"That charm can be overwhelming at times," he said, a note of warning in his voice.

"Well, Matt, nothing's perfect."

She was wrong about that. She was perfect for him.

When they walked through the back door at Sea View House, Matt said, "I'm going to check out the upstairs apartment while you do whatever it is you have to do. Bart left a message that The Crow's Nest is rented for the summer. A professor from California."

"Summer? Time's flying, isn't it?" said Laura.

He heard the trace of anxiety in her voice and lay the roses on the kitchen table before reaching for her. He held her against him, rocking her gently. "We're in charge of our own timeline, sweetheart. Even though Sea View House is special, there are other rentals on the beach, if it comes to that."

He felt her body relax. Good. She didn't need any additional stress in her life.

A half hour later, Matt was back in Laura's kitchen having entered The Crow's Nest from the separate side entrance. He had a report of his findings ready for Bart Quinn.

"I'll be right there." Laura's voice from the bedroom reached him faintly just before she joined him. Blond tendrils around her face, crisp jeans, boots and a long navy turtleneck sweater that hugged her every curve. Large gold hoop earrings and a gold chain belt around her hips completed the picture.

"This is dressy enough for The Lobster Pot, isn't it?" she asked.

Matt gulped and nodded. Couldn't say a thing because his tongue wouldn't work. He took a deep breath and escorted her to the SUV.

Once in the restaurant, Matt gave up on any privacy at all. Maggie Sullivan greeted them at the door like long-lost friends, and her husband, Tom, found time to chat with Laura. Tom Sullivan helped out at The Lobster Pot on weekends when he wasn't coaching a high school team.

Then Bart Quinn showed up with Lila and Katie, who wanted to know where Brian and Casey were. Thea Cavelli, Maggie's sister and partner, stopped by to say hello. Seemed like it was a Quinn-Sullivan-Cavelli night.

Matt looked at Laura and shrugged his shoulders. "Can't do a damn thing about it," he said.

"It's fine, Matt. I like it."

He felt his eyebrows touch the ceiling.

"No, really," explained Laura. "Boston has lots more people, but you can feel lost in a crowd. At The Lobster Pot, everyone knows your name. It's just like the old television show, *Cheers*. It's comfortable here."

"Part of that small-town charm?" He smiled, tossing her words back at her.

"Exactly." She pointed to her empty soup bowl. "And look, all our company hasn't interfered with my appetite in any way."

He nodded, although for the first time in his life, he barely tasted his lobster dinner. How could he, when Laura held him mesmerized, her tongue brushing her lips with each bite of lobster meat, a trace of butter glistening against her skin. He inhaled deeply as his imagination took flight. There were other places for her tongue.

Finally he leaned across the table, placed his fingers under her chin and kissed her. Thoroughly.

"Hmm," she purred, when he sat back down. Her

eyes opened slowly, the irises so large no blue was visible.

That was all the encouragement he needed. "Are you prepared to continue this conversation elsewhere?"

"Oh, I'm prepared this time. Very prepared."

He laughed out loud. "Well, that makes two of us."

And suddenly his tension dissipated. She wanted him as much as he wanted her. He could afford to be generous. "Take your time, sweetheart. Have some dessert."

She stared him down, her eyes smoky-blue just like her voice. "Oh, I intend to. Without delay."

Matt flagged the waitress. "Check, please."

CHAPTER TWELVE

SHE LOVED MATT, and she wanted to make love with him and feel like a normal woman. She *looked* almost normal. Her major scar was low on the underside of her breast. Matt might not even notice. And if she didn't quite fill out her bra on one side, so what? She didn't look lopsided.

"Lock up."

Laura heard the impatience in Matt's voice and chuckled as she closed the front door behind them and turned the bolt. His impatience matched hers. Wonderful. "Like to give orders, do you?"

He reached for her. "I'd rather lead than follow."

"We'll see about that," she whispered, rising on her toes for a kiss.

His embrace was tight, his lips hard against her mouth. Somehow, their coats landed on the floor, and Matt led them to her bedroom, to her bed, kissing her every step of the way.

A partly cloudy sky allowed only a few shards of moonlight through the window. But Laura could see Matt's taut features, his eyes on fire for her. She tugged at the corner of the spread, but Matt yanked the thing out of her hand and pulled it down. Then she reached for the buttons of his shirt, and he stood unnaturally still, watching her. Her fingers connected with skin and she heard him gasp. The only sound in the room.

The top button slipped through the opening. Then the second one. Her fingers brushed against the coarse hair on his chest, and now her breath caught in her throat, her insides tightening. She stroked him again, enjoying the sensation of smooth and rough. Slowly she reached for the next button with trembling hands. But Matt took her hands into his own warm ones, lifted them to his mouth and kissed each finger and palm in a million places. She searched his face and saw the heat in his eyes soften, revealing something else.

"I'm falling in love with you," he whispered. "The way falling in love is supposed to be. I never thought it would happen to me...in fact, never thought about it at all...but you...you're special."

Sunshine filled her. All she saw was Matt. He filled her vision, filled her heart and filled her soul. She felt a tear wend a path from the outside corner of her eye, and cupped her hands around his face. "I *already* love you, Matthew Parker. Now make love to me."

Matt didn't need a second invitation. With eagerness and with care, he undressed her in the shadowed room before tearing his own clothes off. But she shivered in the April night.

"I promise you'll be warm soon," he said, pulling back the covers.

He stroked her beautiful body, finding her pleasure points. He heard her gasp as she shivered, felt her arms tighten around him, as the shivers became shudders that surged and receded like the ocean waves outside their window. And he rode those waves with Laura, as though searching for the perfect one, until finally, delightfully, he found it and crested...with her...together. As though no other lovemaking had ever existed in his life. He'd come home in more ways than one.

Careful not to crush her, he collapsed on the mattress next to her as he tried to catch his breath.

"Not bad."

His eyes snapped open as Laura rolled on her side toward him, but he noticed her insouciance, and he chuckled.

"I'll give you excellent next time," he replied, leaning forward to kiss her. She pulled up the top sheet and lay against the pillow, her thick hair like a halo around her beautiful face, and he could have stared at her forever. Instead, he kissed her lips, her neck, and draped his arm over her.

To his delight, she scooted closer. "I love the cuddling part."

"I love all the parts!" he replied. "Hands, feet, legs, breasts..."

Suddenly her eyes darkened, her lids closed. "Laura? What's the matter?"

She blinked up at him and looked fine again. "Nothing. Nothing at all. Just catching my breath."

"Good," he said. "Because you have a beautiful body, kiddo." He leered. "Breasts included."

Now she blushed, and he felt better. It was a normal reaction to teasing. Funny that she'd react at all. Laura seemed so comfortable with her body. All the outdoor exercising, figure-flattering clothing, and almost no inhibition making love. He mentally shrugged. Maybe all women were self-conscious about their breasts. Even Valerie had complained a lot after the boys were born.

Laura laid her head on his shoulder, one arm falling across his waist, and he wrapped his arm around her, relishing the comfort of her body against him. She was right. Snuggling was part of the fun. He'd allow himself the pleasure for a while longer, and then he'd leave for home.

He closed his eyes and listened to the night. It was quiet. The faint sound of the surf dominated, with an occasional cry of a gull. He kissed the top of Laura's head and she purred, almost asleep. He felt the rise and fall of her chest against him. Soon, her breathing matched his rhythm, and he smiled to himself. For the second time that evening, they were one.

LAURA SHIVERED, pulled the cover higher and reached across the bed for Matt. She felt only empty sheets with a faint lingering warmth where his body had been. She opened her eyes and confirmed his absence, then looked toward the window. The pale moon was almost at the horizon line, so several hours had passed. Morning would break soon. No wonder Matt had gone. Although she felt wide-awake now, she must have been more tired than she'd thought after her trip to Boston. Not to mention last night's activity and quiet admissions of love.

Her thoughts stopped right there. Matt was falling in love with her, and last night had been wonderful. Making love with him had been everything she'd thought it would be. Everything she'd hoped it would be. Except…she hadn't told him.

A knot started to form in her stomach, and she took a deep breath. Her next appointment with Dr. Berger was in a few days. She'd tell Matt after her blood work proved normal.

She turned on her bedside lamp, scanned the room for her flannel bathrobe and forced herself out of bed, naked, to retrieve it from the back of the rocking chair. Not sexy at all, but the New England nights were chilly even in April. She put the robe on and headed for the bathroom and a hot shower. She was ready to start her day.

The heat of the water felt delicious and Laura lingered under the spray after shampooing her hair. She tugged at the strands and grinned when they stayed put. So different from the long, straight style she used to wear.

She stepped from the tub, started drying off and

automatically swiped a towel against the fogged-up mirror.

Her arms dropped to her sides as she stared at herself. She hadn't planned to pause. She'd seen herself many times, and mostly didn't think about her scars or how she looked. They were part of her now and would fade eventually. But they *were* definitely part of her history. The cancer had been real.

Suddenly her reflection shimmered in the mirror. She felt the trickle of tears rolling down her cheeks, but she blinked them away and her vision cleared. And then she studied the image of every woman's nightmare.

A trembling finger traced all three scars, seventeen months old, and still visible. One sat above the un-affected breast where a special catheter had been inserted to facilitate her chemo treatments. The second was under the arm next to the affected breast where the sentinel lymph node had been biopsied to see whether the cancer had spread, and of course, the largest cut had been to the breast itself. Surgery. Chemotherapy. Radiation. With no warning, she'd become a statistic.

She continued to stare at herself. No family history, she ate right, she exercised…so why? Why? She wanted logic when there wasn't any. Why had it happened? Why her? She shook her head and took a deep breath. And another. And heard echoes of Bridget McCloud's loving voice answering the unanswerable. "Oh, my dear daughter. Why wasn't it me?"

And that's when she cried. And yearned for her mother's arms to hold her, yearned for the reassurances that only mothers could provide—that she was still beautiful, still worthy of love, that everything would be all right.

Laura cried hard, but not for long. The need to run on the beach pulled at her. She knew her exercise regimen was a natural defense against depression. The grief for her mom came in unexpected spurts, but she handled it by chatting with Alison frequently and by running on the beach for miles.

She dried her hair and pulled it back with a set of combs, then put on a sweatsuit and running shoes. On her way out the back door, she saw the note on the kitchen table.

Morning, sweetheart,
Back at 5. Concert at 8. We'll ferry.
Looking forward to another wonderful night.

"So am I," she whispered, fanning the paper against her cheek. "So am I."

Matt remained in her thoughts as she jogged along the shore. Her pace was more leisurely than usual, but her hour outdoors seemed to pass more quickly. Just proving the old adage, she thought, about time flying when you're having fun.

She reentered Sea View House, reached for some cereal and put the kettle on. Tea always seemed cozier than coffee when mornings had a bite of winter in them. She was pouring herself a cup when the door-bell rang.

Lila Sullivan stood on the threshold and burst into speech the moment Laura opened the door. "I'm so sorry to disturb you this early on a Saturday, but at the last minute, Matt had to go out of town for the day. He might not be back in time for your date this evening. I'm sorry."

"So am I," said Laura, "but no harm done." She opened the door wider. "Want a cup of instant?" she asked automatically. "Matt's not in any trouble, is he?"

"Oh, no. Not at all," said Lila, stepping inside and walking to the kitchen with Laura. "The Chief got a lead on Jason. Or rather, *maybe* he got a lead. We've searched for him before…and nothing. Today, Matt's gone to New York. Chief O'Brien's buddy saw a guy playing in a piano bar last night. Called Rick this morning. Thought the man looked like the pictures of Jason we've given out."

Lila shrugged off her jacket and put it over a kitchen chair. "Of course, our pictures are eight years old. Jason must have changed."

Laura reached for another mug and set it on the table. The other woman was tense, on edge, and Laura's heart went out to her.

"Matt's such a great guy," said Lila. "He's special to us. To all of us in the family. And he hasn't had it easy."

"Seems to me, none of you have had it easy," said

Laura, pouring hot water into the second cup, instinctively wanting to deflect the conversation from the subject of Matt.

"But he's the one holding things together—even for me. My mom—well, she wants me to forget Jason. Thinks I'm still a romantic eighteen-year-old living in a dream."

Laura took a breath. "I never knew Jason, so I have no opinion. But is it possible that your mom is right?"

The girl's brow creased. She bit her lip and looked aside. "At this point, I don't honestly know." Then she lifted her chin, her eyes flashing. "All I do know is that every time we follow a lead, I get chills. My heart thumps like a bass drum until I'm about to explode. Poor Jason. He's never forgiven himself for Jared's death."

Laura saw pain. Heard pain. Lila's world was real, not fantasy.

"He probably doesn't even know his mom passed away," continued Lila in a soft voice, "unless he somehow saw the obituary in the *Cove Gazette*. Maybe online. Who knows?"

Laura's thoughts cascaded one over the other. "Then he doesn't know about Matt's wife, either."

Lila shook her head. "No, he doesn't. Matt's mom dies. Then Valerie gets cancer and Matt handles everything. Two years of living hell. So, Laura, please...he's so happy these days. If you're responsible, then I'm glad. But please, if it's not for real…please don't hurt him.''

But Laura didn't hear anything Lila said after the word "cancer." Her mind almost closed down. She stared at Lila as though she'd never seen her before. "Cancer?"

Lila nodded. "I'm sorry. You didn't know? Ovarian cancer. It's not a secret, but it's damn scary, isn't it?''

Laura nodded.

"Anyway," continued the other woman, "if Matt's late tonight, you'll know why." Lila stood up. "Saturdays are busy in real estate. I have to get to the office. If Matt calls, I'll let you know. And you do the same. Okay?''

Laura nodded. "I'll walk you out.'' She uttered the words automatically and moved like a robot. When she returned to the kitchen, she dropped into a chair as if she weighed a thousand pounds, glad her shaky legs had held her up for as long as they did.

Matt's loving note still lay on the table. "…another wonderful night.'' Oh, God! How could she tell him the truth now? But how could she not?

Her hand trembled as she reached for her calendar, checking the date of her next medical appointment. Tuesday—Dr. Berger. Her brain started to kick into gear again. Nothing really had changed as far as what she had to do. Despite the additional pain and risk, she would stick to her earlier decision to tell Matt after her blood tests, and after Dr. Berger pronounced her one-hundred-percent healthy. The rest would be up to Matt. Her eyes filled, thinking about his reaction. Life was so damn unfair sometimes. To everyone.

"YOU'RE LOOKING GOOD, Laura. More than good. How are you?"

Laura shook her doctor's hand and watched Dr. Evan Berger take a seat in the examining room. He was young, bright, full of energy and loved his work.

The doc smiled and leaned back against the wall…as though he had all the time in the world, as though no other patients were waiting for him. But Laura knew better. She also knew that his "how are you?" really meant how she was getting along in life as well as how she was feeling.

"As a matter of fact," she replied from her seat on the examining table, "I feel great. Life is good. Better than good." Her mind was on Matt. Only on Matt. His search for Jason had proved disappointing. The pianist in New York had turned out not to be Jason.

They hadn't made it to Symphony Hall, but had spent the evening together on the beach and in Sea View House where she'd prepared a simple dinner. He was exhausted, and they'd cuddled on the couch, just "recharging their batteries," as Matt had said.

Dr. Berger's eyebrows shot up. "There's a look on your face…I like it."

"Yeah, I've got news. But…"

Suddenly she pressed her lips together, frightened to hear his response to her announcement. Not because he wouldn't be happy for her, but because he knew the statistics. *Survival statistics for relationships.*

"But?"

She met the doctor's eyes. "I've met someone. Someone special. A single dad. Widowed four years ago."

His warm smile said it all. "That's wonderful! He's a lucky guy to have found you. I couldn't be happier."

"But…" she began again, then hesitated for a second time.

"But what?" prompted Dr. Berger.

"I haven't told him yet…you know…about my situation. But I'm planning to after I get the results of today's blood work." She inhaled, exhaled. "On top of that, I just discovered that his wife died of ovarian cancer. So what do you think his reaction's going to be?"

A concerned expression replaced the doctor's smile, and he leaned forward in his seat. "I won't lie to you about this, Laura, just to make you feel better. Just like I've never lied about anything else. I think, though, that you probably know the answer yourself." He paused. "Even without a prior firsthand experience, a lot of men can't handle it. Not only boyfriends, but husbands, too. They walk."

She swallowed past the lump in her throat. "I know," she whispered. "Been there, done that."

"I remember," he said with a nod. "And he hurt you when you were down, and the situation stank. But here you are, Laura, a year and a half later, full of life, *with the potential for a full life.* You know that your particular situation couldn't be better. You understand that, don't you? Make sure he understands that, too. Bring him in to see me if he has questions. My door is always open to family and significant others."

"Thanks," she whispered, her voice deserting her as she realized Evan Berger was not only her doctor, but her friend.

A half hour later, she left the office with words of support not only from the doc, but from his staff of nurses. She'd come to think of them as her three fairy godmothers. They performed their delicate tasks with their hearts, souls and intelligence. She was impatient to call them for the outcome of the blood work and yet reluctant for Friday to arrive, when she'd get the results.

It was a sunny afternoon, the promise of real spring in the air. Her spirits lifted as she made her way to Rowes Wharf. She was heading back to Pilgrim Cove and dinner with Matt and the family.

"DO YOU GUYS THINK we can clean up a bit in here?" Matt stood in the family room looking at scattered books, pencils and domino tiles. A general mess. "Laura's coming to dinner."

"So what?" replied Brian, lying prone on the floor. "She's been here before."

"Yeah, yeah, Dad,
We're not bad.
She knows us,
Don't make a fuss."

Casey had discovered rap sometime during the last week. He was pounding the sides of his little fists against the coffee table, choosing his own rhythm and repeating the words over and over again. Most of the time, his stuttering lessened. The kid was evolving every day, figuring things out for himself—what worked, what didn't. Matt never knew what to expect each evening, and was always amazed. Word repetition was standard therapy, but the musical addendums were all Casey. The Parker genes hadn't skipped his younger son.

"But I am making a fuss, boys," said Matt. "I don't want to scare Laura away."

"Aw, Dad. She likes you." Brian's exasperated tone revealed that he considered his dad clueless. "She doesn't care if a bunch of books are on the floor."

"Yeah, yeah, Pops. She thinks you're tops."

Brian rolled his eyes, and Matt had to laugh. He reached for Casey, hugged him and swung him around the room. "She does, does she? Well, I think she's pretty special, too."

Casey's eyes widened and he looked at his brother over Matt's shoulder. Brian nodded. "See," he said. "I told you."

So the boys had been talking. Matt slowly lowered Casey to the floor and motioned for Brian to come closer. He hadn't planned to have a heart-to-heart with the boys without speaking to Laura first, but the opportunity was too good to pass up. Suddenly his mouth felt full of sand; he couldn't formulate a coherent sentence.

He sat the boys on the sofa and stood in front of them. No good. He didn't want to loom over them. He lowered himself to the coffee table.

"Dad! You can't s-sit on the ta-able."

Fine time to follow the rules, Casey. But he nodded at his son and pulled the rocking chair over to the couch.

"So, guys. Here's the thing," he began.

"Excuse me," said a voice from the kitchen. "Can anyone join this party, or is it private?"

"Come on in, Pop. I'm glad you're here." Two adults would be better.

"It's not a party, Grandpa," said Brian. "It's a talk. Dad wants to tell us about Laura. He thinks she's special."

"That's nice," Sam said, walking into the room.

Nice? Matt stared at his father. What an insipid word. Sam was more articulate than that. But his face gave nothing away. The older man, who had expressed concern in the past, wasn't showing his cards now, wouldn't influence the conversation.

Comprehension dawned. The subject was too important. Too delicate. Matt was on his own, the way it should be.

"Remember, a couple of weeks ago, I said if anything new happened between Laura and me, you'd be the first to know? So, here's what's new. I like Laura a lot," he began slowly. "And she likes me. So, she'll be hanging around more often. I'll be asking her to more of your games..." He paused to smile at his boys' beatific expressions. "So you can show off, if you want."

"Aw, Dad. She cheers for everyone, even if you strike out," said Brian.

"I know," Matt responded in mock horror. "It's a terrible thing." He laughed silently when Brian's eyes narrowed. "The point is that I'd like you to get to know her better. And she would like to know you better. So, you'll be seeing her a lot in the future. Including dinner with us this evening."

Casey looked at his brother, ready to follow his lead. Brian's expressive face revealed some heavy thinking going on.

"Bri?" said Matt. "What's on your mind?"

His son looked him square in the eye. "Are you going to marry her?"

Might as well lay some groundwork. "It could be headed that way."

"Oh." More thinking.

Casey's voice interrupted. "Hey! We get to keep Midnight!"

Matt glanced at Sam. "Seven is a good age." His dad nodded and gave him a thumbs-up sign.

"So she'd be our stepmother?" asked Brian.

"But not a wicked one like in the fairy tales she's reading," said Matt.

"Dad! I know that."

Casey giggled. "But she'd be in our family."

"Exactly," said Matt. "Families are really about people loving people. People who love each other want to live together and make a home."

"Dad—you love Laura?" Short and to the point. That was Brian's style.

"Yeah, son. I do."

"But, Dad—" Brian stopped short.

"What, Bri?" prompted Matt.

"What if she gets sick like Mommy did?"

Matt should have seen the question coming. He searched for the right words. "The odds of that happening are really small, son. Laura's very healthy."

"Mommy was healthy when I was little…"

"You're right. She was. We had very bad luck then."

"You know what I think?" Casey asked. "I think only very, very, very old people should die. Much older than Grandpa."

"I think so, too." Brian rose from the sofa and started gathering the scattered books. "Help me, Ca-

sey,'' he said. ''Laura's going to visit a lot now, and
ladies don't like messy houses.''

NORMAL. The most beautiful word in the world.
Laura hung up the phone at Sea View House that
Friday afternoon and danced around the kitchen. She
hadn't expected any other outcome, but confirmation
was reassuring.

She reached for the phone to call Alison. At least
this time, Alison wouldn't tell her about how many
condos she'd lined up for Laura to see.

''Great news, Laura! I'm so glad. Of course, it's
just what I expected.'' Her sister, the cheerleader.

''Me, too.''

''And how's the romance coming along?'' asked
Alison. ''Is Matthew Parker still as handsome, intelligent, kind…hmm…what else did you say…oh, was
it, hot?''

Giggles escaped her. ''I didn't call him that!'' But
she could have. Laura felt the heat steal into her
cheeks, a phenomenon that occurred every time she
thought of Matt.

''The romance is…is…wonderful. I was with his
whole family earlier this week at their house, and the
kids were adorable. Couldn't do enough for me. Acting so polite. I tried not to laugh, and Matt told them
to relax and act normal. So they did, and in two
minutes were squabbling.''

''Sounds serious to me…'' Alison said. Laura
heard the question in her sister's voice.

"Oh, I think so," she replied. "Later this evening, I'm making dinner for two at Sea View House."

"The kind of dinner with candles on the table?"

"Oh, yes." Laura closed her eyes, picturing the scene. "Matt's bringing wine—a merlot, I think…and I'm supplying nice thick steaks, oven roasted potatoes…"

"Wow! You're cooking a real meal? This *is* serious. Matthew is a lucky man."

Laura chuckled. Her sister's idea of cooking stopped at boiling hot dogs. "Well, I think he's pretty special."

And then only silence came from the other end of the phone. "How special, sis?" asked Alison quietly.

Laura gripped the receiver tightly. "I guess," she said, "we'll find out tonight. Much later tonight." With the proper motivation, she could procrastinate with the best of them.

"I'm here for you, Laura. Anytime. No matter what."

Beautiful words. Now, if they'd only come from Matt…

"I know, Ali. Thanks. I'll call you tomorrow."

"You'd better. I'll be waiting by the phone.

THE DOORBELL RANG just as Laura finished preparing the salad. She ran to the front of the house and flung open the door, surprised Matt didn't come around the back through the kitchen.

The first thing she always noticed was his eyes.

Black-as-coal eyes that glowed hot whenever he
looked at her, as he was doing now. Tonight he was
clad all in black. His knit jersey covered a broad chest
with shoulders that seemed a mile wide. Short sleeves
revealed a set of biceps men strove for and women
dreamed about. He was one rugged-looking specimen
of masculinity.

She held the doorknob and stared.

"Uh, may I come inside?"

"Yes—as soon as I stop drooling."

He kissed her on the mouth and slammed the door
closed with his foot.

"You are definitely good for my ego, sweetheart."
His deep voice rumbled between kisses. "Want to
start with dessert?"

Oh, she was tempted! She looked toward the
kitchen, then back at Matt...and her stomach
growled.

"The woman's hungry," Matt declared to the
empty room. "We'll eat a meal first." His eyes captured hers. "The wait will only make what we have
sweeter."

He handed her a bottle of wine, and she led him to
the big kitchen. "We could eat in the dining room if
you prefer," she said, "maybe more like a date?"

"Nah," replied Matt. "Can't hear the ocean from
in there...you'd be miserable."

He was right, and she was startled by his percep-
tion. Had the temperature outside been warmer, she
would have suggested a dinner picnic on the sand.

"My goodness," she said, placing the wine on the table, "you're getting to know me better than I do myself."

He turned her around to face him. "If that's true," he said, "it's because you're on my mind all day long. Just sitting here—" he pointed to the back of his head "—keeping me company."

She walked into his chest and snuggled. "That's so nice to hear." She loved the way his arms automatically came around her and held her. Loved how affection was mixed with desire.

She leaned back, then kissed him quickly. "The steak has been marinating, the grill is lit…let's do it."

"Sure," he said with a wink. "But I really liked that little appetizer."

She did, too.

And she liked working alongside him preparing the simple meal. She liked hearing about the boys' days, about Matt's work, his customers, his employees. Conversation over dinner never faltered.

"What's your schedule for next week?" Matt asked as they were cleaning up. "Going into Boston again?"

She reached on top of the refrigerator, where she'd placed her calendar and studied it. "Yes, I am. For the taping of *Snow White*. I'll probably come home with another script or two to work on. And I have a dental appointment."

"That's at least two days in the city, maybe more if something else comes up. Is it becoming a drag for you, Laura?'' he asked, looking at her with uncertainty. ''The commuting?''

''You mean using the ferry? Absolutely not! It's no hardship at all.'' She leaned closer. ''The secret is that it's easier not to drive a car in Boston.''

Living in Pilgrim Cove would not be a problem. She and Matt would have no conflicts being a two-career couple. *If they remained a couple after tonight.* The thought persisted at the back of her mind.

Soon. She'd tell him soon. After they made love…so he could see clearly what had happened to her. She'd turn on every light to show him her three scars and try to answer any question he might have. She'd try to make him realize that her case was different from his wife's. She'd been diagnosed early. She and Matt could have a future.

''Come on, sweetheart,'' said Matt, nodding at the door. ''We're finished in here. Want to take a moonlight stroll? Walk off an ounce of steak?''

Laura looked through the window. A full moon shone in the clear April sky. Stars twinkled everywhere. ''It's a gorgeous night. I'd love to.''

''I've got running shoes in the van,'' said Matt, walking to the door.

Two minutes later, Laura put her hand in Matt's. He clasped it, squeezed it and led her to the water's edge.

She couldn't have asked for a more romantic setting. The ocean reflected the rays of the moon and there was enough illumination to light their way.

They kept a comfortable pace with each other. Conversation came just as easily as it had at dinner. They talked about Laura's mom and about Matt's mom. About movies they saw and books they read. They talked about Casey and Brian. Laura spoke of her sister's family in Atlanta. They talked about growing up in Pilgrim Cove. And about growing up in Boston. A world of discovery and satisfaction.

They'd covered the familiar three-mile loop by the time Laura led Matt up the back porch steps. She halted at the door, looked up at him, at the man she loved, at the man she wanted to spend her life with, and prayed for a miracle.

"Ready for dessert?" she whispered.

"If you're on the menu—yes." He brushed his fingers through her hair and kissed the top of her head. "What about you?"

As ready as I'll ever be. God knows, that was the truth.

But his eyes shone for her, and her heart beat a staccato rhythm. She led him inside.

And loved him. With passion, with tenderness, with hunger.

And received his love. His kisses. His caresses. She reveled in his joy, and in his pleasure at having given her pleasure.

When they floated back to earth, she delighted in his possessive embrace, his arms circling her as their breathing returned to normal. She cuddled against him, head on his shoulder, in what was quickly becoming her most favorite position of all.

"The perfect ending to a perfect evening," sighed Matt, kissing her quickly on the brow. "You are incredible."

"I guess I'm happy."

"And I'm very glad about that."

Laura sighed, then took a deep breath. "I had some great news today."

CHAPTER THIRTEEN

GREAT NEWS? Matt's mind whirled with possibilities. "Let me guess," he said with a laugh. "You've gotten three more voice-over assignments, every book publisher wants you to narrate and you've been voted the queen of advertising." He squeezed her gently, kissed her again and heard her emit a soft chuckle.

"Not quite. But I'll keep those goals in mind for the future," said Laura.

She squirmed around next to him, and he loosened his hold as she repositioned herself. He glanced down into her big blue eyes peeping up at him through her lashes.

"Beautiful," he said, and watched a faint blush color her cheeks.

"And healthy," said Laura.

"I know, sweetheart. You just proved it."

Her faint pink deepened to rose, and he laughed again. Teasing her was one of his favorite activities.

"Hey, Matt," said Laura, placing her palm on his cheek. "I'm trying to share something here." A slight impatience tinged her clear voice and snagged his attention.

"Sorry, sweetheart. I'm listening." He saw a shadow darken her eyes before she spoke.

"I had a checkup in Boston this week and got the results today. I'm happy to report that everything's normal."

Why wouldn't it be? He started to shrug his shoulders and give her a glib response until he noticed how still she'd become as she looked at him. The mellow, relaxed Laura—the Laura in the afterglow of lovemaking—was gone. In her place was an immobile woman with a furrow on her brow, more serious than he'd ever seen her. But then she smiled at him, and her eyes lit up again.

"Isn't *normal* a beautiful word?" she asked.

Did she expect an answer or was she merely being rhetorical? "Sure it is," he replied, deciding to follow her lead and see where it went, "especially in a doctor's office. Honey, were you worrying about anything in particular?"

She turned from him and reached toward the bedside lamp. He heard two clicks of the switch, and was instantly bathed in the brightest level of illumination the lamp had. He blinked against the sudden light.

Laura sat up against the pillows, pulling the top sheet with her. "I waited until after my checkup to show you something."

Show him what? He'd explored her silken body, had enjoyed every inch of it, and had loved every inch of it. Granted, they hadn't made love under glaring spotlights, but freckles, birth marks, a scar—so what? Everybody had a few blemishes on their skin.

"Give me your hand," said Laura.

He complied. And she led his fingers across the underside of her breast and back again.

"Feel that?" she asked. "That ridge?"

He brushed his hand across her again, slower this time, trying to absorb what his sense of touch was telling him. "Yes," he said slowly. "I feel it now. Scar tissue?"

"That's right," she said softly. "I had some surgery a year and a half ago. To remove a small cyst, but…it turned out not to be a friendly little thing."

Now he couldn't move. Chills radiated from his gut to his extremities. He pulled the sheet down and stared at her. He saw one…two…and another one. "Are you telling me…" he began, with a lump in his throat so large he could hardly get the words out. He looked into Laura's face, and saw it all—fear, hope, and…pride?

"I'm telling you," she said, "I had a lumpectomy, chemo and radiation. But I'm also telling you," Laura continued, "that my ten-year survival rate is ninety-six percent. I'm looking forward to narrating stories when I'm a very old lady."

But his brain had stopped functioning with the word, "chemo." The rest of what she said sounded like jabber. He couldn't process it now. Maybe later.

"Breast cancer! You had breast cancer." He felt the horror invade his entire being. Buried memories resurfaced and writhed in his brain like a cluster of undulating snakes. "Maybe the lab made a mistake. Maybe it was someone else's slide." He fell back on his own pillow, barely breathing, and stared at the ceiling. Nauseous to the core. He couldn't look at her, and he heard her breath catch.

"That's just what I said. It's what everyone says when that call comes in." Her voice cracked and then faded.

"Why did you keep your breast?" he asked. "And the survival rate? How do they know?" One question ran into another before he was able to shut up.

"Long-range studies. In my case, the survival rate—and I repeat, ninety-six percent—was exactly the same with mastectomy or breast preservation. So I chose to keep my breast."

He shook and shivered from head to toe, then jumped out of bed. The air was choking him. Breast preservation! Fancy words.

He searched until he found his underwear and put them on. Then he grabbed his shirt. Images of his kids popped into his mind, his kids who were crazy about Laura now, who wanted Laura in their lives. Hadn't Brian just asked about this very thing? What if Laura got sick like Mommy? God damn it! Why had he gotten involved with her? Love was for other people, not for him. He'd known that. And yet... when he met Laura... And now, another woman would disappear.

He whirled around. "Why the hell didn't you tell me this earlier?"

She stood next to the bed, looking like a Roman goddess wearing the sheet as a toga. Her chin was raised and she regarded him unflinchingly. "Because, until now, it wasn't any of your business!"

Was she nuts or what? "You want to explain that?"

Silence resonated as she watched him pull on his pants. He looked at her in time to catch the changes in her expression. Sadness and disappointment replaced the strength. She was blinking rapidly. The corner of his heart tore, but then he patched it. What had she expected? That he'd jump for joy over her news?

"When would have been the right time, Matthew?" Laura asked in a steady voice. "I've been in Pilgrim Cove about six weeks. Should I have announced it upon my arrival? When we went to the Lobster Pot? Maybe in The Diner with the ROMEOs in attendance? When, Matt? When was the right time?"

That was easy to answer. He stepped toward her with leaden feet. "Anytime would have been the right time, Laura. Anytime, before my kids and I fell in love with you."

Her eyes widened. A tear dropped and trickled down her beautiful face. He'd scored a hit, but it didn't make him feel victorious. There were no winners tonight.

He kissed her lightly on the cheek. "I'll call you."
She nodded.

He turned and didn't look back. Didn't draw breath until he was outside. And then he wanted to howl.

LAURA REMAINED STANDING in the same spot long after she heard the door close. She felt the tears roll down her face but couldn't brush them away. She was numb. She couldn't move, couldn't think and couldn't feel. Yet.

She knew herself well; her defense mechanisms were hard at work. Either that or she was in shock. She caught a glimpse of herself in the wall mirror, her complexion as white as the sheet around her, her large blue eyes burning in their sockets. If she could maintain her frozen state, she'd postpone the pain and desolation that were sure to follow.

But with that thought came a kaleidoscope of mental snapshots—Matt laughing with her, Matt kissing her, Matt's eyes filled with desire for her as they made love. Matt cheering for Casey and Brian at their baseball games. The ice began to crack, and she gulped hard to hold back a sob. She couldn't. And soon deep sobs racked her body, and she crumpled to the floor like a broken doll.

Matt would never call her. "I'll call you" was the line men used as a brush-off. That line plus a peck on the cheek. The oldest one-two punch in the dating game. She'd have to accept it and live with it. She'd have to adjust.

She took a corner of the sheet and scrubbed her face. Where were the tissues? Slowly she looked around and spotted the box on her dresser across the room. So far away. She carefully unfurled herself, stood up and took a step. The "toga" started to unwind and she allowed the sheet to fall away as she retrieved the tissues. She caught her reflection in the mirror and shrugged. She knew what she looked like. Finally Matt knew, too.

She'd gambled and lost, but it had been the only thing to do. At this point, Matt had a right to know. She could never have continued their relationship without revealing the truth. Love had to be based on truth and trust, or it was worth nothing.

The thought comforted her. She'd had no choice but to be honest. She searched a dresser drawer for flannel pajamas and wool socks, and then retrieved her bathrobe. She'd thought Matt would be warming her that night. A tear trickled down her cheek again, and this time she impatiently brushed it away.

No more crying. She could handle this situation. Hadn't she been down this road once before? Wasn't that why her sister was expecting a phone call in the morning? Why Norman had shown some concern?

Well, Laura McCloud was a survivor. She had a fabulous career ahead of her. She had friends and family who cared about her. And, ironically, she had her health. Ninety-six percent was nothing to sneeze at!

She'd call Alison in the morning. And she'd be calm. But right now, she needed a cup of tea. Very, very strong tea.

"WHAT'S WRONG, MATT?"

His dad's voice jarred Matt's concentration, but the interruption didn't really matter. He'd become used to running into brick walls. Since leaving Laura, his thoughts either went around in circles or hit dead ends. Not that he hadn't tried to understand Laura's particular condition. But his experience and Internet exploration hadn't helped. The Internet had loads of information about breast cancer, but in practical terms, he couldn't learn anything specific because he didn't know the details of Laura's case. Size of tumor. Location. Type. Stage. Grade. He'd run away from Laura before asking any questions. So, all he managed to do while online was scare himself into a stupor.

And now Sam had come downstairs at half past midnight to find out why Matt hadn't gone to bed. For the third night in a row, Matt sat in front of the wood-burning stove, staring at the flames and saying nothing. Last night, he'd fallen asleep on the couch in the small hours of the morning.

"I'm fine, Dad. Go back to sleep."

But Sam entered the family room and eased himself into his rocking chair. "You're my son. I've known you for thirty-four years. And you're not fine."

Matt grunted and looked away, back into the fire that reminded him of the night of the storm. Laura had enjoyed being part of the family that night. She'd loved cuddling in front of the stove, toasting marshmallows with the boys.

"Seems to me," said Sam, "that the weather's too warm for all the fires you've been lighting."

His father's words rolled over him.

"It must be that the cold is coming from inside of you." Sam's chair squeaked as he rocked. "And that's all I've got to say."

His dad was a man of few words. Sam's friend, Bart Quinn, even with a case of acute laryngitis, could outtalk Sam Parker. But Sam Parker slammed in home runs with his pithy statements.

"Cold? Like a block of ice," said Matt, leaning forward.

"Laura?" asked Sam.

Matt faced his dad. The lines on his face seemed deeper tonight, the brown eyes filled with worry. "Yeah," Matt finally replied. "It's Laura. She's been sick."

The rocking chair stopped. "She's all alone in Sea View House, sick?" Sam's voice reflected horror at the idea. "Why didn't you bring her over? Get her to a doctor? Or ask Max Rosen. Doc wouldn't mind coming out of retirement for Laura."

"Slow down a minute. It's not like that. She was sick…a while back…before she came to Pilgrim Cove."

"I don't understand."

Matt looked at his confused father, his loving father, the man who'd suffered some awful knocks himself, and now only wanted Matt to find happiness. The man who was allowing Laura into his own heart. He owed his dad the truth.

"You won't believe this, Pop. I still can't. But Laura's had breast cancer."

Sam's eyes widened, then narrowed, and the rocking chair began to squeak again. "Tell me about it."

"There's nothing to tell. We've been down this road before."

"Not necessarily," said Sam. "That road splits in many directions. We've only been down one of the paths." He rocked quietly for a moment. "Look at you. Your fear is bottled up. And you're wound so tight you can barely function. The boys are wondering what's going on. I'm not a doctor, but I know some things about living. I know that the more you talk about a problem, the less power it has."

Matt shrugged his shoulders and told Sam what little he knew. Surprisingly, he felt himself relax a degree or two as he spoke.

"Women survive this, Matt," said Sam quietly. "Take Doc's wife, Marsha, for example. She had breast cancer some fifteen years ago. Why don't you talk to Doc about this?"

Matt was startled. "What? Mrs. Rosen? She just came into the store yesterday." He'd known Marsha Rosen forever and never knew about that problem. But now he wanted to know. He wanted to know more about the early stages of the disease.

Fifteen years ago! For the first time in three days, Matt started to feel something shake loose inside of him. It wasn't talk that shed the fear. It was information laced with hope.

The tiny fragment of hope pierced his despair. He'd go on an information quest. He'd talk with Doc first. And then he'd return to the source. To the only one who could answer all the questions that really mattered.

Laura.

DR. MAX ROSEN and his wife lived on the beach side of the peninsula, almost two miles west of Sea View House on a large corner lot. Once Doc Rosen and his family had used the house only as a summer place, and Doc had wanted to be right on the water. But now the Rosens lived in Pilgrim Cove full-time, and the house had become a structure of beauty inside and out. Their married children lived in Boston, but spent lots of time at the beach with them. "We have the best of both worlds," Doc was fond of saying.

As Matt parked his van in front of the Rosens' remodeled house the next afternoon, he prayed that despite Doc's new state of retirement, he still read all the medical journals. Matt slammed the vehicle door closed, grateful that the afternoon had finally arrived. The morning had seemed to crawl by especially since he'd purposely avoided having breakfast at The Diner earlier. The ROMEOs knew him too well and would detect his unease. And there was no way in hell he was going to discuss Laura's situation in front of them.

He rang the bell, hoping that Doc hadn't made plans with his cronies and was home. The door opened and Marsha Rosen looked up at him, her warm brown eyes smiling as she greeted him.

"Lucky guy! I hear life is going well for you recently," she said.

Ouch. Matt tried to smile back. "Is Doc around?"

Suddenly Mrs. Rosen's eyes became sharp and assessing. She squeezed his arm. "In the kitchen. Come on."

As he followed her, Matt remembered that this was the woman who'd survived Laura's illness fifteen years ago. He looked at her in awe, trying to find evidence. She looked like an ordinary, regular woman. Very pretty and stylish. And discreet, Matt mentally added as she left him alone with Doc.

"I'm scared, Doc."

And Max Rosen listened. "You fight fear with knowledge and action," he finally said. "Seems to me that Laura's already done both. She learned what she had to learn and took the action she needed to take. She didn't pull her statistics out of a hat!"

"They are good numbers, aren't they?" asked Matt.

Doc nodded. "My wife…" He looked toward the hallway where Mrs. Rosen had disappeared.

Matt nodded. "Yeah. I know. My dad told me."

"She leads a support group. She's been doing it

for years in Boston and goes back every week. A few years ago, she became involved with a group right here in Pilgrim Cove. You can tell that to Laura.''

''Maybe Mrs. Rosen should call her. I'm not sure...'' Matt stood up and started pacing.

Doc leaned back in his chair, his eyes following Matt's movements. ''A lot of men can't take it, and you've been through it once.'' The doctor's quiet words jelled with Matt's thoughts. ''And you're not even married. In fact, you've only known her for a couple of months.''

Matt whirled. ''That's right, I'm not married. Why should I subject myself to all this? Why is it tearing me apart?'' In horror, Matt heard his voice break, felt tears run down his face. He dashed them away, but more flowed when he blinked.

Doc Rosen didn't answer for a moment, just stared at Matt with the intensity of a judge searching for the truth. ''I cried, too, when we got the news,'' he finally said.

Matt studied the doctor as though seeing him for the first time, picturing him as a younger man with a growing family and busy career. Picturing his tears.

''Do you know why you're crying, Matthew?'' Doc Rosen's gentle voice grabbed Matt's heart.

''Because I'm a coward?''

''No, son. We're all cowards in the beginning. That's normal. I was scared witless, too.'' He paused. ''You're crying, Matthew, because you love her. You love her so much you can't think straight.'' The doctor cleared his throat. ''I know how it feels. You're not alone.''

BUT DOC HAD BUILT a life with Marsha before they got the bad news. Matt and Laura hadn't spent years together. He would *not* be in love with Laura anymore. That's all there was to it. He'd talk himself out of love before it was too late.

However, Matt found himself heading toward Sea View House. He'd call Laura when he was a block away. He stared ahead, driving on automatic pilot, when suddenly Valerie's sweet image appeared in his mind followed immediately by Laura's beautiful face. Valerie, with her big dark eyes. Laura, her blue eyes filled with disappointment. The two portraits alternated in a picture frame, one over the other. Valerie. A rich, dark mane of hair to her shoulders. Laura. Short blond curls blowing in the wind. Valerie. Laura. Valerie. Laura.

He shook his head and pulled to the side of the road. Then Valerie's dark eyes pleaded, and pity filled his heart for the death of such a young woman. A woman he'd loved.

And now there was Laura. Laura! Always on his mind. Thinking about her made Matt smile. Made him grin. Doc was right. Of course it was too late to turn his back. Of course he loved her. He loved her with all his heart, and for some crazy reason, she loved him. If she got sick again, would he want her to be alone?

No way!

He dialed his cell phone…and heard her beautiful voice.

His heart squeezed, his throat closed. "I'm miserable without you," he managed to say. "Can I come over?"

"The door's open."

He disconnected the call and sat in the truck, shaking with relief, just trying to breathe. So much for withholding emotion. The four days without her seemed like a lifetime. He could hardly believe how much their separation was affecting him. He gunned the engine.

Two minutes later, he parked in Laura's driveway and got out of the car. She stood on the front porch, framed in the doorway, waiting for him.

He walked to the steps and examined her. A wide blue band held her hair back. Her pale complexion was void of makeup, and her shadowed eyes held questions that belied the assertive thrust of her chin. Oh, she was a fighter! His heart began to race, his hands began to tingle. And he felt himself smile.

He climbed the five steps, never taking his eyes from her. His legs felt heavy, as though he were fighting his way through quicksand, until finally he was level with her. His heart filled. He couldn't speak.

He opened his arms.

And she walked into them.

"Thank you," he whispered. He squeezed his eyes

shut and tightened his embrace. She belonged there, close to him. Always. "I love you, Laura McCloud."

He felt her arms tighten around him, felt her head nodding against his chest. Felt her shoulders shake and heard her quick sobs.

"Oh, please don't cry, sweetheart." But her sobs continued. "Let's go inside," he said, and still holding her, followed his words with action. But he got no farther with her than the entrance hall. Laura was crying too hard.

Matt cradled her, rocked her, and finally carried her to the sofa and held her on his lap.

"Lord, I've put you through hell," he said as he kissed the tears away.

She nodded and snuggled into him. "Four days or forty years. Didn't seem to be any difference to me. But I sure wasn't this emotional after the first night. While you were running away, I was training myself to be numb."

Matt shook his head from side to side. "The numbness would have worn off, baby. Love's an emotional sort of thing. Powerful. In fact, it's got to be the strongest feeling of all. You can't run from it!"

Her big blue eyes studied every inch of his face. "And when did you get to be so smart?"

"When I realized it was too late to run from you. But, baby, I've been through this before, and I'm scared stiff."

She reached up and kissed him on the mouth. "Your imagination's running riot now...so, why don't we concentrate on something else, then I'll allay your fears.'' She kissed him again, her tongue tracing the outline of his lips. ''Hmm,'' she whispered, ''it's awfully nice being cuddled on your lap.''

''I hadn't noticed,'' Matt replied under his breath as he moved his mouth over hers, exploring every corner. Having Laura in his arms again was a lot more than nice. It was wonderful.

''Hadn't noticed?'' repeated Laura. ''Is…that… right?'' She drew out the words as she wiggled her bottom against him.

Matt shut his eyes, feeling the heat travel to every part of his body, feeling beads of sweat building everywhere. He took a deep breath. ''Laura? Sweetheart…don't start what you don't want to finish.''

Laura rolled her eyes. ''I always finish what I start,'' she replied in a throaty whisper. Her fingers traced the outline of his ear and she felt him shiver. Good.

''Come here,'' she whispered. He lowered his head and she gently snagged his lobe with her teeth and bit lightly. ''Hmm…'' she murmured. ''I'm thinking of…an afternoon delight…do you…?''

She never got to finish her question. Suddenly Matt stood up, still carrying her, and strode toward the bedroom.

''Afternoon delight?'' he said. ''I swear, there's not another woman like you in the whole world!'' He kissed her in mid-stride. ''And sweetheart, you'll never have to ask twice.''

He paused in the bedroom doorway. "But this time, Laura, we use the brightest lights. I want to see all of you. Every square centimeter—silky or smooth or scarred."

She'd thought she was through with tears, but now she had to blink them back. She looped her arms around his neck. "All right, Matt. Every square centimeter."

She had nothing to hide anymore. Nothing to be afraid of. She'd gambled again on life, and this time, she'd won. The relief was indescribable. She felt weak, she felt strong. But mostly, she wanted to shout her happiness from the rooftops and share it with the world.

"You can put me down now," she said.

"I'm never letting go," Matt replied. "Never again." He carried her to the bed as though her five-foot-seven-inch frame weighed nothing at all. But when he leaned over to place her on the mattress, she tightened her clasped hands and pulled him down on top of her.

"Now I've got you where I want you," she whispered. "Kiss me again."

He obliged immediately. And somehow, between kisses, his shirt came off and hers did, too. Then pants, and bra and briefs. And then, she was skin to skin with Matthew Parker, the man she loved, and the tears threatened again because she thought she'd lost this kind of shared magic forever.

"Shh, darling. Don't cry." Matt's deep voice rumbled in her ear.

"Just let me…do…wonderful things to you."

How could he know what she was feeling?

"I love you, sweetheart." And he showed her how much with his hands and his tongue, as she thrashed and squirmed until she couldn't move at all, until she felt as taut as a violin string.

"Matt, Matt…" Her breath came short and hard until…until the string finally broke, and she was able to drag in deep gulps of air. She reached for him, pulled him on top of her and wrapped her limbs around him.

"God, you're beautiful," said Matt.

How could he notice at a time like this when all she wanted was to feel him inside her?

Seconds later, she did. And then lost track of time altogether as she soared once more to the music of a violin that only she heard.

And when she finally floated back to earth, she turned toward Matt, who'd shouted his pleasure just moments before, and said, "You're beautiful, too."

He grinned. "The word's 'handsome,' darling. Men aren't beautiful."

Matt was beautiful to her, but she didn't argue the point.

And he was beautiful as she gave him a tour of her body, explaining each scar and what had happened to her. He asked questions, winced at times and kissed each part of her that had been affected.

"Even as we speak, Matt, more breakthroughs are happening. Early detection is the key."

He nodded. "Valerie never had a chance."

"I'm so sorry, Matt. So sorry." She'd never discussed Valerie with him before. Never expressed her sympathy. She stroked his arm. "But my situation is different. I found my lump when it was small."

She studied Matt carefully and detected the fear that was still there. He'd need more time to process everything and arm himself with knowledge. He'd need more time to relegate her experience to the back of his mind, instead of allowing it full rein at the front.

"When's your next checkup?" he asked, confirming her thoughts.

"It's six months away. Relax!"

"Easy for you to say," he grumbled, taking her in his arms again.

Easy? She shook her head at the absurdity and twined herself against him. Being wrapped in Matt's arms was the best place of all for her.

"I'm so lucky," she whispered, and felt Matt's arms squeeze her gently.

"That makes two of us."

Laura smiled to herself. Surely, all the hard times were behind her.

CHAPTER FOURTEEN

TWO WEEKS LATER Matt stood in front of his bathroom mirror and tried to reknot his tie for at least the hundredth time. Good Lord! It had been so long since he'd had to follow the convoluted twists and turns that he'd almost forgotten how. And he wanted to look perfect. Well, as perfect as a hands-on small-business owner and single father of two boys could look. He sighed and pulled the tie off completely. Matthew Parker was not graced with the talent to look perfect. But he knew someone who could help out.

"Pop," he called as he ran down the stairs.

"In here," said Sam.

Matt walked into the kitchen to see Sam setting up for one of his Friday-night poker games with the ROMEOs. Good. His dad would be pleasantly occupied while Matt was out with Laura at a concert in Symphony Hall. It was a beautiful May evening. He had visions of a romantic cruise into Boston Harbor.

"Well, look at you! Special night?" asked Sam, running his eye over Matt. "Haven't seen you in a suit since I can't remember when. But you're a good-looking boy."

Only his father would still refer to him as a boy! Matt held out the tie. "Can you help?"

"Sure," Sam replied, reaching for the material. "Going to pop the question tonight?"

Matt swallowed. "How can you tell?"

Sam's laughter was all the response he got. "Do the kids know?"

"Nope. They'll be too disappointed if she turns me down."

Suddenly Sam stopped moving. "Any chance of that?" he asked quietly.

Matt didn't think so, but the unexpected potholes on his romantic path had left him less than a hundred-percent sure. "She's been happy with the way we are since getting everything out in the open. The last couple of weeks have been…well, almost like a honeymoon. But I want more. I want marriage. I love her, and I want a life together, every day."

"Then go for it!" Sam leaned forward and hugged him. "And good luck." He stepped back again. "And, by the way, don't worry about me. If she's concerned at all about privacy, I'll rent an apartment."

Stunned, Matt stared at his dad. "Where did you get that crazy idea? You're staying right here with us."

But Sam put up his hand. "I don't want to be in the way, son. Things change. You do what you have to do."

His dad was sincere, and Matt's concern grew.

"What I have to do," said Matt, "is give you a shot of Scotch and bring you back to your senses. You're not just a convenience to this family, Pop, you're vital to this family. We love you. Now, stop the nonsense."

Sam emitted a long sigh. "We'll see, Matt. We'll see. Now give me that tie."

Ten minutes later, Matt was out the door and in the car after getting a lot of oohs and aahhs from the kids. Apparently they weren't used to seeing him dressed up either except for weddings and funerals. And there hadn't been either of those in a long time. But that was changing. Next month, the Chief and Dee would tie the knot. And hopefully, he and Laura would follow suit.

He sucked in a big breath at the thought, then forgot to breathe altogether when Laura answered his knock on her door. He had the same reaction every time he saw her no matter what she was wearing, but tonight she'd surpassed herself. Royal-blue beaded dress that matched her eyes, glittering long earrings and high-heeled shoes that showed off her long, shapely legs.

He exhaled hard and, with a lingering glance at calf and ankle, refocused on Laura's face. "You look… great," he said. "You're gorgeous."

She laughed and shook her head. "Only in your eyes, Matthew Parker. And that's good enough for me."

"It is?"

Laura squeezed his hand and pulled him inside the house. "Of course, it is." She studied him. "I love you, Matt. Yours is the only opinion that matters—in addition to my own, of course."

"Then why won't you marry me?" The words fell out of his mouth, echoing the uncertainty that plagued him earlier. Laura's shocked expression had him reeling. What had he done? He'd ruined everything!

"Why won't I marry you?" she repeated in a small voice, peeping up at him from under her lashes. "Maybe because you…haven't…asked…me?"

It took a moment to sink in, and then…pure joy! From deep inside him, happiness welled to a crescendo as big as the highest wave ever surfed on any ocean in the world. Like flying without a plane. He opened his arms and when she walked into them, he held her close, vowing never to let go.

"Laura, Laura, Laura," he murmured between the kisses he showered on her. "There is no one else for me."

Her arms tightened around him, and when she looked into his face, her eyes shone with gladness and love.

LAURA STEPPED into the shower at Sea View House a week later, a week after agreeing to marry Matt, eager to feel the hot water against her tired body after a late-afternoon five-mile run. The expression on Matt's face at her response to his proposal still had the power to make her laugh out loud.

As she reached for the shampoo, her left hand crossed her line of vision. She paused, staring at the ring on her fourth finger. A twinkling diamond that reminded her of how the ocean waves sparkled in the afternoon sun. She'd argued with Matt about the expense. She didn't need diamonds to know she was loved. And she didn't want funds diverted from his business if cost was a problem. He'd kissed her arguments away, and when she'd looked into his loving eyes, she saw the pleasure that it gave him to give her the jewel. Now she wore it with comfort and ease.

She rinsed her hair and started lathering her body, her hands sliding over slippery skin. Arms, legs and breasts. And then she paused. What the heck was that? Her fingers explored something new. Something that hadn't been there last week, and shouldn't have been there today. Not on her breast. Dear God! Not again.

She couldn't breathe. Fear slammed her, top to bottom, inside and out. Her stomach clenched. She doubled over and grasped the spigots as much to keep her balance as to shut the water.

"No, no. Oh, no!" Her throat was tight, her protest choked, unrecognizable. Déjà vu. Been there, done that. And she couldn't…she just couldn't go through it all again. The baldness, the queasiness, the surgeries, the radiation.

Breathe! Breathe. She inhaled. Exhaled. It was a start.

Think! Use your brain. It can't be happening again. It's too soon. And most lumps are not cancerous.

Laura clutched the shower door and stepped out to the bathroom floor. The cooler air shocked her already stunned body, like an unexpected fall into a frozen pond, and she shivered all over, breathless again.

Grabbing a towel, she wrapped her dripping hair, then reached for a second cloth to dry her body.

"Buck up, girl. Buck up." Talking aloud helped. "It can't be anything." Of course, that's what she'd said the first time, too.

"You just had a checkup a month ago. You just had blood tests. They were negative. And you are *not* a coward. You come from strong stock, Laura Mc-Cloud." Okay, she was breathing again. And touching a small protrusion on the side of her breast. So, what the hell was it?

Only one way to find out. She dressed in a hurry, went to the kitchen, and pulling her calendar toward her, picked up the phone. Dr. Berger's office answered in two rings.

Her appointment was for ten the next morning, and relief filled her. She'd expected that Dr. Berger would want to see her. And as usual, his staff had been calm and professional, exactly what she needed.

Laura walked to the stove and put the kettle on to boil. If ever she needed a strong cup of tea…maybe with a dash of good Irish whiskey…if she'd had any, which she didn't. But Matt probably did.

Good God! Matt! What was she going to tell him? Laura grabbed hold of the chair back and focused on the floor. What *was* she going to tell him? A moment later, the answer came. The only answer.

Absolutely nothing.

He didn't need to know. There was not one good reason for him to know. He couldn't fix the situation; he couldn't change it. Why should they both have a sleepless night when tomorrow would come soon enough? And when the cyst proved to be nothing, she'd tell him about it, and they'd laugh together in relief. But now...no. Too much uncertainty. Wasn't this Matt's worst nightmare, too?

She pictured him in her mind's eye. Those eyes that glowed with raw heat seconds after seeing her, his broad smile and broad chest. She heard his deep laughter, his voice in song. He was a moving picture in her imagination, tossing Casey into the air, pitching a baseball, hugging Brian.

How could she possibly throw him a curve ball so soon after he'd found his equilibrium? So soon after he believed in love again. So soon after he fell in love with her. No, it wouldn't be fair.

The kettle whistled, and she poured the hot water into her mug and wrapped her hands around it. The warmth helped. A little. Wrapping her body around Matt would have helped a lot more. But she shook her head. Not tonight.

She sat at the table and dialed the phone again.

"Matt? Hi. It's me. Slight change of plans. I've got

an early appointment in Boston tomorrow, so I'm going to do a little work now and get to bed early, too…oh, yes. I'll be back by midafternoon. Maybe earlier if all goes well.''

She chatted a while longer before saying goodnight, pleased with her performance. All those acting classes had come in handy. And she hadn't lied a bit. Just left out the details. And if Matt believed she was going to meet with her agent or a recording crew, so be it. In this case, ignorance really was bliss.

Laura brought her cup of tea with her into the den where her equipment was set up. She did intend to work.

But first, she paused in front of the mirror. She raised her hands to her head and combed her fingers through her hair. Her wavy, thick, wild hair that Matt was crazy about. She pulled it back, gathering it tightly at the nape of her neck and stared at herself.

"Only babies should be bald." She watched a lone tear travel down her cheek as her engagement ring sparkled in the mirror. "Dear God, I'll never… complain about wavy hair again…if only…"

She swiped the tear away. Forget it. If God-bargaining really worked, her mom would be alive, and no one would have cancer. She reached for a new script. At least in fairy tales, she could count on a happy ending.

THE PHONE AT PARKER PLUMBING rang early the next morning as Matt was overseeing a delivery of new inventory at the store.

"It's Bar-thol-o-mew Quinn," said Blanche Gold, with raised brow and accent on Bart's first name.

Matt grinned, making a silent bet that the older man needed a little favor and that Matt was just the guy to do it. A proud man, Bart often used his whole moniker when in a pinch because he really didn't like asking for favors. The big name reminded folks that Bartholomew Quinn was a person to be reckoned with, a person who had done lots of favors for others over his lifetime.

"Good morning, Mr. Quinn," said Matt.

"It will be a very good morning, Matthew, if you have a spare minute to check out a little problem at Sea View House. Laura left a message yesterday on my office machine. The window in the master bedroom's bothering her. Said it keeps her up at night. Maybe it's the shutter, maybe it's the frame. Would you take a ride down there, check it out…being as you're a constant visitor anyway!"

Matt frowned. He'd been in that house two nights ago and didn't remember hearing anything. "Sure, I'll go, Bart." He checked the progress the delivery men were making. "Laura's out this morning, so I'll pick up the key in about twenty minutes. Not to worry."

"Thank you, my boy. Don't want to let anything go. We've got a new tenant for the summer already. Starting with the Memorial Day weekend."

Matt tripped over Bart's announcement. The month

was flying by. But the older man was right. Laura's rental agreement ended before the holiday weekend. She'd just have to move in with him and the family. No hardship there!

Their wedding was set for the third weekend of June. Laura wanted a sunset ceremony on the beach with a champagne toast, and a reception at the Wayside Inn right here in town where her sister's family would be staying. Matt would have agreed to anything. All he wanted was Laura. But in his heart, he liked the idea of taking his vows at the water's edge, at the beginning of infinity, where anything and everything was possible.

The store was quiet. Matt blinked and looked around. Blanche and Ethel were staring at him and grinning.

"Off in those daydreams again, Matthew?" asked Ethel.

"The wedding can't come soon enough," said Blanche. "We'd better recount the new stock. Come on, sis."

And he'd better get out of their way. He selected some extra long nails he might need and waved to the ladies. "See you later."

"Take your time," they responded together.

But there would be no reason to linger at Sea View House. Laura was in Boston.

He stopped at Quinn's Realty, chatted with Lila for a moment and got the key from Bart. "The house is in good shape, Bart. I've checked the upstairs and downstairs plumbing recently, fixed some small leaks, too. And submitted a bill, don't forget.'' He loved to tease the man.

Bart harrumphed. ''I did the paperwork. Funds come from the trust, you know.''

Matt knew very well. He and his dad had been watching over Sea View House for years and were familiar with the payment process.

''I'll have Ralph Bigelow check the electricals,'' said Bart. ''It's standard procedure whenever we rent to a new tenant.''

''And a good idea.''

Matt took the keys and ten minutes later let himself through the back door of Sea View House. Midnight greeted him in the kitchen. He quickly put his toolbox on the kitchen table and scooped up the big kitten and placed her on his shoulder. ''Okay, girl. Let's keep each other company.''

Midnight's purr of contentment vibrated through his ear, and Matt chuckled. Seemed they both missed Laura.

He reached for his toolbox and glanced at the calendar on the table. Such neat handwriting. Such organization. Maybe she had an unexpected audition today. He pulled the calendar toward him and pinpointed the date. The one box where the handwriting was big and shaky.

Dr. Berger. 10:00 a.m.

What? He flipped the pages backward. Hadn't she told him about a great checkup a month ago? Yes.

There it was. A neatly notated appointment in April. He turned back to May and stared at the current date with the messy writing. Messy writing…which meant…good Lord!

He spotted the doc's number at the top of the calendar and grabbed the phone.

He got the address. He made the nine-thirty ferry. A never-ending thirty minutes. Then a cab ride. And Laura wasn't in the waiting room when he finally reached the place.

"Where is she?" Matt loomed over the appointment desk and watched the gal behind it open her eyes in fear. So he looked like a madman. He felt like one, too. But decided to soften his voice.

"Laura McCloud," he said. "She had a ten-o'clock appointment, and now—" he glanced at his watch "—it's ten thirty-six." He felt like he'd run a marathon. And perhaps he had with all his pacing on the ferry.

"She's with the doctor at the moment," came the soft reply.

"I want in," he said slowly and distinctly. "Call the exam room. Tell them Matt Parker is here and I want in *now*."

She nodded and spoke into the phone, but he couldn't hear what she said.

His adrenaline was pumping, he had enough energy to bash down every door in the place until he found her. But he made himself stand still. For all he knew, the receptionist could have called Security. He glanced around. People were staring at him. Hell, *he* would have called Security.

"Here's Grace, thank God," said the appointment clerk, nodding in the direction of a nurse who was walking toward them.

Her arm was outstretched inviting him to follow her, and Matt felt himself relax.

"So, you're Laura's boyfriend," the nurse said, giving him the once-over. Her hazel eyes were as sharp as razor blades, and Matt thought he'd relaxed too soon. Thank goodness he was one of the good guys.

"No," he said, pumping her hand. "I'm not her boyfriend," he said, emphasizing the word "boyfriend". "I'm her fiancé. The man she's going to marry."

"Congratulations," the woman replied without missing a beat. "You've got a winner." Her assessment continued. "I'm hoping she does, too." Then she smiled, and her eyes warmed. "Come on in, Matt. Meet the team."

He didn't care about a team. He only wanted Laura! But he followed the nurse down the hall without another word.

WAS IT REALLY Matt causing all the ruckus out front? Was it Grace's voice she heard with him? Laura nodded at Dr. Berger and his nurse, Janet, when the call came in that a wild man named Matt Parker was asking for her. No, not asking. Demanding.

Maybe it was just as well he was here. He could see what she experienced. And would probably experience again.

A knock sounded and the door opened. And there was Matt, filling the exam room with his six-foot towering presence. He stared at Laura. ''I'm furious with you, but we'll put that on hold for the moment.''

She shivered in her medical gown and slacks, and watched in disbelief as her normally warmhearted, loving, kind man turned on Dr. Berger.

''What the hell's going on here?''

Dr. Berger was no slouch, either, as Laura well knew. He was used to dealing head-on with truth. His questioning eyes met Laura's and she nodded. The doctor rose from his stool, looked Matt squarely in the face, and said, ''She's fine.'' The doctor nodded at the vacated seat, and Matt collapsed into it.

''Proof once again that the bigger they are, the harder they fall.'' Dr. Berger, who was shorter than Matt by a good four inches or so, winked at Laura while Janet and Grace grinned.

Then the doctor addressed Matt. ''She has a thickened milk gland. It's common and definitely not cancerous. But I'm glad she came in. She should never delay with anything that bothers her.''

Matt nodded. ''Just…just a milk gland?'' No mistaking the fear in his voice.

The doctor nodded.

''And lots of women get this?'' Matt repeated.

''Yes.''

Laura watched as Matt just sat and breathed. She knew how he felt. An exquisite release of tension, like a snapped rubber band. "It's okay, Matt. I'm fine."

But when he raised his head and stared at her, her stomach tightened. In his expression, she saw sadness and…disappointment.

"No, Laura," Matt said. "*You* may be fine, but *we* are not fine. Why didn't you tell me the truth about where you were going today? I thought we were partners. I thought we were in this together. I don't need or want a martyr!"

Laura couldn't move. Couldn't speak. Matt's unexpected accusations robbed her strength. Under his prolonged study, she felt like disappearing. Her fear grew along with the silence. In her effort to protect Matt, she'd risked their entire relationship in a way she hadn't thought about. And now she had to reconnect with him. She forgot about everything and everyone in the room except Matthew.

She reached toward him from her position on the examining table. "Please, Matt. Don't be angry. I thought I was doing you a favor. I'm not used to asking for help with this. Not even too much from Alison. And I guess I'm not used to people wanting to take care of me. With my mom, I was always the caregiver."

Her arm dropped. She didn't have any more words. She didn't know what else to say.

Matt had leaned back in the chair, his eyes closed.

Was he thinking about forgiveness? Or was he trying to find words to say goodbye?

"I used to think all my fear was rooted in the cancer," he finally said, looking at her again. "I was so afraid of loving you and losing you. I'll take blame for that. But now I see that there was more. I was afraid of something else."

She stared at him, trying to absorb every word he said. Trying to understand what was on his mind.

"A real relationship requires communication," continued Matt. "Sharing. Talking. Give and take. You're the one who said that Dee and the Chief wasted five years because of poor communication. Well, I'm sick of silence between people. I'm sick of people running away. For God's sake, I have a brother I haven't seen in eight years. And what has his disappearance accomplished?" He waited a beat and then answered his own question. "Absolutely nothing good. Only empty spaces in people's lives."

He stood up and stepped closer to her. "I love you, Laura. And I want our marriage to be one of sharing—the good and the bad. Running away scares me more than anything, so you can't do that. You can't just up and leave people who love you. It's not fair. Do you think you can talk to me, trust me?"

"Thank you, God," she whispered to herself before she looked up at the man she'd love forever.

"Oh, yes. Of course I can. Because I love you, too. With my whole heart."

And then he kissed her, and her world was right

side up again. Music should have been playing; birds should have been singing.

She did hear something. Simultaneously she and Matt broke the kiss and looked around at their audience. Grace, Janet, Kate, the third nurse, and Dr. Berger. All hands clapping and soft sounds of ''bravo'' for good measure.

''What a story to tell the other patients,'' said Kate.

''Just make sure you tell them that it's not about the cancer.'' Matt nodded at Dr. Berger. ''That's the doc's department.''

Laura leaned forward, not wanting to miss a syllable of whatever Matt would say.

''Tell them it's all about the love around you. The love and the support and the caring.''

''Amen,'' said Grace.

One by one, Matt looked at each person standing in the room. ''Thank you,'' he said, ''for everything. And especially for not throwing me out of the office.''

''Our specialty is listening,'' said Evan Berger. He indicated his nursing staff. ''Would you say we've seen and handled just about everything over the years?''

The women chuckled.

''I wish we had more like him,'' said Grace, with a nod toward Matthew.

Laura started laughing as Matt's face turned a deep red, and wasn't surprised when he abruptly turned to her and then to the doctor. ''Is she good to go?''

The doctor nodded.

"Great," replied Matt. "We've got two kids who'll be getting out of school about the time we get home."

Might as well ask now. Laura slid from the table and looked at Dr. Berger. "Any problem with changing that to three kids in a year or two?"

She heard Matt's gasp.

"In your case, no problem at all," replied Dr. Berger. "We'll talk next time."

"All three of us will talk next time," said Matt, a frown on his brow.

Laura squeezed his hand. "Of course. I wouldn't have it any other way. It'll be a joint decision."

He kissed her again. "Come on, my love. Time to go home. Time to celebrate."

"Time for you two to get on with your lives!" The doc had the last word. And a big grin on his face.

WORDS WERE SUPERFLUOUS in the taxi. On the ferry. But touch wasn't. Holding hands was as necessary as breathing. A caress on the cheek, a gentle kiss on the forehead, on the mouth—all vital to life.

With Matt beside her at the railing, Laura raised her face to the May sunshine. The rays warmed her, and she felt all the remaining cold disappear. His finger traced the outline of her lips, and he kissed her again.

"God, I love you so much, Laura. I couldn't let you run away without trying to understand."

She rose on tiptoe, wrapped her arms around his

neck and kissed him with everything she had inside. "I'm so glad you came after me, Matthew Parker. I like a man who'll make a big scene because he loves me!"

His eyes gleamed. "Baby, you ain't seen nothing yet!"

He proved it an hour later at Sea View House in the master bedroom. But making love was different this time, Laura noticed. Just as the boat ride had been. Quiet, more intense and passionate, as though a brush with death had to be overridden by experiencing life at its most exquisite. By experiencing the act that gave life.

"Why," Laura gasped at the end, "is this called 'the little death' when I've never felt so alive?"

"Let's try to figure it out during the next hundred years."

She cuddled against him, then felt herself doze off. Until she heard the familiar *click, click, click.* "The damn shutter is driving me nuts," she mumbled as she wrapped her naked limbs around Matt. "Bart was supposed to send someone to fix it."

"He did, sweetheart. It's how I found you today."

She looked up at him as his words fell into place. "I'm glad he called you and not someone else."

"Not a chance. Sea View House has a lot of history that Bart won't mess with. Only a trusted few can work here. Did you know that he keeps what he calls an "official" journal of stories connected with this house? It's really amazing at how many people have lived and loved here.''

"He's told me…and—'' she peeked at him ''—are you ready for this?''

"What?"

"There's a new story being added to the journal.'' She stared at him until the light of understanding flickered in his eyes.

His index finger pointed at her, then back at himself. His comical expression made her laugh.

She nodded. "Yes, indeed. I just have to write the ending.''

Matt fell back on his pillow. "I swear, this is why everyone knows everything about everybody in Pilgrim Cove. We write it all down!''

Laura giggled. "Bart said the book is kept under lock and key for posterity.''

"Just make sure you write a very happy ending.''

"That's easy. I'll just tell the truth.''

He kissed her and got up. "Why don't you finish the story this afternoon and give it to him at The Lobster Pot tonight. I'm taking the whole family to celebrate how much I love you.''

WITH A BOY on each side of her, and Matthew and Sam behind her, Laura's visit to the popular restaurant that evening was as different from her first visit as it was possible to be. Thea and Maggie greeted *her* before saying hello to the men, as if *she* were the lifetime resident of Pilgrim Cove.

"Is this guy treating you right, like a bride-to-be is supposed to be treated?" asked Thea as she gave Laura a hug and winked at Matt.

Before Laura could respond, Maggie added her voice. "What a time this town is having with two weddings right next to each other. It's something happy to talk about. That's for sure." Then Katie's grandmother turned to the children. "You're taking it easy on Laura, aren't you? Not driving her crazy yet?"

"No-o," said Casey, looked at his dad. "Are we?"

"Of course not," Laura answered quickly, without giving Matt a chance to reply. She looked at Maggie. "They're wonderful kids. The best!"

Casey grinned and so did Brian.

"Of course they are," said Thea. "Now come on in and sit down. We need help with something we're working on for Rick's bachelor party Sunday night. Both you guys are going, aren't you?"

Matt and Sam nodded.

"Good," said Maggie while Thea disappeared. "Most of the police force is going to be here, too. Current and retired. The place will be rocking with the stories they'll tell about Rick." She sighed with contentment. "I can't believe he and Dee are finally getting married. And in only two more weeks! Memorial Day is sneaking up on us."

As the family followed Maggie to their table, Laura puzzled over how they could possibly assist with

Rick's bachelor party. She didn't imagine Thea or
Maggie would want help preparing food.

Thea returned quickly. "What do you think of
this?" she asked, displaying an unframed sketch that
very soon would be destined for a place on the wall.
The top half of the paper was a caricature of Rick
O'Brien riding on a big fish and wearing a policeman's hat on his head. The caption read: He wanted
to *snapper* up...

The bottom half was a cartoon picture of petite
Dee, sitting demurely on a dock at the water's edge.
The punch line read: Because she *smelt* so good!

Laura laughed and groaned at the same time. "No,
no, no. Good wordplay, but not fair to Dee."

"I thought it was too much, also," sighed Maggie.
"Can you think of something else?"

Laura glanced at the menu in front of her. A slew
of fish names. "How about..." she said slowly. "He
wanted to *snapper* up...because she lived inside his
sole."

"All right!" said Maggie with enthusiasm. "That's
better."

"Friendlier," said Thea.

"Glad I could help," said Laura. "By the way,
who's the artist? This stuff is great."

"Oh, that's Maggie," said Thea. "She's better at
drawing than cooking!" Thea grinned at Maggie's
outraged expression and then made a quick getaway.

"That sister of mine! She's the one who comes up

with the ideas. And no one's ever gotten sick from *my* cooking!''

Laura kept her mouth shut. No way was she getting involved with a sisterly squabble despite their obvious devotion to each other.

''Hmm. Is your dad here tonight?'' asked Matt. ''Laura's got something for him.''

Laura's eyes met Matt's. He winked.

''Dad's in the kitchen, stirring chowder,'' said Maggie. ''I'll tell him you're here…after I show you our other etching.'' She grinned at them. ''We're not done yet.''

''Uh-oh,'' said Matt. ''I don't like that look in your eye, Maggie Sullivan. What's going on?''

''Oh, hush. It's not so bad. But I did say there were *two* weddings coming up, didn't I?'' She raced off.

''Now what?'' asked Laura. ''What do you think they came up with?''

Matt shrugged.

''Anything's possible,'' said Sam, ''but it's all in good fun.''

Laura nodded, and caught sight of the two sisters returning to the table with their newest offering. It was a caricature of Matt wearing a big tool belt, one hand raised high in the air, holding a huge wrench with Laura sitting balanced on top. His other hand was fisted on his hip, and he was winking at the viewer. The caption read: Matt Parker loves his *wench!*

Sam applauded.

Matt exclaimed, "True! How true!" And leaned across the table to give Laura a quick kiss.

Brian looked puzzled.

Casey yelled, "I don't get it!"

And Laura laughed until tears ran down her face. She loved them all! She opened her arms to Matt's sons and motioned them over. "Come on. I'll explain everything."

Casey plopped into her lap. "Okay, La-La-L-Mom! Tell us."

EPILOGUE

BART QUINN SALUTED Rick O'Brien as the retired police officer stood sentry at the door to Pilgrim Cove Elementary School on the morning of the Memorial Day program. The Chief usually volunteered his services to the town when extra help might be needed. But today, with his wedding only two days away, the man was either extremely conscientious or needed to keep himself busy.

Bart maneuvered down the crowded center aisle of the auditorium searching for his family, amazed but satisfied at how a children's event prompted such a big turnout. There wasn't another town on the New England coast that could hold a candle to Pilgrim Cove, not in his mind.

"Granddad, over here." Bart recognized Lila's voice and spotted her hand waving at him.

"Is our Katie set for her debut?" he teased as he sat down.

"You mean, did she let me pull a comb through her hair?" replied Lila.

"She looks gorgeous," chimed in Maggie Sullivan. "Cute as a button, bright as the sun. Anyone can see that, not just her doting grandmother! She and Casey are going to knock 'em dead with their duet.''

"Of course they are," Bart replied. "Never thought anything else. Now where's Sam and his crew?'' he asked, scanning the crowd.

"Right across the aisle, Dad," replied Maggie. "You'll see them when everyone sits down. Laura's the nervous one in that group.''

"She's worried about Casey, is all," said Lila. "Casey singing in front of all these people. She's wonderful with him and with Brian, too. She loves them. Each one of them, including Sam.''

"Good. Good," said Bart. "That's the way it should be.''

"Did you know I'm showing Matt's house to a potential buyer this afternoon?'' asked Lila.

Bart shook his head. "He's decided to build a new one after all?''

Lila nodded. "Or buy—if we can find the right house. And that means a stone's throw from the beach.'' Lila sighed, a wistful note in her voice. "Oh, Gramps. He's so in love with Laura. He says his wedding gift to her is the Atlantic Ocean!''

It was the "Gramps" that made Bart look hard at his granddaughter. Her tender word for him, used only in times of unexpected emotion. Lila didn't often comment on romantic love, but now her expression looked dreamy, as if she might actually believe in it. His granddaughter had loved only one boy in her life. And he had let her down.

He glanced at his friend, Sam, father of the boy who'd disappeared. A good man who'd lost too much family. A wife. A son. And then a living son whom he hadn't seen for eight years. Bart shook his head, awed by how one person's actions could affect so many. He sighed heavily, as he'd done so many times in the past. Jason Parker had simply vanished from their lives.

He leaned across the aisle. "Good morning, Sam."

Sam Parker turned to greet his friend.

"We've got Sea View House rented starting tomorrow," said Bart. "Both apartments. Did Matt tell you?"

Sam nodded. "We've moved Laura into our house, lock, stock and barrel. No problem there. She's also selling her house in Boston. It's been a real busy month. Everybody coming and going."

"A wonderful thing, those two."

Sam's smile was of pure happiness, and Bart felt his own heart lighten. "One of my prayers has been answered," said Sam. "I'm a lucky man."

Bart glanced at Lila. He knew darn well what Sam's second prayer was. But Bart had little faith about a happy outcome there. He changed the subject.

"There'll be two new people in Sea View House for the busy season," said Bart. "They each need the healing they might find there."

"Who's in The Crow's Nest? Matt didn't tell me any details."

"Upstairs, we have Daniel Stone, hailing from California. A very sharp guy, but he's hurting something fierce inside. However,'' Bart added, ''he's not hurting in the pocketbook, so he's paying full freight.''

''That's fair,'' said Sam. ''You have to follow the rules of the William Adams Trust.''

''That's what I said to myself,'' replied Bart. ''But downstairs...that's another story. Her name is Shelley Anderson. She's got two small kids and a serious problem with her ex-husband. I'm glad Daniel's a strapping fellow and that Shelley's not totally alone in the house.''

''Sounds like the ROMEOs should mosey on down there every so often,'' said Sam.

Bart nodded. ''I think the ROMEOs will be busy.''

Sam pointed to the stage. ''Look, the children are about to start.''

Bart settled back in his seat, ready to enjoy himself.

LAURA MCCLOUD WAS NOT enjoying herself at all. She'd bitten both her thumbnails to the quick. No one had warned her that giving her heart to the children would be so...so...exhausting. Not physically, but emotionally. She glanced at Matt. How could he sit there smiling and chatting with people as though his two precious boys weren't going to be front and center in a few minutes?

Casey, Casey, Casey. The child's name echoed in her mind. He had to do well today. He just had to! Or else, what? She asked herself. Worst-case scenario? He'd be totally mortified. And that was definitely not an option.

"Would you relax," said Matt for the third time. "He'll be fine. He's singing, and he's great at that."

"But there's only two of them, not a whole chorus."

Matt sighed, but wrapped his arm around her and squeezed. "You're going to wear yourself out, sweetheart."

"This motherhood thing is…"

"Is what?" prompted Matt, a line creasing his forehead.

"Is so important! It's like I'm on a roller coaster. One minute life is smooth, and the next I'm a nervous wreck." She considered herself an articulate person, but today that botched explanation was the best she could do.

"Things will settle down after the wedding and your permanent move to Pilgrim Cove." His voice was calm and reassuring, but her thoughts were on Casey.

She felt Matt's strong fingers massage her shoulder, the nape of her neck, and she allowed herself to relax. Lucky, lucky woman to have connected with Matt Parker. She rolled her head back, enjoying the pressure of his hands against her muscles.

"Show time," said Matt.

Laura straightened up immediately, her eyes on the stage, her heart in her stomach.

The kindergarten and first grade sang "Yankee Doodle."

"Okay," Laura whispered when the smallest children were done. "Here we go."

But it was the fourth grade, not the second grade, that followed with a skit about World War II and soldiers going off to war. They did the lindy hop and sang "Don't Sit Under the Apple Tree." Very adorable and appropriate, but Laura was on edge.

And then there was the fifth grade, and Brian as...Paul Revere! "I thought he wanted to be John Adams," Laura whispered to Matt.

"And Benjamin Franklin. Then he decided that Paul had all the action!"

Verses of the famous Longfellow poem, recreating Revere's midnight ride, were recited as Brian and his classmates acted out the revolutionary story. And then Brian put a small drum around his neck and tapped out a marching rhythm. The high notes of a piccolo sounded and there was little Casey, on stage with his big brother, the beginning of a fife-and-drum corps. Other children joined the drumming and fluting until about ten kids of different ages were playing altogether. In unison.

"Amazing," said Laura, allowing herself to smile for the first time.

"They picked the musical ones," said Matt. "It comes easier to some than to others."

Laura glanced at him. "It comes easy to the Parkers, you mean."

"Only the gift. Perfecting it takes work."

"The boys practiced?"

"Every day." He leaned in and kissed her. "You've been running back and forth so much between the Boston house and Sea View House, you didn't notice."

She had noticed sometimes. "But I thought they were just making noise."

Matt laughed. "Be glad they're not playing violin."

The third grade went next with two poems commemorating the Civil War and World War I.

And only the second grade was left. Casey's grade.

Laura watched the entire class line up on stage and face the audience. Casey and Katie stood side by side in the center of the first row. They stepped forward and looked at the pianist, who nodded. And they began to sing. "'Oh, beautiful for spacious skies...'"

The sound of angels. Laura felt tears well. Any child who could sing like that...surely she could find more ways to help his speech along. She glanced at Matt, but his eyes were only on his son. Eyes that looked awfully shiny to her.

He reached for her hand and pressed it gently, then leaned close to her and whispered, "I love you so much, Laura. We all do. Thanks for loving us back and for just being you."

Her tears flowed and she bowed her head. Love surrounded her. Life flowed through her. She couldn't ask for more.

Please turn the page for an excerpt from
NO ORDINARY SUMMER,
the next title in Linda Barrett's
heartwarming PILGRIM COVE *series.*
Coming in August 2004

CHAPTER ONE

BARTHOLOMEW QUINN LEANED BACK in his oversize leather desk chair and rolled it and himself to the large open window. A spring breeze tinged with sunshine and ocean had been teasing him all morning, and he'd resisted its lure until now. He closed his eyes and inhaled the best perfume in the world. If he were a younger man, he'd close his Main Street office for an hour and hit the beach in full stride. In fact, he had the urge to do it yet. At seventy-five years, he still walked with a spring in his step! Plus a twinge in his knee.

He continued to dream, his mind's eye like a movie camera, capturing every foot of shoreline on the peninsula. He knew the seashore in every season, the ocean in all her moods. The fair ones and the foul. Just like he knew every street in Pilgrim Cove. He chuckled at the thought. Since he'd lived here all his life, he'd be hard-pressed not to know every street, road and thoroughfare. He'd be a lousy real estate agent to boot!

Finally opening his eyes, Bart stood and peered out the window. Main Street was quieter today than it was in the middle of the week. Most of the businesses were closed on Sunday—Parker Plumbing and Hardware, the Pilgrim Cove Savings & Loan—but not Quinn Real Estate at the start of the busy season. Bart and his granddaughter, Lila, had been answering a constantly ringing phone since the beginning of March as people yearned for sunshine and summer vacations after a long New England winter.

Bart sighed with satisfaction. Life had been good to him. His parents had emigrated from County Cork long ago with not even a potato in their pockets, and now their son ran the business they'd established—the oldest and largest real estate sales and property management company in town—in partnership with their great-granddaughter! Now, how many families could boast that?

He turned from the window and started to push his chair back to the desk, but the slam of a car door made him pause. He retraced his step and focused on the street directly outside. A woman was gathering two children from the back seat of a sedan. He glanced at his watch. Probably his noon appointment arriving at almost one o'clock.

He watched as she bent close to the children, talking or listening, he couldn't tell. She had a cap of short dark hair, red highlights dancing whenever she moved her head. Then she straightened, took a child's hand in each of hers, and looked up at the sign on the agency's front door. She didn't move for a second; in fact, she stood very still as though gathering courage, before leading the children up the few steps to the doorway.

Bart shook his head. Poor girl. Could be she'd gotten lost. She certainly looked lost. Lost and scared. But also determined. A not-so-brave mother lioness.

"We'll see. We'll see," he murmured, checking his appointment book for her name before walking out to greet her. He turned right and right again ten feet down the corridor toward the front of the building. The distance to the front door was the price he paid for the corner office with the cross ventilation, and he didn't mind a bit.

His granddaughter stood at the entrance, already chatting with their visitors and leading them down the hall toward him. "Oh, there he is," Lila said. "Granddad, this is…"

"…Shelley Anderson," Bart completed, extending his hand to the young woman with the shiny hair. "Welcome to Pilgrim Cove."

"I'm sorry we're late," she began, a frown creasing her brow, a shadow darkening her eyes.

"No matter," said Bart quickly. "We're a little slow today anyway. In fact, right now is better for me." Lila's astonished expression would have made him laugh if he'd allowed himself to look at her. So he didn't. Bart knew people, had learned to trust his instincts years ago. Right now, Bart would have said anything to put Shelley Anderson and her children at ease.

He watched Lila head back to her office, and then

turned toward the boy and offered his hand. "And you are…?"

"Josh." One word, sullenly given. Limp handshake.

"Fine jacket you have. My great-granddaughter plays baseball, too."

That got the boy's attention. His hazel eyes came alive.

"But she's a girl!"

"That she is, boyo. She's a girl on second base."

Bart let Josh mull that over while he focused on the beautiful little girl hiding behind her mother's legs with her thumb in her mouth. He walked to Shelley Anderson's side and bent down until his knee protested. "And who's this little princess?"

A pair of chocolate-brown eyes, as big and round as any he'd ever seen, peeked up at him. Bart glanced up at the mother, but her attention was solely on her daughter.

"Are you Esmeralda Hossenfeffer?" Bart asked with a wink as he looked at the little girl again.

A tiny giggle emerged from behind the child's thumb. A sweet sound.

"Are you Isabella Farmer-in-the-della?" The gentle teasing came easily to him, a man surrounded by family, where five grandchildren and one great-grandchild had filled his daily life from the moment they'd been born.

The thumb popped out of the girl's rosebud mouth, and she shook her head fast.

"Are you—"

"I'm Emily Joy Anderson!"

Bart snapped his fingers. "That's just what I thought all the time," he said, pleased to see the spirit hiding inside the child. He extended his hand to Emily and she took it before disappearing behind her mother again.

Now Bart centered his attention on Shelley Anderson, who sported a lovely smile as she hugged her daughter. "You have two beautiful children, Mrs. Anderson," Bart said.

Her smile widened and she nodded. "I certainly do. They're beautiful, they're smart, and well, they're just the best." She kissed them each on top of their heads.

Josh made a face. "No mushy stuff."

"Sorry," Shelley said in a light, musical tone.

Bart chuckled under his breath. The woman wasn't sorry at all. No shadows darkened her eyes now, no frowns marred her smooth forehead. And he silently applauded. It was a pleasure to see some confidence overtake the worry he'd seen on her face earlier.

He led the little family to his sunny office and invited them to sit down. He was ready to learn all he could about Shelley Anderson and her children. Not because he was an old gossip with time on his hands. Not at all. In fact, his meeting with this family carried great responsibility.

For twenty-five years, Bartholomew Quinn had been charged with leasing a particular waterfront property on a sliding financial scale when appropriate. He answered to the William Adams Trust, named for the founder of Pilgrim Cove, about his choice of tenants. And so far, he hadn't missed a step in identifying those who qualified.

The instincts of a lifetime had awakened when Shelley Anderson had called for the appointment. Now they crackled in his belly. Sea View House was certainly what she needed; he hoped it was what she deserved.

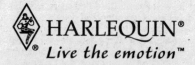

Nothing Sacred
by Tara Taylor Quinn

Shelter Valley Stories

Welcome back to Shelter Valley, Arizona. This is the kind of town everyone dreams about, the kind of place everyone wants to live. Meet your friends from previous visits—including Martha Moore, divorced mother of teenagers. And meet the new minister, David Cole Marks.

Martha's still burdened by the bitterness of a husband's betrayal. And there are secrets hidden in David's past.

Can they find in each other the shelter they seek? The happiness?

By the author of *Where the Road Ends*, *Born in the Valley* and *For the Children*.

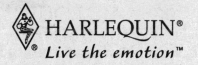

HARLEQUIN®
Live the emotion™

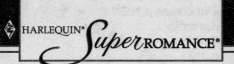

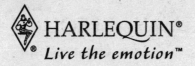

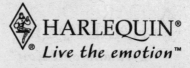

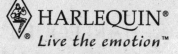

HARLEQUIN *Super*ROMANCE®

For a Baby
by C.J. Carmichael
(Superromance #1203)

On-sale May 2004

Heather Sweeney wants to have a baby. Unfortunately, she's in love with a married man, so that's never going to happen. Then one lonely night, she turns to T. J. Collins—who always seems to stand by her when her life is at its lowest point—and a few weeks later, discovers that she's about to get her greatest wish, but with the wrong man.

The New Baby by Brenda Mott
(Superromance #1211) On-sale June 2004

Amanda Kelly has made two vows to herself. She will never get involved with a man again. She will never get pregnant again. But when she finds out that Ian Bonner has lost a child, too, Amanda soon finds that the protective barrier around her heart is crumbling....

The Toy Box by K.N. Casper
(Superromance #1213) On-sale July 2004

After the death of an agent, helicopter pilot Gabe Engler is sent to Tombstone, Arizona, to investigate the customs station being run by his ex-wife, Jill Manning. Gabe hasn't seen Jill since they lost their six-week-old child and their marriage fell apart. Now Gabe's hoping for a second chance. He wants Jill back—and maybe a reason to finish building the toy box he'd put away seven years ago.

Available wherever Harlequin books are sold.

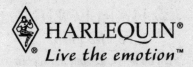

HARLEQUIN®
Live the emotion™